# ON HURRICANE ISLAND

"*On Hurricane Island* is unflinchingly political, unashamedly suspenseful, and, above all, deeply human. Here is a writer who knows how to ramp up the tension while never sacrificing the spirit of her conviction, the sense of grounding in the natural world, or the heartbreaking complexity of her characters."
—Naomi Benaron, Bellwether Prize winner for *Running the Rift*

"*On Hurricane Island* is a chilling, Kafkaesque story about what happens when the United States does to citizens at home what it has done to others abroad. Meeropol puts the reader right into the middle of these practices through characters about whom you really care and a story you can't put down; a really good book."
—Michael Ratner, Center for Constitutional Rights

"In *On Hurricane Island*, Ellen Meeropol takes on the complexities and dangers of contemporary life in a novel that starts fast and ratchets up the tension all the way to the end. She brings to her writing a sharp, observant eye, great skill in characterization, and, best of all, a talent for taut, suspenseful narrative in the style of Graham Greene."
—W. D. Wetherell, author of *A Century of November*

"Ellen Meeropol can be counted on to write with intelligence and heart. In *On Hurricane Island*, she also manages to give us characters who we care deeply about, perfect pitch dialogue and a gripping story about civilian detention centers designed for the likes of you and me. Thoughtful and compelling."
—Jacqueline Sheehan, author of *Picture This*

# ON HURRICANE ISLAND

*Ellen Meeropol*

 RED HEN PRESS | *Pasadena, CA*

Book design and layout by Jaimie Evans
Cover design by Mark E. Cull
Author photo by Ellen Augarten

Library of Congress Cataloging-in-Publication Data
Meeropol, Ellen.
  On Hurricane Island / Ellen Meeropol.—First edition.
    pages ; cm
    ISBN 978-1-59709-300-2 (softcover : acid-free paper)
  1. Military interrogation—United States—Fiction. 2. Terrorism investigation—United States—Fiction. 3. Terrorism—Prevention—United States—Fiction. 4. Political fiction. I. Title.
  PS3613.E375O5 2015
  813'.6—dc23
                    2014037120

The National Endowment for the Arts, the Pasadena Arts & Culture Commission and the City of Pasadena Cultural Affairs Division, the Los Angeles County Arts Commission, the Dwight Stuart Youth Fund, the Los Angeles Department of Cultural Affairs, Sony Pictures Entertainment, and Ahmanson Foundation partially support Red Hen Press.

First Edition
Published by Red Hen Press
www.redhen.org

# ACKNOWLEDGMENTS

My home is in Massachusetts, but my muse lives in Maine. I fell in love with the state when I first visited Vinalhaven, one of the Fox Islands in Penobscot Bay. I started writing seriously in Maine, I received my MFA there, and my stories keep wandering back. In the service of fiction, however, I've taken major liberties with the geography, landscape, residents, and history of the Fox Islands.

I am indebted to the friends and writers who have generously offered their feedback on this manuscript. The talented and thoughtful women in my manuscript group—Jacqueline Sheehan, Marianne Banks, Dori Ostermiller, Kris Holloway, Rita Marks, Brenda Marsian, Lydia Kann, and Anne Kornblatt—helped me see this story more clearly. Thank you always to the Vanettes for their support and critiques—Ginnie Gavron, Sharon Arms, Perky Alsop, and Sarah Stromeyer. I also greatly appreciate the comments and expertise of friends; thank you, Bill Newman, Liz and Jim Goldman, Jane Miller, Neil Novik, Beth Crowell, and Jon Weissman.

I feel incredibly lucky to work with my amazing agent Jenny Bent, my "fairy godmother" publicist Mary Bisbee-Beek, and the gifted and passionate team at Red Hen Press, particularly Kate Gale, Mark Cull, Samantha Haney, and Billy Goldstein.

Finally, I am deeply grateful to my family. Robby, Jenn, and Rachel read many drafts and shared their knowledge, critical reading, and ongoing love and encouragement. This book is dedicated to them, and to my grandchildren Josie and Abel, in the hope that people of good conscience can prevent events like the ones I've made up in this novel.

# PROLOGUE, 1914

The wee-hours explosion rattled the bed.

Margaret was still awake, matching her breathing to her sister's soft snores, hoping to quiet her internal battle of grief and blame. At the blast, she threw off the covers and ran to the open window. The night glowed orange. Within seconds, men's shouts filled the air and the island fire horn blared.

Carrie sat up. "What happened?"

"Fire," Margaret said, pulling her skirt over her chemise.

Mother herded the little boys into the sisters' bedroom. Tommy was sobbing. He held out his arms to Margaret, who picked him up and jiggled to comfort him.

"Stay inside," Mother said, "and keep the little ones with you. I have to help with the brigade."

"What's burning?" Carrie asked, lifting the quilt so the twins could climb under.

"The quarry office."

Margaret's heart battered her ribs so hard that Tommy must have felt the thumping. "I'm coming with you," she said. "Carrie can watch the boys." She let her brother slide from her arms onto the bed and reached into the pocket of her nightshirt for Angelo's carving. Her finger found the rough, broken part.

Mother frowned, then nodded.

"Be careful," Carrie said.

They grabbed the metal buckets hanging by the door and hurried down Main Street. The air was harsh with smoke, and the bucket brigades were at work. Mother joined Father in the longer line snaking up from the public pump at the dock. Margaret found two classmates at the rain cistern near the church and pressed into line between them.

"They say a bomb started the fire," one girl said.

"No one would do that the night before payday," her friend interrupted. "Now they'll close the quarry for sure."

Taking shallow breaths against the smoke and the nausea, Margaret dunked her bucket deep into the cistern, and pulled it out sloshing with water to pass down the line.

The bomb couldn't have anything to do with Angelo or his union, could it? Not possible, since he and the other foreign stoneworkers had been sent back to Europe. Margaret moved down the line, closer to the blaze where two men dragged cartons of burning papers from the building and others doused them with water. Grabbing buckets, passing them along, she tried to think about the granite company and her father's job, but her own ruin engulfed her. How could Angelo have allowed the quarry company to deport him, leaving her alone to face the shame of the next few months, and forever?

Another small explosion flashed, and the fountain of flames forced the islanders back for a moment. The blaze sizzled briefly with each splash of water before surging hotter and bigger. Sparks danced with the flames before floating into the night sky.

# THURSDAY

## SEPTEMBER 8

# 1. GANDALF, 8:06 A.M.

Her name is ridiculous. All because her pregnant mother clung to sanity during six weeks of forced bed rest by reading *The Hobbit* and eating lime jello. Gandalf despises jello and rarely uses her given name. She is Professor Cohen at work and Gee to acquaintances, but there is no way to avoid the absurdity of her first name when confronted with bureaucracy.

"Please have your photo ID and boarding pass available," repeats the TSA clerk.

Gandalf shuffles six inches forward in line. Maybe this clerk only reads nineteenth century Persian novels and has never heard of Tolkien, but that is probably too much to hope for, even at JFK.

On the large-screen monitor, CNN hypes Hurricane Gena, now turning north as it approaches the Florida coast. At work, Gandalf has been gathering data on its path. What a pity she will be away from New York when it storms through. Not to mention ironic that most of the top weather mathematicians in the country are heading to the Ann Arbor conference and will miss the fun. Assuming the teenager bumping his rolling suitcase into the back of her legs does not sever an Achilles tendon, the biggest excitement of the trip is likely to be academic backbiting.

She hands her documents to the security clerk, who scans the bar code on her driver's license and waits, tapping his fingers on the wooden podium. An amber light flashes. The clerk glances from license to boarding slip, passes them to the officer who appears at his elbow, then finally looks at Gandalf.

"What's up, Wizard?" He drops his gaze from her cropped, graying hair to her chest. His smile is provocative, bordering on offensive; it is the kind of look she does not tolerate from a colleague or a student, but this man is not worth challenging. "Hey," he adds. "Isn't Gandalf supposed to be a guy?"

Gandalf forces a small smile; it never helps to show annoyance. She follows the guard's pointing finger to the short line on the far left. Travel has become infuriating, especially in the lead-up to the anniversary of the Twin Towers on Sunday, but this will be over shortly. After she clears Security, she will find her gate, leave Jess a reminder message about tomorrow's vet appointment, and settle down with another cup of coffee to review the equations for her talk. She lifts her carry-on and pocketbook onto the conveyer belt, then arranges her laptop, sandals, and quart bag of bottled liquids in the plastic box with her watch and phone.

"Move inside the scanner, please." The guard's eyes never leave the monitor screen.

Gandalf steps onto the bright green feet decals on the raised platform and the scanner doors close behind her. A humming fills the small chamber, more vibration than sound. She has heard rumors that these machine images are so precise they have triggered a new pornography sideline. It is creepy that a machine can digitally undress you and you do not even feel a breeze. Not that images of her stringy sixty-year-old body are likely to bring big bucks at cyber-auction.

When the whirring stops, when the doors slide open and Gandalf steps through to gather her luggage, two airport cops on Segways block her path. They are twin studies in brown: dark cocoa pants, deep beige shirts, and the hue of their faces halfway between the two. Gandalf suppresses a smile; it is hard to take cops on scooters seriously.

A third officer wearing blue nitrile gloves steps forward and speaks in a low voice. "Come with me, ma'am."

Gandalf glances at her left wrist, at the pale band of skin where her watch would be if it were not with her other belongings at the security station. Relax, she tells herself. There is plenty of time before her flight. Swinging her arms, she follows the officer down a narrow hallway, past a female TSA employee moving a wand up and down the body of a teenage girl in Muslim dress and headscarf. How odd it feels, how naked, to be in an airport unencumbered by computer or rolling bag. Or shoes. Or notes for her lecture.

She turns to the officer. "Please, I need my bags."

"They're being evaluated."

Evaluated? Does that mean searched? "Why?"

The officer takes Gandalf's elbow and steers her around the corner towards a white metal enclosure. "Just routine."

Gandalf takes a deep breath and lets it out slowly. This does not feel routine. It does not feel like a joke because of her name either, like the time in Montreal when a Tolkien fan decided to have some fun. At the entrance to the enclosure Gandalf stops and turns to face the officer.

"What is going on?" She keeps her voice calm, professorial.

"I don't know, lady. Someone must've flagged your name."

"Someone?"

"Homeland Security."

She almost laughs with relief; it is so clearly a mistake. "That is not possible. I'm a mathematics professor."

"Just following protocol. Step inside, ma'am."

Gandalf shakes her head. "No. I demand to be told what is going on."

Is that a smirk that flashes across the officer's face, or maybe she imagines it.

"Sorry, Ma'am. Under the Terrorist Screening Database regulations, I am not allowed to give you any further information."

"Then I must speak with your supervisor."

"Certainly." He opens the door of the white enclosure and gestures. "After you."

Once she is inside, the officer shuts the metal door behind her, cutting off the small familiar sounds of airport business. She stands alone in the center of the silent room. It is the size of a small screen tent advertised in the Sunday paper, a place to enjoy suburban backyard picnics without the mosquitoes. She taps a fingernail against the wall. Metal. This tent will heat up quickly in the summer sun; it is already uncomfortably warm.

The back door snaps open and two soldiers enter in full battle gear, guns and masks. Before she fully registers the threat, one soldier grabs both of her wrists. He holds them together behind her back, binding them tight enough to hurt. It does not feel like metal handcuffs, something plastic. The second soldier faces her, his cornflower blue eyes lock with hers for a moment. She opens her mouth to call for help, but he covers her mouth with a gloved hand.

"Don't," the soldier behind her commands in a gravelly voice. When she nods, the blue-eyed man removes his hand.

She twists her shoulders side to side, pulling against the wrist restraints, but the only effect is that her fingers tingle. When she stops, the circulation returns. The soldier behind her still grips her shoulders. She kicks backwards, feeling her heel connect with his shin. He grunts.

The soldier in front places his boot across her feet, pinning her bare toes. Now she cannot move any limbs. He holds a black cloth in both hands. In the moment before he pulls it over her head, she stares again into his eyes, promising herself that she will never again tolerate that shade of blue. Then everything is dark. Her feet throb even after he removes his boot, but the pain bothers her less than the hood snugged taut around her neck. She breathes fast, deep, sucking air into her lungs and her heart races. Will she be able to get enough oxygen through the fabric?

The soldier behind her places a hand firmly against Gandalf's back. "Move."

His raspy voice is like the troll persona Jess uses to read *The Three Billy Goats Gruff* to her grandson. Gandalf closes her eyes and recites quietly, mimicking Jess's singsong cadence. "Who's that tripping over my bridge?"

"Shut up." The gravelly voice guard pushes her forward.

Do not panic, Gandalf instructs herself. If you cannot use your eyes, use your brain. She will name this guard Troll, the other one Blue Eyes. She will keep track of everything; she will memorize every detail of these people, so that later she can make a full and accurate report to the authorities.

Troll shoves again and Gandalf stumbles forward. Her feet ache; they feel scraped raw from Troll's boots. Without sight, her balance is more off kilter than she would have expected. A door squeaks open and she is pushed through. Outside. The September sunlight burns miniscule bright squares through the coarse weave of the hood. Her bare feet find soft grass and shuffle over the uneven ground. Her head spins. Dizzy. Probably from breathing too fast, hyperventilating; that explains why her ears are buzzing and her lips tingling. She tries to slow her respirations, to gain control. She tries to take small measured breaths, but the attempt sticks in her lungs and grows into a lump of dread that sucks up every molecule of available air. The dark panic bursts, explodes in her chest and the pieces of it spiral around her throat. She is going to die, to asphyxiate. She will never rub the silky fur under Sundance's chin again, or make love to Jess.

No. She will *not* give in to fear. Breathe slowly. Use her senses and her brain. She notes the stale coffee on her breath, trapped by the hood and mixed with the tang of fear. She must think clearly, make a plan, and extricate herself from this mess. It is all a mistake, of course, but where are they taking her and why? Jess will call someone if she does not hear from

Gandalf tonight. Where is her phone, her laptop, the galleys for her article? Breathe. And what about her presentation tomorrow? Sandra and Ahmed will be furious if she does not give the paper. Breathe. Jess will be worried, but she will take care of it. Who do you call in a case like this? The airport? The hospitals? And what kind of case *is* this, anyway? Breathe.

The pressure on her back ceases suddenly. A hand grasps her upper arm and guides her up two short steps, pushes her onto a seat, warm like leather through her pants. Another hand grips her elbow.

"Got her." A female voice this time and the turbulence in her chest lessens a notch.

The grinding of gears drowns out Troll's response. They lurch forward, then settle into a slow, bumpy motion like the golf cart her father used to drive at Leisure World. Gandalf wants to laugh at how Mickey-Mouse it feels, except she is not at all sure her constricted throat can manage any sound at all. And ridicule, laughing at these people whomever they are, probably will not help the situation.

The ride ends shortly with an abrupt stop. Someone grips her arm, pulling her up a short flight of metal stairs, hot under her bare feet. She stumbles and trips, stubbing her big toe. Then she is out of the sunlight, walking on carpet, pushed around a corner and down into an upholstered seat. Her hands are released from behind her back, but the right one is immediately bound to an armrest. Her free left hand reaches across her body and feels along the upholstered wall to the plastic window. Think deductively, she tells herself. She is at an airport, so this is likely a plane, too small to warrant a jetport.

"Keep your hand in your lap, or I'll have to tie it down," her captor says, leaning over Gandalf to fasten the seatbelt across her waist. The guard's hair brushes against Gandalf's hood; it smells of fruity shampoo. Peach maybe? No, it is apricot. A series of small clicks and rustles must be the woman settling in her seat, against the background racket of propellers revving.

"Hey," Gandalf makes her voice friendly. Maybe Apricot-shampoo will respond, woman to woman. "Do you want to switch seats? The window is wasted on me. Unless, of course, you are planning to remove this hood."

"No talking."

Is it wishful thinking or does Gandalf detect a very small smile hidden behind those terse words? She has to find out what is happening to her and Apricot is the only available source of information. Her chemist mother, when she wasn't flying off to lecture about the dangers of Strontium-90 in the milk supply, taught Gandalf three social graces: Mind your manners. Hold your temper. Honey catches more flies than vinegar. Gandalf teased her mother about the lack of scientific evidence on which to base her assumptions, but her mother insisted science did not hold all the answers. Over the years Gandalf has accepted her mother's tenets, modifying the third to include humor. Not that there is anything at all funny about this.

Keeping her voice light, Gandalf turns towards her seatmate. "Is this rendition? I thought Obama outlawed that. Are you taking me to Egypt?"

"I said, no talking."

Her voice sounds young, more nervous than angry, so Gandalf continues. "I am not dressed properly. Don't I need an orange jumpsuit to go with my black hood?"

"Shut up."

Gandalf closes her eyes and leans her head against the window. The plane taxies, accelerates, then takes off steeply. Her belly lurches. The dense dark under the hood magnifies every runway bump, every small dip, every minuscule readjustment of the wings. As the small plane banks into a steep turn to the right, Gandalf's breaths come faster, pulling the coarse cloth back and forth against her nostrils. She cannot stop herself. She unclasps the armrest with her left hand and reaches towards Apricot until she finds her arm. She clutches the smooth cotton of a uniform sleeve.

"Please help me," she whispers. "I'm frightened."

## 2. AUSTIN, 8:28 A.M.

Too bad you're scared, Austin thinks. Guess you should have thought of that before you did whatever you did. I'm your guard, not your therapist.

The prisoner is strong for someone old enough to be a grandmother. Well, the hood makes it hard to tell how old she is, but the empty sleeve of flesh on her bony inner arm jiggles just like Gran's. No matter what her age, Austin isn't crazy about holding hands with the woman. Not crazy about any of this, really, but she'll do her job and deliver the detainee securely to Special Agent Henry Ames. She glances at the soldiers in the forward seat. They're ignoring her. What's the harm in letting the old lady use her arm for a security blanket for a minute?

This kind of situation wasn't covered in training. The camp was designed to detain dangerous citizens in national emergencies. This assignment doesn't make sense. Homeland Security is about terrorists. There's nothing in the manual about picking up old ladies who look totally harmless and utterly clueless, certainly nothing about a detainee sniveling. Whole thing is a waste of taxpayer time and money—that's what Pops would say—paying one green-as-grass female guard and two military escorts to bring in one grandma.

"Treat her with kid gloves," Special Agent Ames ordered early that morning at the mission briefing. "She's a mathematician."

"I flunked algebra. Twice," she warned Henry Ames. "I did fine with geometry though, where I could see the shapes. Triangles and rhomboids, you know?"

He'd waved her explanations away, not interested in her high school failures. "Just help the men pick her up and deliver her here in one piece."

"Why are we bringing her in?" Austin asked.

Ames looked at her sternly. "Do you remember the 'need to know' rule?" She nodded. "Good," he said. "Just do your job."

When the plane levels, the prisoner loosens her grip. Austin pulls her arm free.

"Sorry," the prisoner says. Her voice quivers, then she sighs loudly. The air from her mouth blows a small bulge in the front of her hood. It looks really silly, and Austin wishes there was someone to point it out to, to share a laugh with. But forget the soldiers and there's no one else.

Austin is relieved when the prisoner rests her hooded head against the window and is silent. Maybe she's sleeping, though that's hard to believe. At least she's quiet and that's good, because Austin isn't sure how to respond if the prisoner tries to talk to her again. Fraternization is a big no-no, although she's not clear exactly what it includes. She worries that she might have stepped over the line with the other female prisoner, Norah. Just making polite small talk or answering an innocent question in the exercise yard— does that count?

In her three-week training course Austin learned how to overpower and neutralize an aggressive prisoner. SDI: Subdue, Disarm, Immobilize. Transporting with minimum public attention. How to secure, catalog, and safely transport their effects. Effects—what a stupid word for a person's suitcase and pocketbook and computer and stuff. Still, Austin twists around to check that the prisoner's effects are safe on the seat behind her.

She wonders what the prisoner's face looks like under the hood. That's probably irrelevant, but sometimes this whole job feels so lame, so far away from how she wants to live. Not that she knows exactly what she's looking for, but whatever it is, it's not on the island and not in Maine. If she can stick with this for a few months, she'll save enough money to go someplace else, Texas probably. Pops thinks that Texas is a stupid idea, but he makes fun of this job too, even though he's the one who pointed out the Help Wanted ad in the first place.

"It's not like you're in the Army," he likes to remind her, touching his shoulder which still aches in damp weather thanks to the Vietcong's shrapnel gift. "Not like this is a real war."

Thinking about Pops and Gran and home, Austin closes her eyes for a minute.

"May I have some coffee?" The prisoner's voice jerks Austin awake.

"You think this is some demented Starbucks?"

"I'm sorry."

Austin squirms. She's a soft touch when anyone apologizes, maybe because her mother has never, not once in twenty-five years, said she's sorry. Even for not marrying Austin's father or for dumping a four-year-old to live with her grandparents.

It can't hurt to give the old lady some coffee, can it? Special Agent Ames said to treat the prisoner well. The soldiers in the front seat have coffee. She smelled it walking by their seat. If she asks, they'll most likely give her a cup. But they'll probably notice if she gives it to the prisoner and might tell on her.

"I don't have coffee," Austin says softly. "How about water instead?"

"Thank you." The prisoner's voice is ripe with tears.

Austin isn't good with people crying either. She positions the water bottle in the prisoner's free hand, but oops. How is she supposed to drink wearing that hood thing? Why does she need it, anyway? She'll see their faces soon enough. Austin glances at the soldiers—they aren't paying attention to her or the prisoner. One guy, Sam or Stan or something, is studying a porn magazine, his thick thumb smearing the ink of an astonishingly large boob. What an asshole. Cyrus, the one with freckles and blue eyes, is Gran's cousin but that doesn't mean he wouldn't rat her out. He's Army through and through, Pops says, like it's a virtue. Cyrus slouches in his seat, automatic rifle cradled across his chest. She fingers the grip of her pistol. It's not fair that civilian recruits are issued less firepower. They all do the same job. And she doesn't even get to carry her gun most of the time. Cyrus jerks awake from the edge of dozing, then closes his eyes again.

"For just a minute," Austin says, reaching across the prisoner to lower the window shade. She unfastens the Velcro holding the cloth hood tight around the woman's neck and lifts the hood halfway, trying to keep her eyes covered. The woman's hair, half brown and half gray, stands straight out around her ears like a cartoon of a person scared to death. The prisoner tilts her head back to drink.

The engine noise changes and Austin raises the window shade enough to peer out. She must have really slept because they're already over the marshes north of Portland. Ahead, rocky fingers reach for the open ocean. The coastline is the only thing about this stupid state she'll miss when she moves to Texas. Six months of this job, tops, and she'll be able to get out.

"It sounds like the plane is descending." The prisoner's voice slides back into her joking tone. "That was too quick for Egypt. Where are you taking me?"

Austin gazes at the prisoner, wondering if the old woman can feel her pity. You don't want to know, Austin thinks. People say that Hurricane Island is bad news and always has been. Parents forbid kids to go there. Too dangerous, all those old steam engines and stone drills rusting in the bushes. Grandparents whisper it's cursed, because of how the town of Hurricane disappeared practically overnight, a gazillion years ago. Then that wilderness camp for rich kids bought the island and put up "No Trespassing" signs and they didn't last long either.

All the warnings and signs didn't keep her from playing hooky one spring day in high school and paddling over with her favorite cousin Gabe. But the forlorn bits of foundations and vacant cellar holes spooked her out.

"What happened to the houses?" she asked Gabe.

"People tore them down for the lumber."

The emptiness of the village was creepy, but swimming stoned in the quarry was magic, even more so when she found the linked initials carved in the cliff. Playing hooky that day was worth the worst punishment she ever got from her grandparents. Gran was furious about Austin going to the little island but wouldn't explain why. She wouldn't answer Austin's questions about the initials either, even though she looked like she knew something. Her face paled when Austin questioned her and then she left the room. "Let it be," Pops said.

"Where are we going?" the prisoner asks again. Maybe she can feel Austin's pity, because all joking is wrung from her voice.

She'll get her answer soon enough. Austin grabs the bottle, sloshing the last bit of water onto the prisoner's shirt, and shoves it into the seatback pocket. Give people an inch, like Pops always says. She knows she's being rougher than necessary when she pulls the hood back over the prisoner's head and secures it tight. But what does the woman expect? She should have thought about the consequences of whatever she did, beforehand.

"My shoes," the woman says. "I need them."

Making the woman walk around barefoot isn't right. In fact, it's a kind of mistreatment. But Austin is hired as a guard, not a social worker. She leans across the prisoner to slide up the window shade, revealing the edge of ragged coastline and the empty expanse of water. Directly north of the bay's wide mouth, the Three Sisters Islands cluster like misshapen poison ivy leaves. Pops says they're perfectly located for maximum storm damage.

The plane circles to the north and descends. Austin has never seen The Sisters like this before, from above. On Lily Haven, wide-porched summer homes tucked along private coves are linked by gravel lanes and flanked by jewel-tone rectangles of tennis courts and swimming pools. Banking steeply to the south, they fly over the biggest island. Storm Harbor bustles with marine traffic—lobster boats and fishing craft, the ferry to the mainland, a few kayaks gliding single file along the sheltered western shore. A large tidal basin sprawls across the southern third of the land, filling and emptying to the heartbeat of the tides. Austin spots her grandparents' house beyond the town dock, down the street from the school where Gran used to teach.

Hidden behind Storm Harbor's spruce covered hills, the much smaller Hurricane Island comes into view. If Austin squints, Hurricane looks like a girl running away from her sisters—hair blowing, baggy pants billowing in the wind. The plane dips sharply, passing over the one-wharf harbor sitting in the small of the girl's back. The prisoner gasps and clutches both armrests so tightly that the fan of tendons stands up on the backs of her hands.

"Are we landing?"

"Soon," Austin whispers, not sure if that should be comforting or not. Below, a single road leads uphill from the dock—along the girl's waist—with empty foundations and crumbled stonewalls bearing witness to the town that once flourished. Just beyond, in a tight square behind razor wire topped walls, squats the square building of the detention center. To the right are woods, and then the deserted quarry with tall granite cliffs that catch the September sunlight and smolder orange. From this height, the quarry looks insignificant and nowhere near immense enough to contain all her sorrows about Gabe and the initials.

"Please. Where are we?"

The runway comes into view along the backbone of the island's ridge. Austin isn't crazy about landings either. She tries to make her voice sound tough.

"I told you—no talking."

# 3. HENRY, 12:14 P.M.

Special Agent-in-Charge Henry Ames stands at his open window on the second floor of the administration wing. There's no evidence of the hurricane yet. No sound or sight of the airplane yet, either, but he might as well head up to the airstrip. He logs off the secure computer network and sets the encryption program. Good thing he'll have time to process the new prisoner before the hurricane hits.

Professor G. Cohen. He supposes he's ready for her, whoever she is. That morning he visited the women's wing and personally inspected her cell, still smelling of sawdust. The Washington guys think it's easy, rehabbing a decrepit Adventure Camp, making a secure facility from flimsy construction. City folk have no clue what the damp air does to buildings. Let *them* try to deal with wood so rotten a child could kick out the windows.

He rubs his fist against his sternum, pushing away the smoldering ache. Better take a couple of antacids before it gets too bad. He'd be less stressed if the Washington guys weren't so stingy with their information. He likes to know what is coming, not flying blind like this. Why are they interrogating this Dr. Cohen? Too bad she's not a medical doctor; he could ask her about his heartburn. All he knows is that she's a mathematician, an expert on something related to triangles and hurricanes, and that he is supposed to treat her with kid gloves. Mathematics? That just doesn't make any sense, but Henry doesn't dare ask the Regional Chief for more background. Everyone is more antsy than usual, just like every year when the anniversary of 9/11 approaches.

Making a mental note to have someone oil the rusty hinges on his office door, Henry steps into the second floor hallway. Against his strong objections, the disaster gurus at FEMA contracted with a company from the mainland to renovate the rickety building. Henry warned them that a local firm would do better work, cheaper too, but the Chief insisted it would generate less gossip.

As if the entire population of the Three Sisters Islands isn't already spinning yarns about what's going on half a mile off Storm Harbor. They all explored the little island as kids, as fascinated by their parents' prohibitions as by the ruined village and abandoned machinery. The juicy rumor that this godforsaken place, infamous for an anarchist bombing, was chosen for Maine's only civilian detention center is probably wagging tongues and sparking gossip from the suits in Augusta to the crunchy granolas in Blue Hill. There's no way to keep this secret, not with Homeland Security's unholy trinity of the Bureau and Army and FEMA running the camp, plus the tactical necessity of liaising with the local sheriff. Damn stupid Washington guys have no clue. It probably makes sense to have the Army doing Security, but FEMA in charge of Operations? Because they did so well with the trailers?

One flight down, Henry pauses at the foot of the staircase and listens for the airplane. Still nothing. Hopefully the two soldiers assigned to capture Dr. Cohen are competent; he hates working with personnel from other agencies. You don't know their capabilities and can never be certain where their loyalties lie. And Austin Coombs, his new civilian employee on this mission, isn't a known quantity yet either. But what choice does he have? When his only female guard quit suddenly, he had to hire and quickly. The previous guard said the pay was good, but the idea of the camp just didn't sit right with her. Hopefully the generous severance package and gag agreement will keep her mouth shut.

At least Ms. Coombs is Three Sisters born and bred, even if her father was from away, and her mom left her for the grandparents to raise up. The grandmother is a Carter, a distant cousin of Cat's, which counts for a lot. Henry's own family is from Bangor, so he'll always be "from away" even though he moved to the island in ninth grade and graduated from the three-room schoolhouse where Austin's grandmother taught. The girl seems strong, compact and sturdy, and the role is mostly babysitting. Once he insisted that she remove the nose ring and pin her hair back, she looks respectable enough, but why would a girl like Austin want a job like this?

A distant mosquito whine emerges in the southwest sky and deepens into engine noise. Henry hurries by the staff barracks and mess hall to the gravel road, passing the abandoned steam engine used to drill granite a hundred years ago. He slows, out of respect or something, as he walks by the ruins of the old quarry office, destroyed by an anarchist's firebomb and now blanketed by vines. At the top of the hill is the narrow airstrip, slashed from the granite spine of the small island. He argued against that too; there is a perfectly good airport on Storm Harbor. But Army, Homeland Security, and FEMA all insisted that the camp needed its own secure and private landing strip.

Henry stops in the shadow of the spruces at the edge of the field. The day lilies are shriveled brown stalks, but fireweed is in bloom and the season's last raspberries are ripe. He appreciates the natural beauty of the place, but that doesn't mean he forgives the Bureau for this posting. They refused to listen six months ago when he tried to explain that heading up a civilian detention center is not a lateral transfer from running the Bangor office. It's a demotion, pure and simple.

"It's your assignment, Henry," the Regional Chief said. "You know the island. You know the people. We need you there to get things running smoothly, and keep them moving securely."

Remembering the brief, nasty flicker of a smile at the right side of the Regional Chief's mouth reignites the gnawing behind Henry's breastbone. He's probably being paranoid; none of the Bureau guys has ever said anything to suggest that they know, except that one time at the Bangor Tavern. They were celebrating the joint case with the Mounties and the Regional Chief let the nickname slip, spoken in a rude tone: *Hen*. Female, chicken, and full of innuendo.

The plane is now eagle-sized, visible above the treetops to the south. Henry burrows two fingers under his tie, into the space between his shirt buttons, and rubs the gnawing ache behind his sternum. Female detainees pose all sorts of logistical challenges. That's why he had to hire Austin, but maybe the girl isn't up to it. Whatever *it* is, when he figures out what the Bureau needs from the Cohen woman. They will sure tell him PDQ if he doesn't get the info they want. This crap sure isn't what he anticipated when he joined up thirty years ago during graduation week, at the job fair table the Bureau shared with military recruiters.

As the twin-engine plane bumps down the runway to a stop, Henry waves to the mechanics waiting with the portable stairs. No, this assignment isn't what Henry wants, or what he deserves, but he damn well isn't going to screw it up.

He joins Tobias at the edge of the airstrip. Tobias was his second-in-command in Bangor, and Henry brought him along as camp facilities manager. Sometimes the man's zeal makes Henry uneasy, but there's no one he trusts more, which isn't saying a whole lot. He wishes he had a good friend at work, someone to really talk to and depend on.

Together they watch the hooded prisoner start down the metal steps escorted by the two soldiers. Having her hands cuffed behind her back throws her off balance, and she teeters on each step, tapping her bare foot tentatively before trusting her weight to it. It's asinine to keep the hood in place, but it's protocol. Henry probably would do the same himself.

"Orders are, not too rough with this one." Henry wishes he didn't have to say that out loud.

Tobias clears his throat. "Where do you want her?"

"Room 4, Women's Wing."

"Next door to the black bitch?" Tobias says. "But they'll talk to each other."

"Curb your mouth and use your brain. I *want* her to contact Ms. Levinsky."

"Then why not put her in Room 3? Roomies."

"Because then she'd *know* we wanted them to talk." Henry turns away, disgusted. Tobias seems incapable of subtle thinking.

On the bottom step the prisoner stumbles, falling to her knees on the rough tarmac. The soldiers jerk her upright. Henry walks towards her.

"Bring me her shoes," he orders the soldiers. "We'll take her from here."

The prisoner's voice is muffled through the hood. "Where am I? No one will tell me anything."

"Their orders were to bring you here. Not to answer your questions."

"Are you in charge?" she asks. "Can you tell me where I am?"

Henry smiles, even though she can't see it. Being the boss is the one saving grace of this despicable assignment.

"Yes, Dr. Cohen." He grips her arm. "I'm in command of this facility. You're on Hurricane Island."

## 4. GANDALF, 12:22 P.M.

Her knees sting like crazy, but she forgets the pain when he says Hurricane Island. The name does not ring any geographic bells, but the irony is not lost on her: she has spent most of her professional life studying hurricanes. Where is this place? It is impossible to know for certain without her watch, but the flight must have been three hours. Putting the point of an imaginary compass on JFK and scribing a guesstimate circle on a mental map, she must be in northern New England or upstate New York, on the coast or a lake big enough to contain Hurricane Island.

She rubs the bottom of one bare foot against the other shin to dislodge an annoying pebble and breathes deeply. Even through the hood the air smells moist and vaguely marine. The coast then: probably Maine.

She turns in the direction of the man holding her arm, wishing more than light and shadow were visible through the weave of the fabric. Someone else is standing nearby; she can sense the dark shape of his presence. And the man in charge said "we" a moment before, indicating at least one other person. She inhales and exhales slowly, trying to banish the terror constricting her throat.

Footsteps thump on the rough asphalt, then Troll's gravelly voice. "Her shoes, sir."

"Thank you. Dismissed," the man in charge says. When the footsteps fade, he unhooks the Velcro fastening and lifts the front edge of the hood so she can see the asphalt runway. He drops her shoes.

"You can put them on." His voice is quiet, not unkind.

She slips her feet into the sandals and crouches down to adjust the straps. That makes her knees burn again, and she glances at the speckles of blood. Just a scrape, nothing to worry about. Not now, when there is so much worse that can happen.

She turns towards him. "Why have you brought me here?" She tips her head back to peek at him and glimpses an ordinary face, not particularly cruel or vicious.

"Hey. You can't do that," yells a new voice, an angry voice. A hand grabs her shoulder and another yanks the hood down, pulling the Velcro tight around her neck. Her shoulders tense, and her throat constricts again. What if she can't breathe?

"Take it easy." The man in charge loosens the fastener.

She does not need vision to perceive the tension between the two men; it ignites a silent electric charge in the air. She waits, very still, alert and listening, feeling the hairs on her arms standing erect. When the angry man's shadow steps back, she turns towards the man in charge.

"Please," she asks. "What is going on? What *is* this place?"

"A civilian detention center." He drops his grip on her elbow, and she feels him turn away. "No more questions."

A rough hand grips her arm and tugs her along the tarmac and down a long hill. Her escort does not speak to her; she does not ask him anything either, knowing he will not answer. Her throat aches too much to speak anyway. They enter a building, climb one flight of stairs, then stop.

The angry man unlocks a door and kicks it open with his foot. Unfastening the Velcro, he pulls the hood from her head quickly while shoving her into the room, then slams the door closed, all without speaking a word. She has no chance to see his face but does catch a glimpse of the number four on the doorframe, a gold-plated number that could have come from a bin in the Home Depot, designed for a small house on a tree-lined street instead of a prison.

What is a civilian detention center?

She leans back against the door and looks around, but Room 4 does not divulge any answers. It is bigger than a jail cell, at least the ones on television, with a cot and chair on the left-hand wall, a toilet and sink to her right. A pink plastic trashcan is tucked under the sink; she despises pink. Opposite the door, the outside wall has a single barred window. She drags the chair against the wall and climbs up, but can see only blue sky and puffy clouds.

The view is not exactly up to bed & breakfast standards, but she is getting a good rate. She hugs herself, rocking back and forth to interrupt the shaking. "Nurture your sense of humor," she whispers.

She can do that, but she must also keep track of everything, so that she will be able to make a full report to the authorities, later. She has not gathered much data yet. There are two military guys, Blue Eyes and Troll; the female guard, Apricot; the kind-voiced man in charge with his ordinary face; and his subordinate, Angry Man. Not much to go on yet, but she will not let them get away with this.

She walks in a tight circle around the room. Three strides from door to sink, another two to the chair at the window, three more to the bed, and a final three return her to the door. She repeats the circuit. Her brain is sharper when her body moves, and it relaxes her, though it drives Jess crazy. In the evenings, Jess likes to read curled up on the sofa next to Sundance, in a nest of pillows and purring fur. Gandalf paces the apartment, back and forth, her mind racing.

The ache in her throat returns. Right now she would give anything to cuddle with Jess and Sundance. She regrets all the times she was less demonstrative than Jess wanted, wishes she had been able to make Jess happier, maybe even gotten married. If only she could talk to Jess right now. Jess might even know something about civilian detention centers, since she tends to see conspiracies in the random malicious and ill-considered acts of the government. Or maybe it is an occupational hazard; Jess is a literature professor, and she appreciates a well-crafted narrative arc with a strong plot.

Gandalf stops pacing to rattle the doorknob, to examine the heavy-duty hinges and the small heat vent in the ceiling. Climbing again to the window, she grabs the bars and shakes hard, but there is no give. The window is too small to fit through anyway, even if she could remove the grating.

There is no way out of this room, and she will never see Jess again.

No, she tells herself, do not go there. She breaks off her pacing and probing to sit on the narrow bed. She lets her head sink into the cushion of her hands, tries to stop their trembling.

She must figure this out: who are these people and why did they bring her here? It is all an error, of course, and there must be a logical explanation, such as mistaken identity or a computer glitch. But how can she convince her captors of that fact?

# 5. RAY, 12:25 P.M.

Coffee cup in one hand and Fig Newtons in the other, Ray Coombs waits in the shade of the carport off the kitchen door, even though his granddaughter won't be home for hours. Deep blue with puffy clouds, the sky offers no hint of the storm barreling up the coast. He lived through Edna in '54, so he knows how bad it can be. But today his worry-thoughts are stuck on Austin, not the weather.

The mail jeep sputters to a stop in front of the house and Jeannette half-lifts her fingers off the steering wheel in greeting. He walks across the yard while Jeannette digs around in the plastic carton on the seat. She passes a slim pile of envelopes through the open window.

"How're you and Nettie?" Jeannette asks.

"No complaints. You folks?" Jeannette is married to his wife Nettie's cousin Cyrus who's a sergeant in the Army. Ray isn't crazy about career military types, but Cyrus is family and he's stationed at the whatever-it-is out on Hurricane.

"Hanging in there," Jeannette says.

"Good." Ray looks away. It's not nice to pump her for information, but he's got a bad, bad feeling about that place. Maybe Cyrus has talked to Jeannette about the facility.

"And that granddaughter of yours?" Jeannette asks.

"Fine, I guess. You know she's working out on Hurricane?"

Jeannette nods.

Maybe Cyrus can keep an eye on Austin over there. Family matters, even when folks aren't close. It's supposed to be a secret, but everyone knows that something big is going on over there and everyone has an opinion. Some folks welcome the jobs, saying that having a government project out there will erase the stain of the little island's history. Others hate the feds building something ugly on the land their great-grandfathers quarried, the place where fingers and arms and lives were lost. They argue that the facility is only located in their backyard because no one else wants it. "We'll regret this," they predict.

Behind him, the screen door squeaks. "Jeannette," Nettie calls from the stoop. "Can you take your lunch break?"

Jeannette glances at her watch, then nods, and turns off the motor.

Following her to the house Ray thumbs through the mail, by habit checking every return address for one of their daughter Abby's rare notes. He tosses the envelopes onto the kitchen table, then leans against the counter where he can watch the women. Nettie moves the mail, then pours two cups of coffee from the percolator, and tops off Ray's cup. She fills the china creamer with milk from the fridge.

"You ready for the bulb sale?" Nettie sits across from Jeannette. Ray thinks his wife is relying more on lip-reading these days.

"Working on it." Jeannette takes a sandwich from her lunch bag and unwraps it. "You hear anything recently from Abby?"

Ray's hand freezes on the mug handle, mid-air. Can letter carriers mind-read what people are searching for in their stacks of bills and junk mail? No. Jeannette and Abby went through school together and they used to be friends, that's all. He watches Nettie's face, hoping she'll talk about it. Maybe if he leaves the room, he thinks, and starts to push away from the counter but Nettie stops him with a glance.

"Not recently," he says.

"I miss her." Jeannette sips her coffee. "How's Austin doing with the new job?"

Nettie shakes her head. "Don't know. She says she's not allowed to talk about her work. I don't like it. It just tears me up, that she spends every day out *there*."

Ray tries to remember if Jeannette and Cyrus weighed in about the Hurricane Island facility one way or the other when it was being built. Cyrus usually has plenty of opinions and likes to share them. And he's ambitious. But he's probably forbidden to discuss Army business.

"What about Cyrus?" he asks. "What's he told you about that place?"

"Not a word," Jeannette says. "And you know that's not like Cyrus."

Ray opens the refrigerator. While the women's conversation turns back to the bulb sale to benefit the Land Trust, he eats leftover tuna salad from the plastic tub and tries to picture his girl as a prison guard.

Austin acts like she's doing him a favor, taking the job on Hurricane, but the opposite is true. He wishes she never signed on with those people. Nettie is mental about the island, even if half her family works over there. She blames him for Austin taking the job. True, he showed Austin the ad in the weekly paper, but he also pointed out the ad for a dishwasher at the new lobster restaurant for tourists out by Saperstein Neck, and the listing for a part-time clerk at the Historical Museum, even the one for a live-in nanny on Lily Haven. Austin turned up her nose pretty quick at that one. "Won't catch me wiping runny noses and butts for rich folks," she said in that snotty voice she started with at age four and perfected at puberty. Course there's worse jobs than mopping up after kids' messes, but she doesn't know that yet. And she's strong-willed, his girl. His granddaughter actually, but Nettie and he raised her after Abby walked out. Austin is more their daughter than her mother ever was. No, that's not quite true, but maybe raising Austin gave them a second chance, an opportunity to do a better job than they did with her mom.

Jeannette gets up to leave, and Ray walks her out. When he returns, Nettie still sits at the kitchen table, elbows planted on the placemat with drawings of scenic Maine lighthouses, a look of deep worry on her face.

Nettie wore that exact same expression a month before, after Austin announced that she'd accepted the job on Hurricane. Nettie went pale and squeezed her lips together until they pretty much disappeared, the way she does when trying to keep from saying what she's thinking. The way she does whenever Hurricane Island is mentioned.

"I figure six months, tops," Austin said. "Then I'll have saved enough for Texas."

That's another thing. Only natural that the girl misses her parents. But her cockamamie scheme to go find her dad in Texas, when the guy clearly doesn't want to be a father; that's heartbreak sure as winter.

"You've got lots of family right here," Nettie said.

Austin made a face. "That's part of the problem. So many cousins I can't keep them straight. And I don't have a single thing in common with any of them. Gabe was the only one I could stand and he's dead. These islands are full of losers."

Nettie squeezed Austin's arm. "I know how much you miss him."

"What about Evelina?" Ray said. "Is she a loser too?" Cousin Bert's daughter was their Congresswoman, local girl makes good.

Austin pushed back from the table. "You trot that woman out every time we have this conversation. I'm sick of hearing about her."

It was hard to argue with her, especially when he agreed with her about all those cousins. Sometimes, it felt great, like they were connected to something big and full of history. Other times, the extended family felt like a giant multi-winged and sharp-tongued albatross.

"I know you think I'm old-fashioned, but it's more than all those cousins," he told Austin that day, desperately wanting her to understand. "It's this place, this rocky, stormy, foggy, wild and unforgiving place. These islands are members of our tribe, part of our family tree. They're living organisms, and we don't just give up our own. Always been that way, even back in the early 1900s, with all the trouble on Hurricane. You belong here, Austin."

"Do I, Pops? What good is all that family to me, when I have no parents?"

Unable to look at his wife's face, Ray watched Austin take the uniform down and smooth the front of the beige button-down shirt. The girl didn't mean it. She didn't mean her words to come out sounding razor-sharp like that. When she left the room, he took Nettie's hand, limp on the table next to her crumpled napkin, and squeezed. He hadn't been able to think of a single word to make her feel better.


Jeannette honks twice as her jeep pulls away. Ray leans against the mailbox and stares at the muddy liquid in his mug. He doesn't know what tomfoolery they've got going on at Hurricane Island. And he can't come up with a single comforting thing to say to his wife about their girl taking Bert's ferry over there every day. Nettie hates the ill-fated little island with its overgrown spruce and alder groves, the forsaken quarry and rows of ruined stone houses. She believes Hurricane Island messed up her family a century ago, shamed them in the eyes of their community, and now it's going to somehow harm Austin. Maybe she's right, who knows? But, one thing he does know. He wishes he never showed Austin that ad in the paper.

# 6. AUSTIN, 12:37 P.M.

Austin carries the detainee's suitcase and computer bag to the splotchy shade of an alder grove just off the tarmac. She watches Tobias argue with Henry Ames and then march the old lady down the hill. Laughing, the two Army escorts walk towards the mess hall behind the still unpainted guard tower. The whole place feels half-baked, hovering between ghost town and military outpost.

Brushing a crinkly orange leaf off her uniform jacket, she waits. She's hungry, but doesn't know what to do with the prisoner's belongings. As a civilian employee among all the military and security staff, it's not clear where she fits in. At the bottom of the heap, most likely, expected to do what anyone tells her.

She has a niggling feeling about this job, an uneasy sick worry like the dread of a late period, and Tobias is a big part of the reason. Her skin sizzles when he is around—there's something bad-boy sexy about his square jaw and buzz cut and smirking energy. The other guards claim he's a genius at getting inside people's heads and ferreting out their secrets. Every time she looks at him, it seems like he's been watching her and that creeps her out big time. Still, maybe the scary feeling just goes with the territory. Interrogation is part of their work—questioning people who are dangerous to the government. But other than Tobias, in three weeks on the job she hasn't observed anything more exciting than a training DVD on sleep deprivation techniques. The acting was so bad the trainees treated it like a comedy until Henry Ames came in and scolded them.

"Coombs," Henry Ames calls her name from the tarmac. "I'll take those bags. After lunch, report to the Women's Wing. I want you with our professor during her interrogations."

At the mess hall, she buys a cheeseburger. She scans the six or seven employees in the room but there's no one she wants to sit with, especially not the two Army guys from the morning mission. She wraps the burger in a napkin, slips out the side door and across the road. To her right stands the kudzu-choked remains of the bombed-out quarry headquarters. It's an eyesore, even with the magenta flowers still blooming. Why haven't they torn it down? She turns away and takes the path through the woods. If she hurries she can eat by the quarry and still be back in time.

Emerging from the woods, she stops for a moment to look around, to breathe deeply. The afternoon sun ignites the gray-pink cliffs and releases the tang of spruce. The green water sparkles in the sunlight. Too bad quarry swimming is totally off limits to the camp staff. Grounds for immediate dismissal, Henry Ames warned in orientation. Austin walks along the path carved into the cliff face, thirty feet or so above the water level. There's no regulation against taking her lunch break away from the detention center, where other employees aren't likely to wander. She doesn't want to hang out with any of them. Besides, she's been thinking a lot about the initials these past weeks working out here, especially since early this morning, seeing the quarry from the air.

She isn't sure she can even find the initials again. It's been what—eleven years—since she was here with her cousin Gabe. Everything looks different now, smaller and shabbier. The rocky ledge seems narrower and the quarry water a little scummy. She eats and walks slowly, one hand skimming the sun-baked cliff. She studies the cliffs until the rock contours look familiar. She stops at a shallow gap in the rock, deep with shadows. That's the place.

Austin pops the last bite of burger into her mouth and feels inside the tapered crevasse. Nothing. Is her memory wrong? No, this has got to be the place. She reaches in again, a little further, sweeping her hand back and forth in an arc across the smooth stone, hoping no spiders have made their home there. With her arm fully extended and at chest level, her fingers touch the delicate ridges of the leaves, and trace the letters and numbers inside.

MEC + AF. 1914.

She was fourteen the day Gabe convinced her to skip school and paddle over to the little island. He was three years older and so cool. Leaning back against the cliff face, sleepy with the exertion of their swim and Gran's thick cheddar sandwich and the lingering effects of weed, she had raised her arms over her head and caressed the granite wall. She was sweeping her hands back and forth across the stone, wishing someone would touch her with such light fingers, when she felt the cooler stone in the narrow gap. Her fingers found the carving, and she tried to read it like Braille. She couldn't figure it out so she stood up and peered into the shadows to get a better look.

"Gabe," she called. "Over here."

He was dozing, stretched out along the ledge with his arm dangling down towards the water. He opened one eye. "What?"

In another setting, Gabe would have made a smart-ass remark about the carving, like hoping the artist—whoever he was—at least got laid. There were linked initials and Class of Whatever cut into stone all over the Three Sisters Islands. But these were different—the isolated spot for one thing. And 1914—they were so old, almost a century. Plus, Gabe said they were a class act. Like many of his generation, Gabe's great-grandfather had worked in the quarries as a young man, and Gabe was fascinated by the craft of sculpting stone. Even with part of the carved foliage broken off, the circle of intertwined branches and leaves was elegant, full of grace, like something you'd see in a museum. Gabe explained that instead of being cut into the cliff, the stone around the letters had been carefully chipped away. "That's called intaglio," Gabe said. "Someone with real skill carved this."

Austin usually ignored Gabe's history trivia, but the carving intrigued her. For weeks afterwards as she tried to fall asleep at night, she wove sleepy scenarios about the couple who made their affection last forever. Who were they and why was the carving in that place, in that shadowy nook of the quarry cliff, a spot so hidden you'd have to know it was there? Thinking about it made her feel weird, as if their love was a ghost message whispering to her from the distant past. And Gran's anger, her sorrow, about the place just added to the mystery. There was something important about the initials and the cave, and it was connected to her family.

"What happened in 1914?" she had asked Gabe.

"Did you sleep through history class?" he asked. "Ever heard of World War I?"

When he turned eighteen the next year, Gabe announced he was going to enlist and go to Iraq. She hated the idea of him as a soldier and argued so fiercely he finally told her to piss off, that someone had to stop the terrorists. After that, she had to rely on town gossip for news about his deployment. She hadn't had an email from him in months when she heard about the IED.

She still dreamed about Gabe's funeral—his dad Bert expressionless in the front row of folded chairs, the flag folded in a triangle, clutched against his chest. Gabe's girlfriend Lissa sat next to Bert and looked straight ahead. It was kind of spooky that Lissa's father Henry was now Austin's boss. Leaning forward in her seat, Austin had stared at a small clump of earth stuck to one of the white stars. She wasn't sure if she was allowed to touch the flag but the dirt bothered her so she reached to brush it off. Gabe's half-sister Evelina turned around and gave her a nasty look. Evelina wasn't elected to Congress or anything yet back then, just bossy.

After Gabe died, Austin didn't return to Hurricane Island, not even on Senior Skip Day when the class turned the quarry into their own private pool party. She could picture her classmates spreading their beach towels along the mammoth slabs of stone at the north end of the quarry, dropping fishing nets of beer cans into the deep water to keep them cold. She stayed home that day. It would have been a betrayal to party in Gabe's favorite place without him. Would have been a betrayal to Gran too, even though Gran won't ever talk about why she hates the little island so much.

The sun slides behind a cloud, and Austin shivers. Ironic that she ends up working here on the damned little island. But if she's ever going to get out of Maine, it'll take more than bagging groceries at the IGA. The need for a job overpowers the sad spookiness of the place. Checking her watch, she hurries along the ledge and through the woods. Tobias is fierce about punctuality. When she reported tardy to him the first day, when it wasn't even her fault because Special Agent Ames kept her late, Tobias's ears had flushed red as he explained the importance of being on time for duty.

He is waiting for her now on the porch of the Women's Wing, his face dark with anger.

# 7. TOBIAS, 1:14 P.M.

In the basement observation room, Tobias presses the console power button for Women's Barracks Room 4. He studies both views of the new detainee's cell on the split screen. Camera A, hidden in a knot on the pine doorframe, is aimed at the empty bed. From its vantage point at the center of a painted beach plum in the frame of the small mirror over the sink, Camera B provides a close-up of the prisoner. She stands at the sink, hands splayed over her face, staring at the mirror through the spaces between her fingers.

"Hand-painted mirrors?" Henry complained when Tobias brought him the requisition to sign. "This is a detention camp, not a country inn."

Tobias hates having to justify his tactics, especially to a thickheaded guy like Henry. "We need a decorated frame," he explained, censoring the annoyance out of his voice, "to hide the camera lens. Most prisoners stare into the mirror, even talk to themselves. But if you don't want top notch, we can just go with the one camera angle."

Reluctantly, Henry signed.

When Tobias zooms in for a close-up, the red blotches under the woman's eyes become clearly visible between her fingers. He sees the scrap of black fabric at the same moment she reaches for it and pulls it from her hair. It must come from the hood, because she tosses it into the trashcan with an expression of distaste and fury. She pulls up the legs of her khakis and examines her scraped knees, then turns on both taps. She frowns when the hot water knob spins without resistance.

"Sorry there's no hot water, or band aids and antiseptic in the medicine cabinet," he whispers to the monitor screen. "Complain to the management."

He checks the clock. He ordered the new girl to search the prisoner's effects and then come and report to him. Of course, he already examined everything himself. If you want something done right, do it yourself. His staff doesn't get that, not even the two Bureau guys, never mind the turkeys assigned to him by military intelligence. He hears their bitching that he hogs the surveillance camera assignments to himself. They think he's lazy, wants to just sit and watch a monitor, but it isn't that, not at all. He's the most qualified. He's the one the Regional Office sent to the Homeland Security course on advanced domestic surveillance techniques. It takes special training to be able to discover things from observation. Do those other guys know how to ID a terrorist by their gait? Bet they can't look at a suspect's stride length or how he swings his arms and determine if he's planning to blow up an embassy. Okay, so Tobias can't do that either, not yet, but he's working on it, and at least he knows it *can* be done.

Even Henry Ames doesn't understand the fine points of the surveillance-interrogation continuum. It's hard to treat the boss with deference when he doesn't command Tobias's respect. Henry simply lacks the hunger, the craving to know every detail that a really top-notch interrogator needs. Besides, how can you admire a man with such small feet? Tobias smirks to himself. Isn't that supposed to signify a small dick?

The prisoner hasn't moved. Tobias wishes she would sit on the bed, so he can switch Camera A to whole-screen mode. Maybe she'll cry, or take off her clothes or something interesting. Something revealing, he means, something that will help him get beyond the bitch's defenses. Henry calls her Dr. Cohen, as if polite address makes any sense here. Tobias prefers the tactic of taking away their names, stripping them of individuality, and assigning them numbers. When Tobias suggested the numbers, Henry wagged his index finger back and forth and reminded him that these are citizens, not enemy combatants. What's the difference; they're all dangerous, right?

So, he goes ahead and gives each detainee a number. A simple system based on the order in which they're interned. Starting at 500, so the population won't seem so puny. This one—Cohen—she's #524. That's how he labels the surveillance disks and that's how he thinks of her. That's how he will address her tomorrow or the next day, when the time is ripe to start the interrogation. Not too soon. You've got to make them wait. Make them worry about it until they *want* the questioning to start, crave it, so they don't have to wait anymore and because they think reality can't be worse than their fears.

Except, of course, it can be.

At the tentative knock on the door, Tobias puts both cameras on auto-record and turns off the monitors. Need to know: that's the Bureau's key rule about data security. He'll review the tapes later. Exquisite attention to detail, that's what leads to important breakthroughs in intelligence work.

He has no idea why Henry hired this Austin Coombs. She has no experience—not military, not Corrections, not even ROTC at the fourth-rate college listed on her application, where she dropped out before graduating. Just because her family is local, that's no reason to think she'll be useful. Of course, they need a female guard to babysit the female detainees, and she does look strong, though maybe that's just the hardy island stock. She's not really his type, with her olive skin and dark hair, but she has a great ass.

"Enter." Might as well see if she has any smarts at all.

Austin's glance goes immediately to the bank of monitors. Tobias smiles to himself. I'm too smart for you, green-girl, he thinks.

"Okay," he says. "What did you learn about #524 that might be useful in our interrogation?" Might as well train this one the right way.

Austin hesitates. "I think she's . . . you know, queer. I mean, gay."

Tobias looks at the girl. "Evidence?"

"Some photos on her laptop. And her emails, if you read between the lines and use a little imagination. She lives with someone named Jess."

Not bad.

"Could I ask you a question about this place?" She doesn't wait for his answer. "Why build the center here, on this island, instead of like in Egypt or someplace?"

"So we can detain and interrogate domestic terrorists quickly."

"But this place is so dinky." She blushes. "So small."

"Small is good. During the Japanese internment program, the biggest problems were at the larger camps where troublemakers could organize. We have dozens of facilities, easy to hide and easy to control, just like this one." He's proud of the network, all those men ready to keep the nation safe.

"But why not put them on military bases? They're already set up, with security and everything."

"The military has too many rules and regulations. We prefer more flexibility." He stands up. Enough questions.

"Just one more thing," Austin says. "I looked through the prisoner's suitcase and her computer, but her cell phone is gone. It was in her pocketbook when I took her off the plane, but it's not there now."

Damn. Where is it? And how did he miss that? He'll have to find it, before Henry discovers that a critical piece of evidence is missing.

# 8. GANDALF, 5:46 P.M.

It is hard work, not giving in to the sickening waves of apprehension, to the accelerating spirals of fear. Using her brain is her only hope for escape, so she will keep it sharp and agile by solving puzzles. Like determining the time of day: the slanting shadows, at least a 30-degree angle, suggest late afternoon, but then she gives up. Not knowing the latitude makes precision impossible. Whatever the time now, when 6 p.m. comes and goes, Jess will start worrying. Obsessing about exactly when that moment will arrive is marginally easier than anticipating what will happen in this room when it gets dark. There is no lamp, no visible switch on the wall or hanging chain to control the ceiling light fixture. Gandalf isn't exactly scared of the dark, that would be irrational, but at home Jess does not object to having a small night-light in the hallway.

She paces the room. How do people stay sane locked up with no work, no books, and no one with whom to share life? Before Jess, Gandalf would not have added that last necessity. Before Jess, she never understood all the commotion about falling in love; there were always women, and rarely men, available for the occasional get together. Then, sixteen years ago, she and Jess found each other wandering alone through the formal gardens at the university president's house. The mandatory September faculty reception meant two excruciating hours for anyone missing the gene for scholarly gossip or the inclination for brown-nosing. A week later she was in love and she finally did comprehend the fuss.

But until now, she has not begun to appreciate the enormity of the price of human connection. She cannot stop crawling around in Jess's mind, sharing her agony of imagined scenarios. When Gandalf does not call home and interrupt the evening news, Jess will begin imagining an accident. She will picture Gandalf lying at the bottom of a cliff among twisted metal airplane parts, in a ravine, bleeding and stunned with broken limbs akimbo. Or maybe abducted and held for ransom, her bound and gagged body hidden in a dank basement in a Detroit suburb, gagged with a dirty sock. Or even her slim corpse, raped and stuffed into the trunk of a yellow taxicab driving towards the river.

A new idea strikes her, and she sinks to the bed, unable to catch her breath. In addition to picturing all the accident scenarios, Jess might also be fighting off some very different fears: Gandalf lying on a blanket under a weeping willow with a lover she arranged to meet at the conference. Jess might wonder if there is really a conference or if it is all an elaborate deception. If Gandalf is breaking her heart, the way her ex-husband did. Gandalf rocks back and forth on the bed, as if she can stifle the possibilities by not speaking them.

"Pssst."

She must be imagining the noise, but it comes again. Pssst. The sound appears to originate in the floor. She looks around the perimeter of the room, low along the walls.

"Anyone there?" The whisper is louder this time; it comes from under the bed.

Gandalf leans forward until her hair touches the floor. Under the bed, in the center of the shadow where the wall meets the floorboards, is a darker space. Sloppy workmanship left a two or three centimeter gap between two boards in the pine molding.

Swallowing hard, Gandalf answers, "Who's there?"

"Norah. Who are you?"

"Gandalf."

There is silence for a moment. "Is that a code name or something?"

"No. It is my real name. Are you a prisoner too? What *is* this place?"

"Shhhh," Norah says. "They're probably bugging our cells. Come closer to the hole. And whisper."

Lifting the cot away from the wall, Gandalf reminds herself to be cautious and skeptical in case this Norah person is a plant. But maybe she can get some information while taking care not to reveal too much.

What is she thinking? She has nothing to hide.

Gandalf squeezes next to the wall. She sits cross-legged on the floor and brings her face close to the hole in the molding.

"What is this place?" Gandalf asks again. She has to know, while at the same time she does not want to know, cannot bear to know. There is no way it can be good news.

"I'm pretty sure we're in a detention center for citizens suspected of subversive activity," Norah says. "Of domestic terrorism."

Terrorism? Images flood her brain: military brigades, platoons of soldiers with assault weapons sweeping through dusty foreign streets, IEDs and mountain caves. These are images that belong on the evening news, certainly not in her life.

"I do not understand," Gandalf whispers. "I haven't done anything."

There is silence for a moment before Norah answers. "Yeah. Me either."

"Do you know what time it is?"

"Why? You got someplace to go?"

Gandalf feels slapped. Who *is* this woman?

"I'm sorry," Norah says quickly. "My twisted sense of humor. It's just that all the normal things, like the time and what day it is and work and walking the dog, disappear in this place."

Gandalf studies the cadence of the woman's words. Her New York accent is both familiar and disconcerting. There might not be much difference between the two of them and that is even more frightening. "Are you from the city?"

"Brooklyn," Norah says. "Red Hook. You?"

"East Village. How long have you been here?"

"I'm not sure, exactly. I didn't start keeping track right away. I expected to be released any minute. Two weeks, I guess, maybe three."

Gandalf's breath catches. Three weeks? "But why? What do they want?"

Norah's sigh squeezes through the small hole and expands into a bubble of anxious air around Gandalf's face. "I don't know about you, but they probably picked me up to sabotage the case I'm litigating. They don't even interrogate me much anymore. Just leave me to rot in here."

Interrogate? Gandalf's back twists in spasm. She stretches out prone on the floor, her feet under the cot and her head resting on her arm. She pushes aside the wood shavings littering the floor and moves her face closer to the opening.

"So they kidnapped you to prevent your case from going forward?"

"But it won't work," Norah says. "Someone else at the Center will take over."

"The Center?

"Where I work. The Human Rights Litigation Center in Manhattan."

Gandalf idly brushes the wisps of wood curls into a small pile. "So why bring you here?"

"I don't know, exactly. They already tap the Center's phones and monitor our emails. I don't know what more they want."

What more? What did they already get? And what kind of interrogations does she mean? Interrogations suggest a swinging bare light bulb, a single wooden chair bolted to the cement floor. Leather restraints and cigarette burns and pliers, images from every documentary film on torture that Jess ever convinced her to watch.

"They're trying to intimidate us," Norah says.

"Is it working? Are you scared?"

"Terrified." Norah is quiet for a moment. "Why'd they take you?"

Gandalf rests her head on her fisted hand. "It is all a mistake."

"This whole concept is a mistake." Norah's voice grows cross. "I mean, kidnapping U.S. citizens and taking us to some secret prison?"

"But with me, they kidnapped the wrong person. I am a mathematician. I am not political; I don't even sign petitions."

"Maybe they think you have expertise or information critical to national security."

National security? That makes Gandalf want to laugh and cry at the same time. "I develop algebraic models to quantify extreme weather patterns, hurricanes mostly. It is totally benign stuff, equations, of interest only to academic mathematicians." She pauses. "Where *are* we, exactly?"

"Somewhere in Maine, I think. I was meeting with donors in Boston when they picked me up. We drove about five, six hours. Then a boat."

"I was kidnapped at JFK." Gandalf pictures the white metal room, black hood, Troll and Blue eyes. "They brought me here in a small plane. The guy in charge told me we were on Hurricane Island."

Norah doesn't respond.

"What? Have you ever heard of it?" Gandalf asks.

"No." Norah's voice is small. "I was just thinking that I'm glad you're here. It was awful being alone in this place."

The pictures in Gandalf's head have grown too intense, too demanding, and she has to ask. "Norah, did they torture you?"

There is only silence and it stretches forever.

Gandalf closes her eyes to stop the prickling. Something touches her cheek, and she jerks. A small dark finger pokes through the opening in the wood molding. Gandalf hooks Norah's finger with her own, hanging on tight.

# 9. AUSTIN, 6:52 P.M.

Austin pauses in the doorway, blasted by the evening newscast. Pops points to the television screen.

"You seen what's coming at us? Maine hasn't had a storm like this since '54. I ever tell you about Edna?"

Austin groans loudly. Pops's monologues always start with that phrase: I ever tell you about.

He ignores her. "Edna caused forty million dollars' damage in New England. Fifteen million bucks in this state alone. Portland got six inches of rain in six hours, and the rivers went wild, washed out roads and bridges. Eight people drowned. And the oddest thing? It was this very same week in September." He shakes his head. "Got a real bad feeling about this storm. We could be in for a major disaster, and you can bet Washington won't be much help this time either."

"What about your darling Evelina?" Austin asks. "God's gift to maritime Maine?"

"Evelina will do what she can, but one woman in Congress?" He shrugs with an exaggerated gesture. "We'll manage. Hurricanes or nor'easters or lobster poaching, no matter. Mainers take care of our own."

"Hurricane or no," Gran calls from the kitchen, "folks got to eat. Austin, come set the table. And show some respect for Evelina. She's done good things for this place."

"Not to worry," Pops says. "Over dinner, I'll tell you all about Edna."

In the kitchen, Gran hands Austin a basket of rolls. "You know, Evelina sponsored the bill about that new funding for special ed. Ask your cousin Anna and her kid with the sack on her spine what they think of Evelina."

Austin barely remembers Anna or her kid. But admitting that would just bring a different lecture from Gran, the one about the importance of family.

"Sure," she says, taking plates from the cupboard. "Whatever."

Twenty minutes later, Pops looks up from his plate and waves his fork towards the ordinary dusk visible through the kitchen window. "Looking outside now, you'd never believe what's heading our way." His fork jabs the air to punctuate his words. "It was the exact same with Edna."

"Come on." Austin swallows a mouthful of mashed potatoes. "You're making this up, aren't you? Don't tell me you remember the weather on an ordinary September day like sixty years ago? How old were you?"

"I was fourteen, but I remember it like last week."

"Before you get started, Ray." Gran turns to Austin. "How was your day? You left here before dawn."

Austin wishes she could say something about the math professor who doesn't seem like much of a terrorist, or about how creepy Tobias makes her feel when he stares at her. But she's not allowed to talk about work.

"Nothing exciting. I ate my lunch at the quarry. Gran, do you remember that time in high school when Gabe and I played hooky and went swimming in the quarry out on Hurricane? You went ballistic. What was the big deal?"

Her grandparents exchange glances. "It was dangerous," Gran says.

"Come on. You never worried when we swam in the Storm Harbor quarries." Austin can tell that Gran is hiding something. "The funny thing is, that day we discovered an old carving in the granite. Leaves and branches and two initials—MEC and AF—and the date 1914. I saw it again today when I was eating my lunch." She looks back and forth between Pops and Gran. "Do you know who those people were?"

Pops looks at Gran and reaches for the chicken. Gran presses her lips together.

This time, Austin refuses to give up. "I'm curious about those initials. Any idea why they're hidden away like that, carved in a crack so it's hard to find them? What's their story?"

Pops passes the chicken to Austin. "These islands are full of stories."

"I know they are. So what's the scoop on MEC and AF?"

Gran's face morphs into her teacher-know-it-all expression. "Terrible things have been happening over there for a century. The trouble at the quarry, then the fire at the rich kids' camp. If you ask me, those Washington folks are tempting fate, building out there again. Hurricane Island is bad news. Always has been, always will be. You learned about all that in school."

"But who were MEC and AF?" Austin shakes her head. "And how can a pretty little island full of spruce trees and big rocks be bad news? It doesn't make sense."

"A lot of things don't make sense. And the Washington folks' craziness is none of our concern." Pops pats Gran's arm.

Actually, Austin doesn't know exactly what happened on the small island, the trouble at the quarry. In school they learned that the granite industry fell apart overnight, something about foreigners and a strike and a bombing that destroyed the quarry company. Now the ruins are choked with kudzu, and every time she passes them she wishes someone would just tear them down. There'd been terrible accidents too, with injuries and deaths. Pops once told her that every island family had lost at least one member to the quarrying business and the worst disasters took place on the smallest island, so rustic and isolated. But whenever she asks about *their* family—who *they* lost—Gran goes all stony-stubborn and Pops mumbles something about Gran hating to talk about it. Then he changes the subject, just like he's doing right now.

"Why won't you tell me about the initials?" Austin asks. "What do they have to do with us?"

Gran looks down at her lap, and Austin can't see her face. Then she pushes her chair away from the table, stands up like she's a hundred years old, and walks out of the kitchen.

Pops gets up too. "Let it be, Austin," he says. "I know you didn't mean to upset her. And I get it, about your job. They pay good wages and you want to get off this island and see the world." He follows Gran out of the room.

Not the whole world, just Texas. Ever since she can remember, Austin has wanted to go there to look for her father. "He never could get used to Maine weather," Austin's mom used to explain on her rare visits. But she'd get pissy when Austin kept asking and the discussion usually ended with her zinger, "All that man ever gave you was your name."

Maybe so, but that's more than her mother left her. One morning when Austin was four, Mom dumped her with Gran and Pops and took the early ferry to Rockland. The first few years Mom showed up every Thanksgiving, ate enough turkey and pumpkin pie for three lobstermen, and promised to send for Austin as soon as she had a good job, or a bigger apartment, or things settled down with her boyfriend. After a while, she stopped promising. Stopped visiting too.

Austin carries the dishes to the sink and turns on the water. When she was younger, it made her furious to think about her mother abandoning her like that. But recently she feels a kinship with her. More like she's a sister or something. Because now she *gets* it, why her mother had to leave. Some days, Austin thinks she'll die—fade away from boredom—if she doesn't get away.

The window above the kitchen sink looks across Hurricane Sound to the little island. Dusk outlines the dark hill with a rim of peachy orange. Sure, she loves these islands, how sunset reflects on the bay, and the noon sun warms the granite stone against her back. But she needs more than water and rocks in her life. And whatever happened a hundred years ago with foreigners and strikes and bombings, one thing is clear: there's no MEC or AF around these islands for her. Gran and Pops are dear, but they aren't enough. And Gran is hiding something, which makes the secret feel important and weighty, and Pops is helping her hide it. Austin bets it's about the initials and people in their family. Maybe it's even about whatever drove her mother to abandon a four-year-old child, because that's the most unusual thing about her family.

Yes, Austin promises herself as she scrubs a greasy plate with the soapy sponge. She *is* going to escape this jumbled pile of rocks and spruce and go far away. But before she leaves, she is going to figure out what happened to MEC and AF on Hurricane Island, and what it has to do with her.

## 10. HENRY, 6:55 P.M.

Henry has no idea why he took the phone. Sitting in his leather swivel desk chair, he places the device in the precise center of the blotter and stares at it. Why, instead of entering it in the digital Detainee Possessions Inventory with her laptop and other effects, did he omit it from the list and slip it instead into his pocket? He has never before broken the chain of evidence. So stupid, and it's not even his first mistake today. Totally against protocol, he told the new detainee the name of the island. He folds his forearms across the blotter and lets his chin rest on his hands. Inches from his nose, the phone's matte metal trim reflects a red light. Flash, flash, pause, flash, flash.

Damn. The flash is the blinking red light attached to his computer. After the advanced Homeland Security course, Tobias insisted on installing an alert system on Henry's home computer to notify him in emergencies.

It takes three tries to log on to the secure website. He'll complain to Tobias about that tomorrow. There's no question the guy is technologically gifted, but the additional layers of passwords and firewalls are out of control. Ever since Tobias returned from the last course, he's been acting like a television spook. Henry teased him once about his Dick Tracy two-way wrist radio, but Tobias didn't laugh. He takes himself way too seriously, even alienating the military guys assigned to the facility. Recently the other men have been complaining about the assignment rosters, saying that Tobias gives himself all the cushy shifts in the surveillance room. Something else to deal with.

When the Top Secret network finally lets him in, two emails flash *Urgent.* The first is a group message from the Regional Chief in Boston about the hurricane. He expects to read about emergency protocols, but instead JR tells them to review their disaster manual and passes on the announcement from Washington: *In view of the impending high-security window, facility evacuations are prohibited regardless of local circumstances.*

Henry shakes his head at the monitor screen as he checks the *Read and Understood* box, returning the receipt to Boston. Regardless of local circumstances? Maybe this bureaucratic crap makes sense for most facilities, but the men in DC have no clue about the damage a hurricane can inflict with the assistance of Penobscot Bay waves and wind. No clue, and no desire to hear.

A soft knock on the door startles him. Cat's voice is muffled through solid oak. "Open up, Henry. I need to ask you something before I go."

Cat hands him a steaming mug of coffee and holds up her sparkly high-heeled sandals. "Do you have any idea what happened to these? It looks like an elephant danced all night at the prom."

He smiles. "I haven't seen any elephants in your closet."

Damn. He shouldn't have borrowed her shoes. His feet are small but much wider than hers. He should have bought his own pair sooner.

He sips the coffee. "Have a good class."

"Don't forget there's pie."

"I'll wait for you." He kisses her cheek. He wants to tell her everything, about shoes and dresses and all of it. If only he weren't so damn frightened of her reaction. Maybe tonight. She's always in a good mood after spending an evening with her friends, pasting old photos in scrapbooks. Photos of their daughter Melissa jumping off the cliffs into the swimming quarry down the road or the three of them wrapped in blankets on the deck watching the sunset. Maybe tonight.

He puts the mug on his desk, just north of the phone. The coffee will give him energy but make the heartburn worse, an unacceptable trade-off. Maybe coffee laced with Tums. Except that the rodent living in his chest, gnawing on his sternum and nourished by his nerves, seems to like antacids for dessert. Henry switches the monitor back on and stares at the screen.

The second message is also from the Regional Chief, but this one is labeled For Your Eyes Only and signed JR, as if they were colleagues, friends even, two guys who might go out for a beer or three after a successful mission.

*Two things, Henry*, it begins. *First: I haven't received your damage prevention press release yet. Forward immediately. Second: your female mathematician is high priority. The link between her and a Pakistani insurgent appears credible, as does the strong probability of an attack on the eleventh. We've had an uptick in chatter about death to Americans on the anniversary. Read the attached background document carefully. And don't fuck this up.*

Henry rubs his knuckles in small circles over his sternum, marveling at how quickly the buddy-buddy tone dissipates in JR's hands. He reads the attached document, worthless in its circular suppositions, and hits Reply to the Regional Chief's message and types: *We begin interrogation tomorrow morning.* That should hold him.

Damage prevention, that's what the Regional Chief calls it. He wants a reasonable cover story to keep the media from sniffing around the facility. There've already been a few press inquiries and some blogs bleating about the public's right to know. This is the kind of thing the PR team at Quantico usually deals with; the Bureau is fanatic about controlling all information to the media. So why would they insist *he* write this story? Is he being set up? No, that's paranoid thinking. They trust him, and he knows the local scene, that's all. He can do this perfectly well himself.

All he needs is a plausible explanation for the presence of an alphabet soup of federal agencies on a remote island. Something sexy enough to capture the interest of the media, especially the alternative press, because those guys are bulldogs, always looking for a conspiracy. So his story must be a perfectly crafted misdirection that is close enough to the truth to feel authentic.

A shift in perspective might help. He opens the office door and steps through the hallway into the front room. Dusk softens the plain lines of the old farmhouse. The bay window faces the Sound where the last salmon embers smolder on the horizon, outlining the small humpback shape of Hurricane Island. No matter what bad things happened over there in the past, no matter what questionable things his men are doing there now, you can't destroy the beauty of this place.

Every few months Cat brings home brochures from the realtor's office where she works as a receptionist. "It's a great time to sell waterfront property," she says, dropping the brochures on the kitchen counter.

Over his dead body. After all those years working in Bangor and coming home only on weekends, he isn't budging. This is his home, even though having the detention camp across the sound feels like shitting in his own backyard. These islands are—they *should* be—worlds away from terrorism and the mess in the Middle East.

That's it! The Three Sisters Islands are worlds away, but their rough landscape is a perfect location for field simulation training for intelligence operatives before posting them abroad. It mimics the environments new agents will find in hot spots around the world: rugged terrain, unpredictable weather, and unreliable communication technology.

"Maine Weather is just like Afghanistan, right?" He can just hear some smart-ass reporter ask, but he's got the spin-ready answer: "Afghanistan, no. Not Iran either. But it's actually pretty close to North Korea." Yes.

He writes the press release, detailing the critical role of training exercises in successfully waging the war on terror. He proofreads it, then sends it out blind to his select list of press contacts around the state. He sends a separate copy to the Regional Chief, curbing his impulse to address it to JR, then logs off, shuts down the computer, and sets the anti-tamper alarm. Swiveling his chair away from the computer extension, he stands up and stretches.

He's never told Cat that at first JR demanded that Henry live at the camp. He refused, explaining that he could see keep a careful eye on the camp from home. Damn, he could see the island from his porch without binoculars. When they insisted, he told them that it would end his marriage and he'd leave the Bureau before he let that happen. They gave in, but it was another demerit in his file.

Like Dr. Cohen's cell phone, mocking him now from the desk blotter. Breaking the chain of evidence is a huge and ugly black mark, possibly enough to get him fired. He presses the power button on the phone and stares at the screen-saver photo of an orange cat. It was totally out of character for him to take the phone. He prides himself on deliberating carefully and developing a cogent plan before acting. It was just an impulse, he tells himself, but he knows better. His training included psychology and profiling classes as well as media spin. You don't have to be Freud to wonder if an agent who would do something like this, something so clearly against the rules, was having doubts. You would question his motivation, his loyalty even. If an agent under his command took the phone, Henry would fire him.

Damn! Henry slams his fist on the desk. He might question some of the Bureau's current methods, but *his* integrity is mostly intact. And since he has the phone, he should be moving ahead with the investigation; he should listen to her voicemail. The more he knows about Dr. Cohen, the more effective his interrogation will be tomorrow morning. He looks at the three new messages, all from "Jess." Over the years, he has become hardened to the escalating messages from relatives, intensifying from concerned to anxious to frantic, but he still feels uncomfortable handling this phone.

He plays the first message on speaker.

"You're late, Gee. Call me soon as you can."

In the second message, the voice is tighter.

"Gandalf? Sweetheart? What's going on? I got a little nervous when you didn't call from the gate, but I figured you were working on your paper. When you didn't call at six, I checked online and the Detroit flight landed on time, so where are you? Call me. I love you."

He thinks briefly about Cat, wonders how she'd react if he disappeared into thin air. Of course that's immaterial, because why would anyone want to abduct him? He hesitates, then listens to the last message.

"Gandalf. It's 9 p.m. and I'm officially freaked out. I called your hotel, and you never checked in. The airline won't tell me anything. They transferred my call to some security office, and I hung up. The police say it's too early to file a report. Their asinine rule is not to open a case until someone has been missing for twenty-four hours. I just know that something horrible has happened. Please call me the second you hear this. *If* you hear . . ." Her voice breaks, followed by the connection.

Before he can really think it through, his finger touches the "call back" box. A photo icon pops up, a woman with a gray braid and a tabby cat draped over her shoulder. She answers on the first ring.

"Gandalf? Sweetheart?"

The emotion in her voice frightens him. What possessed him to call this woman, presumably the most important individual in the prisoner's world? It's cruel and that isn't like him. His cheeks flame, and he hangs up.

He powers off the phone and locks it in his desk drawer. Whatever came over him, whatever the twisted reason, he's done with it. He'll punish himself; he'll go upstairs and read in bed until Cat gets home. No silk and lace and satin for him tonight. He stands up, feeling weary and shaky and old.

But he can't get comfortable, no matter how he arranges the pillows. He can't read. And even when Cat gets home and joins him in bed, he can't sleep. Like so many other nights recently, worry consumes him. Worrying about the changing protocols of the last few years and how increasingly uncomfortable they make him feel. About Tobias and his increasing volatility. About his daughter Melissa working in Washington where she's being influenced by all the wrong people. About the storm coming and how unprepared they are. Most of all, he worries about Cat.

Some wives are supportive; he devours their posts on the blogs. They understand that dressing in silky fabrics means nothing about manhood. He and Cat have a good marriage. They bicker like any couple, arguing about moving into town or how often to invite her parents to dinner, but rarely disagree about important things. Of course, Cat might consider him wearing dresses important.

Well, it's important to him too. Silk and lace and satin against his skin enlarge him, make him greater than his everyday self. He imagines dancing with Cat in the privacy of their bedroom. Candlelight and soft music. In his fantasy they both wear satin dresses; hers is ruby red and his deep teal. They move together slowly, sensuously, in harmony with the soft crinkle of fine fabric. The waiting, the foreplay, is exquisite. Cat moves first. She takes her time with the long zipper from neckline to hips and slips it off his shoulders. He shimmies out of it. Then he unzips her dress, which spills onto the floor with a satiny whisper. They alternate, undressing each other one item at a time: matching lace brassieres, one nylon stocking at a time, ivory panties of the finest silk.

Except that doesn't sound one bit like his Cat. She's more likely to run screaming from the bedroom, lock herself in her sewing room, and call their daughter in DC. Giving Melissa one more reason to despise her father, one more reason to add to her long list, with what she calls his despicable career choice right at the top.

But tonight he is too tired to figure out any of this. Tonight he just craves sleep. He closes his eyes to the shadows, spoons himself around Cat's warmth, and times his breathing to her muted snores.

# 11. GANDALF, 11:35 P.M.

The rotating searchlight from the guard tower tosses parallel bar shadows into the room. They creep in slow motion along the wall, across the floor, and onto the bed, warping and twisting as they move. For hours, Gandalf has been lying curled up on the cot, eyes wide open and heart racing, staring at the patterns. Her brain tumbles over itself, clumsy, inarticulate, paralyzed.

It is true that nothing truly horrible has happened to her yet, if you don't count being hooded and cuffed and kidnapped. She tries to find that fact comforting, but it just means that the unspeakable possibilities are all in the future, looming over every next second. Tormenting images coil back and forth between imagined scenes triggered by Norah's interrogation, those from her own mental file, and worrying about Jess.

Normally with a big storm threatening, she and Jess watch the Weather Channel together. Looking up from grading papers, Jess might deconstruct the coverage as fiction, identify the emotional uses of landscape and setting, critique the cardboard characters, admire the pacing and rising action. Gandalf might interject her own professional expertise, scrutinizing the science, demanding more rigorous evidence, and criticizing the over-simplification of the weather models' predictions.

Lying in her cell, Gandalf does not need a television to precisely visualize the programming. The earnest members of the Major Storms Team—who thought up these self-important job titles, anyway?—are no doubt alternating between building Hurricane Gena up as the storm of the century and re-marking endlessly on the uncanny resemblance to the 1954 hurricane. Jess will not appreciate the parallels, but it is striking that during this very week over six decades ago Hurricane Edna spawned hurricane watches from Georgia to Cape Hatteras. And now Gena is spinning towards New England along exactly the same pathway. All week at work Gandalf followed the storm, noting the deep trough developing along the eastern seaboard. She never expected to be facing the fury of a major hurricane on a puny island somewhere in maritime Maine without the benefit of her sophisticated computer prediction equations. Without even the weather app radar on her smartphone.

What kind of emergency preparations could they possibly have on this island?

If she were home, she would calmly and carefully explain the weather system, and Jess would roll her eyes at what she considers excruciating detail. But she is not home, and Jess is probably making deals with any remote gods she can muster, promising to never again ridicule Gandalf's geeky enthusiasm for a sudden dip in the jet stream or a back-door cold front.

Right about now, when Jess cannot stomach another second of hurricane hype, she will turn off the television and start roaming their darkened apartment. There will be enough Manhattan nightlight filtering through the tall windows to make lamps unnecessary. Jess might run her fingers along the spines of the heavy hardcover books on Gandalf's shelves. Not a brightly colored jacket in sight; they are esoteric tomes, arranged in a manner Jess finds incomprehensible. Perhaps she will sit at Gandalf's large oak desk, usually bare on top except for a stack of journals and the ceramic mug she uses to hold pens. Jess made her the mug for their second anniversary; she painted the wizard motif to match the tiny wizard charms on gold chains they exchanged when they moved in together.

"Embrace your inner wizard," Jess whispered when she fastened it around Gandalf's neck. And then they both laughed, because nothing in the universe was less likely.

Gandalf's hand flies to her throat and touches the gold wizard.

"Are you awake?" The words, halfway between a whisper and a sob, come from under the bed.

Norah.

Carefully, Gandalf pushes her cot slightly away from the wall. An inch, then two. Finally six inches, making a gap big enough to let her face fall into the crack, her ear and mouth hopefully concealed from whatever snoop devices the guards might be using.

"Are you okay?"

Norah laughs, a smothered, choked-off laugh. "Just great."

"What's wrong?"

"I'm lonely. Freaking-out lonely. Climbing-walls lonely. Would you talk to me?"

Gandalf closes her eyes. Terrific. It is just her luck to be incarcerated on some godforsaken island in the middle of nowhere with a needy, talky-therapy type. If they are going to survive this, whatever it is, it will require more than sharing personal histories.

Hold on just one minute, Jess's voice warns inside Gandalf's brain. Don't be so judgmental. Don't alienate your only potential ally, even if you are not yet totally convinced you can trust her.

"What do you want me to talk about?" Gandalf asks.

"Anything. About you."

"There is not much to tell. I'm an academic mathematician. My work is tangentially related to triangulation theory."

"So, why did these guys pick you up? Is there a military use for your research?"

"Not until we figure out how to manipulate severe weather and that is decades away. My work is only of interest to a few dozen mathematicians scattered around the globe."

"So maybe it's not your work. What about family, friends? Is your husband a double agent for Iran or something? Or maybe your kid is a campus activist?"

Usually her personal life is off-limits. She knows that the younger faculty members consider her cold and aloof. One year at the department reception, she heard a teaching assistant whisper "Ice Lady" in her direction. But this setting and Norah's distress require some disclosure on her part. And it will be easier to talk without seeing reactions on Norah's face.

"I am not married," Gandalf says. "No children." She is fond of Jess's son David and his family but has never felt particularly maternal towards them. "I live with my partner, Jess."

"Jesse?"

"Short for Jessamine. She's an English professor. What about you?"

"Separated. Two daughters, eight-year-old twin girls."

When Norah does not continue, Gandalf says, "You must really miss them," then chides herself for such an inadequate response. She was born missing the gene for girl-talk. Norah is still silent, so Gandalf continues. "Jess always wanted to explore Maine someday. She probably had something else in mind though, like kayaking or hiking. Do you know anything about this place?"

"Precious little. There's another island nearby, but I think we're pretty far from the mainland. Until you told me, I didn't even know this island was named Hurricane. Hey, you study hurricanes. That's got to be a good omen, don't you think?"

"Terrific," Gandalf says. "What else?"

"I get the impression the facility is pretty new. One big building with at least three floors. Of course I've never been outside, except in the courtyard."

"What about other prisoners?"

"No idea. We're kept locked in our rooms except for the exercise yard. Or interrogation. I've never even seen any other prisoners. Except you."

"And you've never actually seen me." Gandalf pauses. "Tell me why they brought you here, if not your lawsuit?"

Norah makes that choked-laugh again. "There are so many reasons. It could be my blog. I do tend to rant. Or my father—I'm a red diaper baby. Do you know what that means?"

"That you have Communist parents?"

"Uh-huh, and grandparents. My dad was a Black Panther organizer in Harlem. He went underground to avoid COINTELPRO. My sister and I were constantly harassed by the feds, in school, on the playground, everywhere. One agent played Scrabble with us, that's how much time he spent at our kitchen table. One day he warned my mom that she was about to be arrested, and she went underground too."

"What happened to you?"

"My sister and I were farmed out to relatives. Eventually my dad gave up on the possibility of democracy in this country and moved to Liberia. Mom said she couldn't stomach one more group of well-meaning people gathered in a living room thinking they could change the world. She and my sister grow orchids in Florida."

"Your family does not sound like much of a threat."

"Maybe I'm just paranoid."

"What's your lawsuit about?" Gandalf isn't actually interested in the legal details, but Norah needs to talk, and maybe the case will shed light on what these people want.

"You've heard of *Posse comitatus*?" Norah asks. "The statute that forbids the military from butting into domestic peacekeeping?"

She should have paid more attention in civics class. "Not really."

"When the Army was called in to crush the lingering rebellions after the Civil War, Congress passed the act to keep the military out of civilian matters. Of course, everyone ignores it. Bush-the-shrub signed funding acts for quasi-military detention camps, poised to receive civilians in the name of stopping terrorism."

"Like this one."

"Uh-huh," Norah says. "Obama claimed he closed them down."

"Maybe he doesn't know about this?" Gandalf voted for him twice despite Jess's warnings that he was corporate through and through.

"That's hard to believe. Anyway, Homeland Security and the military keep the program alive, and the Republicans pump money into them. We filed a lawsuit, but it's a catch-22. They won't let you challenge the statute unless it has affected you personally. Now I finally have a strong case, if I ever get out of here. Ironic, huh?"

Gandalf feels a small rush of hope. Maybe Norah brought her incarceration on herself; maybe her activism got her in trouble. In that case, she herself has nothing to worry about. Bringing her here is a mistake, and the authorities are certain to figure that out pretty quickly. If only they will give her a chance to explain before they start interrogating her.

"Norah . . ."

"What?"

"Did they hurt you?"

Norah doesn't answer.

"The interrogations. Did they, you know, use torture?"

As the silence lengthens, Gandalf tries to control the R-rated images rolling across her retina. And Jess says she lacks imagination.

"They didn't rape me," Norah says, "or tear out my fingernails, if that's what you're asking. No waterboarding."

"What *did* they do?"

"Before every session they kept me in an icy cold room for forty-eight hours. Bright lights, music blaring—vile, awful music. Violent lyrics, misogynist, you know? No food, just water. No clothes, either." Norah's voice is flat. "They questioned me naked. There were a lot of them. All men. They made crude comments. Racist and hateful. About my body." There is another pause. "About what they planned to do to me."

Gandalf tries to think of a comment, some words to offer into the silence, but none come.

"You know what is even worse than the cold and the music? Being alone. Twenty-three hours most days, with one hour in the exercise yard with a guard. Maybe that doesn't sound that bad to you, but it's driving me insane. Even makes me miss my ex-husband and I can't stand the guy. I almost look forward to interrogations, for the company. Pathetic, huh?"

"I am so sorry." Gandalf feels herself blushing; what a stupid thing to say. "Did you, um, tell them what they wanted to know?"

Norah's voice gets steely. "I didn't tell them anything. Anyway, they asked me about people I'd never heard of. Tried to get me to say I knew these people, had been in cells with them." She pauses. "But I worry all the time, every minute, about how far these people will go to get the answers they want. You've heard the stories of prisoners being tortured to death?"

"Maybe in Egypt or Iraq," Gandalf says. "That couldn't happen here, to American citizens. Anyway, I have nothing to hide."

"And you think that will help you?" Norah's voice breaks on the last two words.

Gandalf squeezes her eyes tight, tries to slow her breathing. A picture creeps into her mind: Norah, naked, her body on display to a jeering audience of soldiers. She does not even know what Norah looks like, except that her hand is small and dark. On impulse, Gandalf reaches down, between the bed and the wall, searching for the hole in the molding. Norah's hand isn't there, but Gandalf's fingers touch the shavings on the floor. She brings a clump to her nose and sniffs.

"Norah," she says. "Why do you suppose there is all this sawdust here?"

"What sawdust?"

"On my floor, near the molding." She pushes some through the hole.

"I don't believe it!" Norah's whisper explodes into the silence.

"What?"

"The sawdust. Don't you see?" Norah says. "That means they *cut* this hole on purpose. *After* they built the rooms. So we would talk to each other. I am so stupid. I should have expected this. They're fucking listening to every word we say."

# FRIDAY
## SEPTEMBER 9

# 12. RAY, 10:23 A.M.

Grabbing his green wool shirt, Ray eases the screen door closed behind him, and sits on the stoop to pull on his sneakers. Other than the determined wind chasing swollen clouds across blue sky, the storm isn't broadcasting itself yet. But Ray can feel it. The weather pundits can't display gut feelings on a full-color moving graphic, but any fisherman, even a mostly retired one, recognizes the promise and the warning.

This one is going to be big. He'll remind Austin to pack a bag tonight. No chance she'll get off Hurricane once the storm hits. He sure doesn't feel good about her bunking down there, not one bit. Bad enough she has to spend her days in that place, even with Nettie's cousins working there.

Ray hesitates at the intersection with the harbor road, still thinking about Austin on Hurricane, and Bert and Cyrus too. Maybe he can pry some information from Bert about the goings-on out there. Bert usually ferries back to Storm Harbor mid-morning for biscuits and honey at Mitch & Ruthie's. Bert claims he goes there for the lemonade, but everyone knows how lonely the guy is even though he's kin to half the island. Or maybe because of that. Everyone knows all the miserable details about how his first wife left him to raise Evelina by himself, and then he married a girl from Rockland and the breast cancer got her, not two years after their boy Gabe was killed in Iraq. No man should have to deal with so much pain.

Sure enough, Bert sits at his favorite table in the corner, his chair leaning back on two legs against the pine wall. He sees Ray and raises his fingers half an inch off his glass in greeting.

"Morning, Ruthie," Ray calls to the woman behind the counter. "Coffee?"

"Coming up. Anything doing out there?"

"Just some wind." Ray sits across from Bert. "Crossing bad?"

"A bit. Tomorrow'll be the bitch."

"Yup." Ray pauses. "I wish Austin didn't have to be over there."

Bert tilts his head sideways and closes one eye. "Might be pretty bad."

"Thanks for nothing." Ray sips his coffee in silence for a few minutes. "Storm's not the only thing eating at me. It's that place you work at. What do they do over there?"

Bert shrugs. "I just ferry folks over and back."

"You don't hear anything?"

"Bits of stuff."

"Don't worry you none?"

"They pay well, and I need the job."

"Well, it worries me, Austin being there."

"You know Henry Ames is in charge?" Bert says. "Lissa's dad."

Ray swirls his cup, watching the thin film of oil eddy. Gabe was planning to marry Lissa after Iraq. Good thing the girl moved away, and Bert doesn't have to see her in the IGA with some other guy's kids.

"Is Ames solid?"

"He'll do. Seems a bit off these days though. Him and his sidekick both."

"What about Cyrus? He still working over there?"

Bert nods.

"Can I trust him to look out for Austin?"

Bert does that funny clownish thing with his head again, tilting it and closing one eye, like he can see everything clearly that way. "Cyrus is hard to figure."

"I'd sure appreciate if you keep an eye on my girl," Ray says.

Bert nods but doesn't answer. Ray takes a long swallow of coffee, then tucks a dollar bill under the saucer. He turns to leave.

"Ray," Bert whispers. "I'll watch out for her."

Buffeted by the blustery wind on the sidewalk, Ray studies the dark shadow of Hurricane Island across the sound. Even with Bert's help, he doesn't feel good about this. Austin never was an easygoing kid, any more than her mother was. And the girl was darn persistent with all her questions last night. But no one is more mulish than Nettie, not when she doesn't want to talk about something. He's been trying for decades to get her to talk about what happened to her family out on Hurricane. The only time she ever opened up was when they were teenagers and he got home after riding out Hurricane Edna in the cave. She had been beside herself with worry and fury, certain that he would die out there. When he returned safely, and she was giddy with relief, she told him her great aunt Margaret used to live on Hurricane Island and disappeared. Disappeared how? Ray wanted to know more but Nettie said she only knew fragments of the story. And when he brought it up a few weeks later, she refused to talk about Margaret or Hurricane at all.

The year Abby was born, Nettie's mother died and left her a packet of letters from Margaret. That night Ray found Nettie nursing Abby and weeping over the pale blue papers, her tears dampening Abby's black curls. Nettie wouldn't talk about the letters and the next morning she sewed them into a cloth packet which she hid in the closet in the baby's room.

Ray knows the local history and rumors about the conflicts just before the quarry company folded, about the strike and the bombing blamed on the anarchists or socialists, whatever they were, whatever the difference is and who cares now, anyway. He has his suspicions about what's in the letters, but no matter how many times he tells her it's ancient history, and no one cares any more, no matter how many times he tries to talk about the hole in her family, she refuses. Let it be, she says.

By now he's mostly stopped asking, but he has never stopped feeling shut out by Nettie's refusal. And he has never stopped wondering if that hole in her family might have somehow, he isn't sure how, had something to do with how difficult it was for Nettie to raise up her own daughter.

He scans the sky. Not a drop of rain yet, but the atmosphere is high voltage. Like tiny electrons are zinging interlocking circles in the air around his head, giving off pops of invisible energy. This storm's going to be a doozy.

# 13. AUSTIN, 11:15 A.M.

Clutching the lead to the prisoner's handcuff-to-waist harness restraint, Austin presses her thumb carefully in the center of the security pad. The door to the exercise yard opens with an electronic whirr. She often imagined this kind of scenario during the security-vetting period between being hired and starting training. She pictured herself moving a prisoner from cell to cell, jingling a big bunch of keys on a brass ring. Of course, brass rings are outdated—modern security is all about retinal and fingerprint scans. But she still gets a kick being trusted with such an important job.

Crossing the threshold into the yard, Austin and the prisoner look up. Clouds chase each other across an indigo sky.

"Guess that storm is coming," Austin says. "The hurricane."

"Yes. Gena." The prisoner starts walking the perimeter of the yard.

Austin falls into step beside her, still holding the leash. Once in the secured yard, she's allowed to remove the restraint, but she's more comfortable keeping it in place. No way the prisoner can escape anyway—the building totally encloses the courtyard and for this hour the locks are programmed for Austin's fingerprint. Wait a minute—couldn't a prisoner escape by overpowering a guard and forcing the guard's finger against the pad? But Henry and Tobias must have thought of that. She's silly to worry, especially today. This old lady is not likely to try to disable her with a judo move. She smiles at the thought.

"What's so funny?"

"Nothing," Austin says. "You know, last night at dinner my grandfather couldn't stop yapping about some old-time hurricane that followed the same path as this one."

"Edna," the prisoner says. "September 1954."

"Wasn't that before you were born?"

"Yes, but I study hurricanes professionally."

"Why would you do that?" Can't hurt to talk a little, can it? She might even learn something important. For the investigation.

"They fascinate me. I was visiting my grandparents in Florida when Hurricane Donna hit," the prisoner says. "It's one of my first memories, watching the destruction from their bay window and playing in the ruined yard afterwards."

"Is it really true that there are more destructive storms now, with climate change and all, and they're going to get worse and worse?" Austin heard that on TV and it worries her.

"The data confirm that they are statistically more frequent and severe, but that doesn't predict the future."

"I've always wondered something else. Why do they use those weird, old-lady names, like Gena?" Austin glances at the prisoner. Was that an insulting thing to say?

"Actually now they use both male and female names. But for many years, in their misogynist wisdom, they decided that the way storms shift directions suddenly is a female trait."

"Where do the names come from? I mean, who decides?"

"An international meeting of meteorologists. Every year they vote on the list, following the alphabet." The prisoner pauses, then adds, "If only *we* could choose our given names; I would never have chosen mine."

"What is it?"

"You don't know my name?"

Austin shrugs. "We use numbers here."

"What's my number?"

That couldn't be secret, could it? "524."

"Well, my *name* is Gandalf."

"What does that mean?"

"Didn't you ever read *The Hobbit*? *Lord of the Rings*?"

"Isn't that a movie?"

The prisoner frowns, like Austin is really stupid. "They're books by J.R.R. Tolkien," she says. "Gandalf is a wizard."

"You're named after a wizard? Does that mean you're supposed to be magic or wise or something?"

"Or something. When I was about twenty, I read all of Tolkien's books searching for wisdom," Gandalf says. "I did not find any."

"I have an unusual name too. Austin."

Gandalf looks at her sharply, as if her name triggers a memory. She mumbles something Austin doesn't catch, something about apricots, then asks, "For Jane Austen?"

"For the city. My dad's from there."

It's none of Gandalf's business that Austin's dad returned to Texas two weeks before her second birthday. Or maybe he went somewhere else, who knows. Her only image of him comes from a photo. He's standing in his lobster gear at the town dock with a silly grin on his face. Austin found it when she was about eight and stuck it on the mantel, right between the formal picture of Gran and Pops on their wedding day and an old-timey brown photograph of some children standing stiff and formal in front of a potbelly stove. Gran snatched the snapshot down and gave it back to Austin. "That deadbeat doesn't deserve a place in our parlor."

"It's amazing that your grandfather lived through Edna way out here," the prisoner says. "That was an astonishing storm. Does he remember details? I would love to talk to him about it."

Uh-uh. Leave her family out of this. The prisoner is acting like they're friends or something. This conversation might be getting awfully close to fraternizing. Austin unlocks the prisoner's harness and gives her a small shove towards the center of the courtyard.

"You only get an hour out here. Better make the most of it."

## 14. TOBIAS, 11:31 A.M.

In the basement of the administration building, Tobias studies the monitors. Number 524 jogs around the exercise yard. The new girl leans against the shingled wall, looking pleasingly young and ripe. He is picturing female guards wearing uniforms with short skirts when his phone rings.

"Tobias here."

"It's Henry. I heard from Washington last night about the new detainee. She's high priority."

"Great. I've been thinking we should give her a few hours in the cold box before the interrogation, just to warm her up for the questioning." Tobias wouldn't let himself laugh out loud. Henry was too stiff to enjoy a little joke.

"Are you nuts? What part of 'not too rough with this one' did you not understand?"

Tobias heard Henry's instructions on the tarmac, but that doesn't mean he agrees. Still, he has to keep the whine out of his voice. "Boss, you know that cold cell preparation gives the best results. Why not use what works?"

"It's my decision and it's final: no cold cell. Have her ready for me at 1500. And I want the new guard there. Austin."

"I'd like to be involved."

"Not this time. Make the arrangements."

The disconnection click thunders in Tobias's ear. Why did they bother to build two cold boxes, if Henry won't use them? And why doesn't Henry get it, after all these years of working together, that Tobias is a far more gifted interrogator than Henry will ever be. Henry is missing the pit bull gene.

But wait. Maybe deep down, Henry does understand and he's being devious. He really *does* want enhanced interrogation, but he wants it off the record. That must be why he asked Tobias to make the arrangements, without specifying which arrangements, except no cold box. That leaves Tobias free to use his discretion. He'll follow the SLIC protocol: Strip, Lights, Isolation, Cold. He scoots his desk chair to the master console across the office and adjusts the air conditioning in Room D to Coldest. Hypothermia works best in the cold box, but used right, it can be extremely effective in a regular room.

Tobias turns back to the monitor. The prisoner has been jogging around the exercise yard for forty-five minutes, long enough to get hot and sweaty. Good.

He dials Austin's cell phone and watches on the monitor as she answers. "This is Austin."

"Tobias here. Bring your prisoner to Interrogation Room D."

"Okay, right after her shower."

"No, immediately. The room code for today is 4986."

"4986. Got it."

Tobias can't believe it. "You dolt. Don't *ever* speak classified information out loud in the presence of a prisoner."

"She can't hear me," Austin says. "She's across the yard."

"She's ten feet away. Besides, it's standard operating procedure, and that means no questions."

He watches Austin stand frozen for a moment, surveying the yard. The girl probably hasn't considered before that she and the prisoner are under surveillance, that *everyone* is under surveillance, all the time. In her head, she's probably replaying their sweet little heart-to-heart about hurricane history and embarrassing names. She'll learn.

"Yes, sir."

"By the way." He keeps his voice low although there's no one to overhear. "Those uniform pants look damn good on you."

Tobias disconnects the phone and watches Austin approach the prisoner and reconnect the harness apparatus. When she escorts the prisoner into the building, he switches to the interrogation corridor monitor.

"I need to shower first," Gandalf says.

"There's no time. They want you now." Austin places her thumb against the security pad. When she enters the code, her body shifts slightly to block the keypad from the prisoner's line of sight.

Tobias nods. The girl's smart. She won't make that mistake again, won't jeopardize the code. Too bad he's not doing this interrogation. He'd like to mentor Austin, teach her the best approaches to information extraction.

He switches cameras again, this time to the interrogation room interior, where Austin is clipping the prisoner's restraint to the metal chair bolted to the floor in the center of the room. The prisoner looks stunned, hugging her bare arms. He can practically see the goose bumps rising on her skin and wonders for a moment if her nipples are erect too. Henry probably won't acknowledge it, but the rapid-cool AC unit has been worth every penny. Of course, it's not as effective as the cold box unit and optimally SLIC preparation begins 24-48 hours before the interrogation. But cold will be especially effective after her workout and besides, these academic types are soft. Even for Henry, this woman shouldn't be hard to break. Tobias wonders if a lezzy will react any differently to sexual humiliation.

SLIC: how he loves military acronyms. People ridicule the initials, but he treasures their secret power. He has memorized the instructions from the manual: *Stripping consists of forceful removal of detainees' clothing. In addition to degradation of the detainee, stripping can be used to demonstrate the omnipotence of the captor or to debilitate the detainee. Interrogator personnel tear clothing from detainees by firmly pulling downward against buttoned buttons and seams. Tearing motions shall be downward to prevent pulling the detainee off balance.*

Personally, he prefers knife-stripping to tearing. It's a newer technique he learned at the Homeland Security course. Too bad he won't be doing this interrogation, but there's room for his contributions. He can understand that Henry wants first crack at this math professor. Maybe he's reserving Tobias's expertise for the second round, when the prisoner is worn out and ready to spill her guts. In any case, he bets that stripping will be a particularly effective preparation technique on this perp.

On the monitor, Austin leans close to the prisoner's ear and whispers something Tobias can't hear. He frowns. The guard isn't supposed to get all cozy with the bitch. He activates the overhead speaker, even though it's against protocol. Even though it alerts the prisoner that she is under surveillance.

"Austin," he yells. "Get your lovely ass out of there." He punches the Off icon and adjusts the temperature down another notch. He'll get something to eat and take his own sweet time with it. Then he'll finish preparing the detainee for interrogation.

## 15. GANDALF, 2:15 P.M.

She cannot stop shivering. It has been cold forever; she has been locked in this room eternally. What did Norah say about the cold, forty-eight hours? It feels like hours and days and weeks, although she knows it cannot be that long but there is no clock and no window, and they still have her watch. Not to mention her computer, her files, the page proofs for her article. She must have already missed her presentation; Sandra and Ahmed are no doubt furious and even if she gets a chance to explain, they will never believe a story like this. No one will.

Her body is shaking uncontrollably, but her brain feels incisive and potent. These people made a huge mistake in abducting her, but they might be unwilling to admit it. So she will have to organize her own escape, or at least be ready to seize any opportunity that presents itself. In the meantime, her mind is engaged and ready to tackle the obstacles using the only weapon she possesses: her intellect.

Like perspiration: she has never thought about it before, has never considered if sweat turns to ice on skin, although she has observed how ice forms easily on beards. If a student asked if it were possible for sweat to freeze, she would suggest they work together to determine a formula based on the salt content. She begins to develop the equation in her head, but the cold air blowing from the vent directly above her in the ceiling captures her thoughts and whisks them elsewhere, to another problem: how cold is it? Cold enough to freeze the water in her cells?

She corrects herself; it is actually saline not water, so it requires a lower temperature to freeze her blood and interstitial fluid. Her mind skids again, to the argument she had with Jess last winter as they spread salt on the icy narrow sidewalk leading to the trash cans where the super never bothered to plow. Jess said that since adding salt to water makes it boil at a higher temperature, like with cooking pasta, it stands to reason that salt would increase the freezing point too. That would make the ice on the sidewalk worse. Gandalf tried to describe freezing point depression, using the example of antifreeze. But Jess waved her explanations away, saying who cared about antifreeze, shouldn't science be logical? Then Gandalf muttered something insulting about English teachers and walked off, leaving Jess to finish the walk herself. She ached now with the memory. She should have found a way to explain it. Jess deserved better.

She must turn her brain back to the problem at hand, getting out of this place, and maybe Austin can be persuaded to help with that. The guard seems ingenuous and naïve, incongruous in this ugly place. She seems prickly too, as if she does not expect much from people. Gandalf understands that attitude; she was lonely as a child and adolescent, never fitting in or feeling comfortable with her peers. In a love-hate relationship with her stupid name, she read *The Hobbit* every year on her birthday, looking for a nugget of personal wisdom. But the book was playful and quirky, and she was neither, and still is not.

Besides, Gandalf cannot allow herself to trust anyone in this place. Austin acts sympathetic with her "hang tough" comment, but maybe she is supposed to say that, to make Gandalf think the young woman is on her side. Maybe Austin gave her that drink of water on the plane for the same reason, so she will let down her guard and reveal some important state secret.

Except that she has no secrets to give up, state or otherwise. Gandalf bites her lip, which feels oddly thick and numb. She has no information that could buy her freedom. Norah sounded so proud she hadn't answered their questions, but it is different for Norah. She might really have information the government wants. Maybe she has even done something illegal. But once the people in charge understand that Gandalf just manipulates her equations, minds her own business, they will stop treating her like a criminal. Or if the people at this place are corrupt, their bosses are bound to step in and straighten things out, sending her home with an apology.

If only she could cry. Maybe tears will dissolve the thick clog of frustration lodged in her throat, plugging her swallowing and aching, aching. Tears will at least be warm, but they will not come. Maybe that is lucky; they could freeze on her face. They are probably frozen in her tear ducts.

Enough self-pity; she must think. Think warm. She closes her eyes and pictures the beach in Puerto Rico where she and Jess spent three days last winter. Her brain flickers a few times, transforming the fine white sand into ice, but she steers the image firmly back to beach, and then she is lost in the warmth of the memory of that last evening. Seduced by the tour guide's description of the tiny marine animals with luminous bodies, they signed up for an excursion to a bioluminescent bay. It was already dark when they arrived at the edge of the nature preserve, climbed into a canoe, and paddled under a narrow canopy of mangroves that slowly widened into the bay. Almost imperceptibly at first, the starlight fell from the darkness behind the mangrove leaves into the water. The water shimmered each time their canoe paddles touched the black surface. The flickering grew until the water was on fire with tiny embers. She is warm.

A man bursts into the room; the warm air and sparkling bay disappear. In the moment before he ties the blindfold headache tight around her eyes, Gandalf catches a glimpse of a narrow weasel face. Actually more like a ferret than a weasel. Ferret: she files the name in her mental folder along with Troll and Blue Eyes. And Apricot, even though Apricot now has a real name. Austin, who strapped her into this chair and abandoned her in this freezer.

After Ferret blindfolds her, he removes the straps binding her to the chair. "Stand up," he says, and she knows that voice. Ferret is Angry Man, who argued with the man in charge at the airstrip and brought her to her cell.

Her muscles hurt and they are stiff. Standing blindfolded is harder than she expects, and she wobbles before finding her balance. For a few moments the man does not do anything or say anything. She cannot stop trembling. Then his hand is on her shoulder, another on the front of her shirt. His fingers are warm on her chest, and for an instant the warmth is welcome until the fear takes over. He grabs a handful of the cotton fabric and rips it downward towards her belly, and the cotton tears. The shirt falls to the floor with a faint fluttery sound, and she crosses her arms over her chest.

His open hand presses against her belly; his splayed fingers linger at the waistband of her shorts. The button rips free, and it pings three times on the floor. The zipper gives way with a raspy sound. Then a rustle and a click and cold metal against her belly. A tug and a soft noise, the slicing of a knife through fabric. Her shorts fall onto her toes. She steels herself; her bra and underpants will be next.

Instead he pushes her back into the chair and reconnects the leather strap around her waist.

The door opens and closes. Is he gone? She is blindfolded and cannot be sure. Her nose itches, and she scratches it and realizes that her hands are free, so she could remove the blindfold herself. But she better not. He might be waiting for her to do that. He might come back and take away her underpants. Is she being unreasonable? Is paranoia a symptom of increasing hypothermia? She cannot remember what Norah said about the cold. Norah certainly did not say anything about ripping clothes off piece by piece in this calculated perversion of seduction. Maybe Norah does not know her well enough to talk about something so intimate. No, not intimate, but personal.

Why did Ferret leave her in her underwear? Probably to let her know that he will return, that more humiliation is coming, that there is something left for him to take off. Next time.

The shivering takes over everything, and her hands won't work. She never knew before that shivering could be so intensely painful. She tries rubbing her half-numb hands along the deadened skin of her upper arms but it does not help. Her blood must be pooling someplace, someplace deep inside, because it is no longer circulating, cannot be enticed to the surface to warm her. She wiggles her toes, and they feel slow and fat in their cold-anesthetized stupor. Actually, some anesthesia would be welcome, because her toes hurt, her feet and legs and fingers and hands too. The shaking pain is deep and heavy, like her head.

After a while the pain starts to fade, which does not make sense because she is getting colder, not warmer. Or perhaps it does make sense, and she just cannot find the sense, cannot catch the morsel of logical thought in this icy and slippery place. Time slows down, and her worrying slows down too. And that is good, but then maybe it is not so good, because breathing is harder. Like swimming. Like drowning. She needs clothes, blankets, a long soak in a hot bath. She imagines thick towels to dry off and warm clothes to put on. Wool socks. Maybe even Jess's leather pants. She teased Jess about them: aren't you scared the animal rights' folks will tear them off, leave you running bare butt down 6th Avenue? Fleece pants would be even better. Do they make battery-operated pants, like those mittens and socks for skiers?

She cannot answer her own questions, cannot grasp the concepts long enough to consider them seriously. Words and sentences skid along the frosty synapses of her brain. Her thoughts slip-slide and somersault away before she finishes thinking them. The cold air is a frigid cloud settling on her, seeping into her pores, freezing every thought in her head. Everything except the fierce need to stay warm.

She curls her body into a ball, bringing her feet up onto the seat of the chair. She hugs her legs and lets her chin rest on her knees, where the scrapes are frozen into miniature plowed furrows. Maybe Austin will come back and help. It seemed that Austin liked her when they talked in the yard, when she whispered "hang tough," before abandoning her to this frozen hell. Perhaps Austin was hiding some kindness, some humanity underneath that uniform. But she will not think about Austin now because finally, for the precious time being, nothing hurts any more. Her heavy body drags her down, plummeting her brain into ice-blue patterned sleep.

# 16. HENRY, 3:02 P.M.

Henry sticks his head into the staff lounge and looks around, but the new guard isn't there. He takes the stairs to the basement. Damn, he hopes this girl works out because he hates wasting time interviewing staff and orienting them for nothing. Austin seems sharp enough. Too bad he can't remember the story Cat told him about the girl's family, back when he was doing her background vetting. He was thinking about something else while Cat talked, something more important, but he should have been paying attention. He will have to ask Cat again tonight and confess that he forgot.

Now he has to concentrate on the interrogation. He won't admit it to anyone, not even under torture—well maybe under torture because he hates pain, but not otherwise—but he isn't crazy about this part of his job. He loves the investigations, solving the puzzles and tracking down the bad guys. But since the twin towers, his job has become less detective work and more interrogation. Not only that, the traditional techniques of outsmarting suspects, of building a relationship and extracting information bit by bit, are being abandoned in favor of more aggressive methods. The rules have changed and the new techniques, if he's honest with himself, make him want to puke. Tobias has somehow figured this out and holds it against him; he keeps suggesting that Henry leave the interrogations to him. But he can't do that. Tobias likes doing them far too much.

Henry thumb-presses his entry into the interrogation corridor and pushes the door behind him until the lock clicks. Austin is leaning against the wall outside Room D, looking worried and slightly green.

"Your first interrogation," he says.

He can always tell. Beforehand they look anxious, terrified even, men and women both, almost as if they're the ones facing the intense scrutiny and humiliation, the discomfort. The trick is to inspect the new recruits afterwards. Some still look sick and they usually do okay, eventually became good agents. Others are flushed and excited, as if they just screwed someone on top of the guests' winter coats at a cocktail party, and they're the ones to watch out for. Like Tobias.

"Yes, sir, my first. So what, exactly, is my job here?"

"Good question. Observe. Project a neutral attitude towards the detainee. Later we might need you to take a more active role, befriend her to extract information."

"Like good cop/bad cop?"

Too much television and everyone is an expert in interrogation. Henry enters the entry code on the keypad. "Not really. We're all the good cops," he says. He wishes it were true.

The arctic air in the room blasts Henry's face, takes his breath away. What is Tobias thinking? Henry hurries to the wall console and switches off the air conditioner, then turns his attention to the prisoner strapped onto the chair.

Dr. Cohen is curled into a tight ball. Blindfolded and naked, except for her underwear. Her arms encircle her legs; her head is burrowed into the cave between her arms and chest. Her skin is oddly flushed and mottled. Austin kneels at her side. She pulls off the blindfold, places both hands on the woman's shoulders and shakes.

The prisoner's head lolls back. A blue tinge circles her mouth.

"Gandalf?" Austin yells into the prisoner's ear. "Are you okay?"

Hmm. Henry wonders how the guard knows the prisoner's given name. But the woman doesn't answer, and that's a more immediate problem. He grasps her chin hard between his thumb and index finger and tilts her head to face his.

"Dr. Cohen." He speaks loud and slowly. "Can you hear me?"

Her eyes flutter open, then close.

"Damn." Henry turns to Austin. "Get blankets. And hot tea. Lots of sugar. And quickly."

Alone in the room with the detainee, Henry can't think straight. For a moment he considers calling Cat and asking her what to do but he has already broken enough rules. Maybe his mother was right about medical school. At least then he would know how to help this woman. Massage her extremities to get the blood flowing, or is it more important to get blood to her brain, and how does he do that? How bad is she, anyway? All they need is a confinement-related fatality right now, especially a high priority detainee with suspected links to an insurgent in Pakistan. It would dishonor the Bureau, not to mention spelling the end of his career.

He feels his face flush with shame, glad his father isn't around to witness his disgrace. Dad warned him about the FBI. "Stick with the state police, son," he said at Henry's college graduation. "You'll regret getting mixed up with spooks."

This is all Tobias's fault. Henry isn't a violent person, but right now he'd love to punch the guy. Of course, then Cat would mutter something sarcastic about pesky little Y-chromosomes. Anyway, Tobias would probably knock him cold with one blow, and he would no doubt capture it on tape to shame him forever.

In fact, Tobias is probably watching him right now. Henry stares directly into the camera hidden in the molding along the drop ceiling. Turning back to the control console, he uses his retinal scan mode to override the system, to shut down all surveillance cameras in the room. It's disturbing how much safer he feels, knowing that Tobias can't see him. He pulls a chair next to the prisoner and sits down. He puts his hands on her forearms and begins rubbing softly. Can cold temperatures cause brain damage, or is it just heat that kills brain cells?

"Can you hear me, Dr. Cohen? Austin went to get hot tea. And blankets. Please hold on until she gets back. You'll be okay."

He feels stupid talking to someone who probably can't hear him and would most likely despise him if she could. As well she should; this excess happened on his watch. And here he is, blithering on to her like a cheerleading Nurse Nancy. But maybe talking with her can prevent a deepening coma, or worse.

"Listen, Dr. Cohen," he continues. "I'm sorry about the temperature. It's our job to question you, not harm you. I promise we'll get you warmed up before we proceed with the interrogation."

Dr. Cohen opens her eyes at his last word, closes them again without speaking. But the expression on her face, of contempt mixed with fury, tells him that she understands his intention to proceed with the questioning. Which means that her brain isn't freeze-dried. Relief floods his veins, and Henry wants to sob at the reprieve.

Relief mixed with humiliation.

He removes his hands from the cold surface of her arms and rubs his fist against his own aching breastbone. Maybe Cat is right, and he should have those heart tests before he keels over in the middle of an investigation. Maybe there *is* something wrong with him. He can't imagine questioning this poor woman, not after the way she just looked at him, with the contempt that mirrors his own growing doubts about this mess. But is it a physical condition or mental cowardice?

Maybe he just can't do it today, he tells himself. Maybe by tomorrow morning he will have developed the courage to resume the interrogation, because the woman must be questioned. And because if he doesn't do it, the job will fall to Tobias with his over-exuberance and his fancy new enhanced techniques with their initials and their damn euphemisms.

A kick at the door brings Henry to his feet, and he opens it for Austin. She carries a cup of tea in one hand, blankets over the other arm.

"Stay with her until she warms up," he tells Austin. "Then go home. I'll resume the interrogation in the morning."

In the corridor, Henry sinks back against the cement wall. Maybe Tobias is right that he's getting soft, out of touch. This is so different from the old days of the Bureau, when they questioned guys who had information about bad stuff.

He pulls his phone from his pocket. He should call Tobias right now and let him know that the interrogation is postponed. Tomorrow they'll continue, with appropriate restraint and respect for the rules.

Or maybe he'll just let Tobias take over.

Henry closes his eyes. He has no illusions about culpability. Ultimately, it doesn't matter who is physically in that room with the professor. It makes no difference who asks the questions, who makes the threats, who causes the discomfort. This interrogation is on his watch, and he is responsible.

# 17. TOBIAS, 3:18 P.M.

When the interrogation room monitors go black, Tobias's first reaction is fury. Who's responsible for this fuck-up? Someone's head is going to roll.

He's been searching again through the Cohen bitch's personal effects, looking for the missing cell phone. By now, they should have already downloaded and examined the call log. Any calls to or from Pakistan could be powerful evidence, not to mention potent ammunition in breaking the woman. Not that he expects her to be tough, but you never know, not really. People can surprise you with their stubbornness. And their secrets.

The blank monitors could be a malfunction in the surveillance system. Tobias runs through the troubleshooting protocol and discovers that Henry's retinal scan override has been deployed. Holy shit. Henry turned off the cameras? Tobias hurls the manual onto the floor and watches it skid under the desk. How can Henry treat him like this? It's disrespectful. Not to mention, a stupid thing for Henry to do. A very stupid thing.

Because Tobias knows things about Henry, things the man does not want to become public. Actually, Tobias doesn't exactly understand what he knows, except that it's unsavory and potentially a career-ender. He always suspected that there's something *off* about Henry. A guy can tell these things. Then one night at the tavern in Bangor, must have been four, five years ago, they were celebrating solving a border smuggling case before the Mounties figured it out. They had probably had more rounds than was smart for public servants, even off duty. Tobias had been heading for the john as Henry walked out with the Regional Chief. He heard the Chief address Henry as Hen, in a smarmy tone of voice. Henry's neck and face flamed scarlet, and he sat way down at the other end of the bar. After Henry left, earlier than the rest of them, Tobias asked the Chief what that was about.

The Chief smirked. "Fucking tranny."

Tobias was still married to Lois then, although things had already started falling apart. He probably stank of ale and cigars when he got home that night, and she was already asleep. Still, it wouldn't kill her to show a little affection, would it? He has always blamed Henry for his response to Lois's snub, for the way he slapped her face and blurted out that word. Tranny. He didn't actually know what it meant, but the way the Chief spat the word made it sound bad, and that's what he wanted Lois to feel. Bad, just like he did.

When he woke up the next afternoon, with sewer-breath and a minefield head, Lois was gone. It wasn't until he checked Wiktionary that he understood her confusion, her disgust. But he just wanted to hurt the frigid bitch. He thought the word meant queer or something like that. How did the Regional Chief know so much about it anyway? And how did sicko Henry score such a classy wife? Catherine had always been charming to him at the office holiday parties, the occasional barbecue on their deck. Even Lois liked her.

That's all water under the bridge. Now, he just wonders what's going on in the interrogation room. But he won't give Henry the satisfaction of calling. He can be patient and bide his time, right?

Bending down, he picks up the manual, its pages spread-eagled on the floor. Smoothing the line drawing illustrations of restraint procedures and bruise avoidance techniques, he leans the desk chair back to its limit and puts his feet up on the desk.

People don't appreciate the art involved in this work, the subtlety. Brute force only goes so far; it is the mind-fucking that makes a prisoner want to spill his guts. The art is knowing what kind of fear is likely to unhinge each prisoner, what preparation and humiliation to utilize. That's what leads to success in this business. He closes his eyes and plans his approach to the professor.

The telephone jerks him awake. He swipes the back of his hand across his mouth. Nothing. Lois claimed he drooled when he slept. Another lie.

He glances at the caller display. "Yes, sir."

"I don't feel well," Henry says. "I'm going home early. I'll resume Dr. Cohen's interrogation tomorrow morning. Gently. If she knows anything at all, it's minor."

"Not to worry, boss. Whatever she knows, we'll find out one way or another."

"Are you listening to me, Tobias? We have no evidence this woman has any terrorist ties. She's a U.S. citizen and we are professionals, doing our job. We're not the CIA and this isn't Afghanistan. We don't torture people."

"It's not torture, boss, it's . . ."

"Enhanced interrogation technique. That's semantic crap, and you know it."

Tobias recognizes the edge of scorn. But Henry's the one who's pathetic. Tobias tries to make his voice kind. "Terrorist, activist, communist," he says. "Call her whatever you want. But if she knows something, we'll find it."

"And we'll do it by the rules," Henry says sharply.

"Which rules are those, Boss? The rules have changed."

"You're out of line."

"Maybe I am," Tobias says. "But you're out of touch."

Tobias listens to the click and dial tone for a moment, then scoots the rolling chair to the console. First, he resets the cameras. When he designed the surveillance system he put a fifteen-minute limit on the override function. It's possible he might have neglected to mention that to Henry. He checks that Henry has left the interrogation room and sees he left the Coombs girl babysitting her with blankets and tea. Well, then they'll both be cold. Tobias turns on the AC and the stereo feed. Rap music, full blast. Words and sentiments as foul as he's been able to find on the Internet.

His stomach rumbles, and he glances at the wall clock. He'll wait an hour to make sure Henry has left the facility, let the professor stew for a bit. No way he's waiting for tomorrow. This interrogation is far too important to put off.

# 18. AUSTIN, 3:26 P.M.

Austin touches the scratchy Army-issue wool blanket over Dr. Cohen's shoulder. "You okay?"

The prisoner jerks away. Her hands clutching the mug tremble so hard Austin worries she'll drop it.

Austin squirms under the force of the older woman's gaze and withdraws her hand. It's not a friendly stare, not grateful for the blankets and tea. More like accusatory, as if somehow Austin is responsible for the blasting frigid air and the explosion of nasty music. Can't she see that Austin is freezing too, even in her uniform? Well, who cares if the prisoner isn't grateful? Henry Ames told her to stay with the woman, to make sure she's ready for tomorrow's interrogation. Of course, he said to stay until the prisoner was warm, and that wasn't going to happen now. She pulls the second chair, the interrogator's chair, next to the wall. How will she know when it's safe to leave?

Twenty minutes later Tobias saunters into the room. He switches off the music and air, then looks from the prisoner to Austin and back again, as if he can read the prisoner's accusation and Austin's remorse. He wears a take-charge attitude. Did she misunderstand Henry Ames about waiting until tomorrow to continue the interrogation? She doesn't think so.

"There's been a change of plans," Tobias announces.

He motions for her to stand up, then takes her chair, never removing his gaze from Austin's face. Blushing, she leans against the wall where she has a good view of both Tobias and his prisoner. How does the man manage to make that small interaction so charged with the gutter?

Tobias stands with one foot on the seat of the chair and points his finger at the prisoner. "I need answers from you. Now."

His first questions are routine, inconsequential. His voice is even, without menace. Austin listens carefully but she doesn't get it. Why waste time asking where Gandalf was going on Thursday when they already know?

"Tell me about your work," he says.

"I'm a mathematician, a university professor. I conduct research and supervise graduate students. But you must know this already."

"Yes. What is your research?"

"I analyze cloud patterns."

Austin thinks about lying on the flat rocks of the Basin with Pops on fine afternoons, sharing a bag of Fig Newtons and telling each other made-up stories prompted by the shapes of the clouds. Gandalf gets big bucks as a university professor for studying that? Tobias doesn't seem impressed either.

"Clouds?" he asks. "Folks out here fish. Their lives depend on the meaning of clouds, knowing what weather is coming. What do clouds have to do with math?"

"We develop equations to correlate cloud pattern with weather models. Destructive weather, mostly. Other people in my field examine tornados and thunderstorms, but I am interested primarily in hurricanes."

Tobias smiles. Austin isn't sure if she's ever seen him smile. What's funny about hurricanes?

"Can you predict their paths?" he asks. "That might come in handy this weekend."

Ah. Austin gets it—a joke about the hurricane. Tobias is trying to disarm the prisoner and put her at ease.

"So you should probably thank me," he continues. "This basement is a pretty safe place to ride out the storm. That is, if the predictions are right, and Gena is heading right at us."

"Prediction models have become quite reliable," Gandalf says.

"What about manipulating storms? You know, sending fifteen feet of snow and ice to bury a Taliban outpost?"

"Not yet," she says. "We're at least a decade away from that."

"The military must be interested in your work."

"My research has been in non-military areas, but one of the mathematical tools we rely on heavily is triangulation, which has significant military importance."

"Triangulation? What's that?"

"On the most basic level, it is a geometric process of calculating the distance to a point, using the length of one leg of a triangle and two angles."

Austin has no idea what they're talking about. How can the prisoner be so smart about this stuff after freezing half to death?

"Didn't the military invent that, for GPS?" Tobias asks.

The prisoner nods. "They developed the global positioning concept in the 70s, before it became commercially viable for consumer use. But the work we do involves complex real-world observation and large systems of simultaneous equations. At this point, with no likely commercial utilization for our research, there is little funding available."

"Not even from the armed forces? Have you ever been approached by them? I bet they'd be interested in funding your work, even if success isn't close."

Austin tries to understand. So what if our own Army funds the woman's research into hurricanes? What does that have to do with terrorism? None of this seems important enough to kidnap the woman, fly her to Maine and almost freeze her to death.

Gandalf pulls the blanket tighter. "There is always Defense Department money available; everyone in research knows that. If you want it, you simply write your proposal slanted towards the potential military application of the work, like night navigation or weaponry direction systems. But that has never been my interest."

"Are there a lot of people doing this kind of work?"

"Hardly anyone, actually. A handful of investigators."

Tobias nods, as if that's what he expected. "Okay," he says, "now let's talk about these colleagues of yours."

"In my department?"

"No. I want to talk about Sandra Myerson and Ahmed . . ." He removes a post-it note from his uniform shirt pocket and reads it. "Ahmed Makhdoom. Tell me about them."

Ah. Austin leans forward.

"The three of us met in graduate school. We were interested in similar questions and began collaborating. Our dissertations explored different aspects of the same problem and we published them as a group. That's rare for mathematicians; we are usually a solitary sort."

"And you were close personally as well?"

"Not since graduate school. I see Sandra at meetings every year or so. She has an endowed chair at Stanford. Ahmed returned home to Pakistan to teach. I have not seen him face to face in twelve, thirteen years."

"Where was that?"

Does Gandalf hesitate, just a bit? Austin isn't sure. Maybe it was just a pause as she reached to touch something—a gold necklace?—around her neck, then set her empty mug on the floor. Or maybe the temperature is getting to her, slowing her down. What information is Tobias looking for?

"It was London, 2003, at the international symposium."

"If you haven't seen these people, how do you write papers together?"

"We have a secure private website where we can work jointly online, in real-time."

"Yes, of course. We found that site on your laptop, Ms. Cohen. Very instructive. We were especially interested in the archived emails between you and Mr. Makhdoom."

Gandalf's eyes widen slightly, but Austin notes that she keeps her expression bland. Perhaps not as secure as you think, Professor?

Tobias scoots his chair closer to Gandalf. "Tell me, what other work do you do together, online?"

Gandalf looks puzzled. "Nothing else. What do you mean?"

"Political work."

"I am not at all interested in politics."

"What do you know about your friend Ahmed's political leanings?"

"We never talk about politics. I don't think he cares much about it either."

"Your friend is a practicing Muslim, right?"

"I believe so, but Islam is a religion, not a political position."

"You just said you don't know about his politics."

"I don't."

"But you do know that your friend Ahmed is from a small village in South Waziristan, one of the most politically volatile places in the world?"

"We never discussed our backgrounds."

"I'm sure you know that his uncle was a founding member of a radical jihadist party in Waziristan, right?

"No, I did not."

"And that Ahmed's brother is in a microbiology graduate program at MIT?"

"I did not know that either."

"Perhaps you know that ten days ago your good buddy Ahmed's uncle, a politically powerful man and extremely anti-American, and his pregnant wife were killed by a U.S. drone attack?"

Gandalf looks down. "No."

"Are you aware that shortly after that accident your friend Ahmed was observed in his uncle's village near the Afghanistan border. The village where Ahmed was born, where his brothers and sister still live with their families."

"Perhaps he went home for the funeral?"

"Did he tell you that?"

"I told you that I have not heard from him."

Tobias shakes his head slowly. "You don't know much, do you, Professor? Well, what do you say to this: we have credible evidence that a terrorist cell is planning another attack, a significant attack, on this country. Your country. The planning cell is located in Ahmed's home village. We think he may be part of the group."

Gandalf looks stunned. Either she is genuinely surprised, or a better actress than Austin would have guessed. Tobias's performance isn't too shabby either. He stands up, throws his cap on the floor and speaks to Gandalf with clear disgust in his voice.

"When's the last time you got a telephone call from your friend Ahmed?'

"Never. We communicate by email and our website."

Austin shifts her weight to the other leg and glances down at her watch. She is exhausted and she's just an observer. Gandalf must be dying. How does Tobias look so fresh?

"Maybe so, Ms. Cohen," he says. "Maybe so. But I suspect you're not being totally truthful. I admit I'm disappointed in you. I had such high hopes for our little talk. I might have to ask some of my slightly less, well less *refined*, colleagues to join us. You might want to reconsider your lack of cooperation."

Austin looks away. She doesn't want to see the reaction on Gandalf's face. Tobias must be referring to the "guys." She's heard the male guards bragging about how they terrify female detainees.

Tobias refastens the restraint around Gandalf's waist. At the control console, he stares into the retinal scanner. Austin can't see exactly what he does next, but she hears the air conditioner click back on. And the music. He walks to the doorway.

"Perhaps our guest needs some time alone to think about things," he tells Austin. "Take away the blanket."

Is she imagining it, the way his voice lingers on "blanket," as if it has another meaning, something secret between the two of them?

Then he faces Gandalf, and his voice gets hard. "I'll be back. You might want to consider cooperating fully. That is, if you are interested in going home. Jess is quite worried about you."

Austin takes the blanket from Gandalf's shoulders and gathers it in her arms as she follows Tobias to the door. She wants to look back at Gandalf, to communicate some sort of comfort, to apologize even. But it's possible the woman does know something about this Ahmed guy, something she won't tell. Besides, Tobias is watching.

In the corridor, Tobias double-checks the lock, then crosses his arms and looks at Austin. "We'll resume in one hour."

After returning the blanket to the storeroom, she stands in front of the outside door at the end of the corridor. Wind-flung raindrops batter the barred window. Almost two hours left on her shift, two interminable hours before she can walk down the hill to the ferry and go home to supper and Gran and Pops, far away from this place.

## 19. TOBIAS, 5:00 P.M.

When they return to the interrogation room an hour later, the prisoner is a marble statue posed on her metal chair. For an instant, Tobias sees her as beautiful, almost as art. He feels a shudder of something like shame, but it passes quickly. He notes that she hugs ashen legs with goose-bumped arms. Good. Cold temperature is effective preparation, and warmth makes prisoners grateful, ready to talk. But this one turns ugly. She refuses to look at him, doesn't respond when he turns off the music and changes the flow of air to warm. She ignores him when he turns his chair around and straddles it. He leans his elbows on the top rung and stares at her. Either she's catatonic or royally pissed off. Fine. Either way he's getting to her.

"Are you ready to work with us, Professor?"

When she doesn't answer, he slaps her face.

She flinches. Austin cringes too, and reaches for the towel on the desk. He stops her with a glance before turning back to the prisoner.

"Now do I have your attention?"

The prisoner dips her chin, a small gesture of defeat. A speck of blood blossoms on her lower lip. It grows in size until it drips onto her bare thigh. She doesn't move to wipe it up. Playing it tough, is she?

He scoots his chair closer. "Let's talk some more about your friend Ahmed."

She moves her lips, then speaks slowly. "Not a friend, a colleague."

"I don't believe you." Tobias drums his fingers on his legs. He loves this part, when he knows something they don't know he knows, and he is about to pounce on them, claws out and ready to draw blood. "Because the letters and emails I read sounded more personal than that. Intimate, even."

"Intimate?"

"How about this note he sent you in 1988?" Tobias closes his eyes and recites. "'Our minds are so compatible. Do you ever wonder if we might find other kinds of solace in each other?'" He cocks his head and grins at the woman. "That sounds like a rather intimate invitation to me."

She flushes. "When Ahmed returned to Pakistan after graduate school, he felt out of place. Lonely. He flirted with me some by mail, but not seriously." She looks at him then, full face. Which is actually pretty ridiculous with that bead of blood hanging off her lip. "He knows I like women."

"Don't play me for a fool. This message is some kind of code, right?"

She shakes her head. "No code. After that one exchange, he never mentioned it again."

He can feel that she is lying. The trick now is to make his questions circle around, and catch her by surprise. "But you were turned on, weren't you? By his desire?"

"I felt only embarrassment."

"Then why save the correspondence?"

"It's our work archive. It's supposed to be private."

"Do you consider yourself a patriot?"

The detainee looks surprised. That always throws them off-balance, the quick change of subject. Tobias glances at the girl, Austin. He hopes she's paying close attention.

"Of course," the woman says.

"So, if there is an immediate and dire threat to your country, and you are one of the few people who could prevent a major terrorist disaster, you would do so, right?"

"Naturally, if I could."

"Well you can. We have reason to believe that your colleague is part of a Pakistani cell and they are planning an attack on a critical U.S. target. The anniversary of 9/11 is in two days. A likely date for something big to happen, don't you think? Now you're a smart lady, a professor. Surely you can see how important this is. You're our only direct link to Ahmed Makhdoom."

"But I only know him through our mutual work. I know nothing about this."

The woman is hiding something. He can always tell.

"This information is crucial for our national security, and we don't have much time left. You've left me no alternative. First thing tomorrow morning, I'll bring in some additional interrogators. To help jog your memory."

He studies the effect of his threat, how her nostrils flare and the muscles around her mouth stiffen. Good, she has lots to ponder all night long.

Austin's face changes too. He watches her mouth constrict, squeeze in on itself as if something smells bad. Her eyelids droop like she's exhausted and can't wait to go home to mama. She might be too soft for this job, but he can think of other activities she'd be just right for. Don't let her distract you, he reminds himself.

He isn't the slightest bit tired. On the contrary, he feels zingy and jazzed up and full of energy. He doesn't plan to go home tonight. Someone in charge has to stay at the camp, just in case, with the big storm coming. Henry doesn't think about things like that, doesn't plan ahead. It's one of his faults. Still, everybody has a vulnerable place, if you look for it, and his job is to search and find those weak spots. He's convinced this prisoner is hiding something related to the Ahmed fellow, but her major weakness is her lady friend. He's read their archived emails and felt the passion, though the messages are carefully bland on the surface. Maybe it's time to bring Jess back into the room.

He leans closer to the prisoner and lowers his voice into the dead-serious range. "Listen to me, Professor. I know Ahmed is your friend, and you're loyal. That's an admirable quality. But think for a moment about your *other* friend. We can pick Jess up as easily as we got you, and she might not fare so well."

The prisoner's eyes fill again. She sits silently for a minute, then speaks. "I'm cold. May I please have the blanket back?" She glances towards Austin, who returns her look with something like pity.

Very interesting. There's something between the two of them, something more than who brings the blanket. Tobias holds up his index finger, wags it back and forth. "Nope. Not until you give us something, anything, to help us stop this attack." With a flourish he brings both hands to his thighs and resumes playing drumbeats to accompany the rumble of thunder outside.

## 20. GANDALF, 5:34 P.M.

She watches Ferret's fingers drumming on his legs. His nails are squared-off and very clean; his hands small and neat, full of tension. They are rattle-snakes ready to strike. His words are frightening too but they make no sense because Ahmed is not a terrorist. He is a math geek, like Sandra, like her. She is willing to tell these people anything she knows, but she will not fabri-cate evidence, not about Ahmed or anyone else. She will not let herself dwell on Ferret's rattlesnake hands, either, or his threats to Jess. She will not think about the guys he mentioned; they must be the men Norah talked about, the men who said ugly things about her exposed body.

Gandalf shudders. Her body, which moved from violent shivering pain to dead-tired and mostly numb, is starting to hurt again in the warmer air. She glances at Austin leaning against the wall. Her face is an icy, dismal mask; what could the girl be thinking about all this? Her eyes follow every move Ferret makes with something softer than fear, almost desire? But that cannot be right; she probably cannot stomach this either. How could she? Ferret seems comfortable and at ease in this room, except that he is not get-ting what he wanted which is why he is threatening her with Jess and the guys, trying to intimidate her. He is bluffing.

Maybe Ferret can read her thoughts, because he turns his chair around and leans back, extending his legs straight out in front of him, as if he is re-laxing in his living room. That is better; she hates it when guys sit straddling chairs, legs opened wide as if their scorching genitals need all that extra breathing space.

"So, tell me," Ferret asks, looking up at the ceiling vent. "What got you interested in clouds?"

That is an easy one. She was doing her homework in front of the picture window looking across the Hudson River towards the Palisades. The river was the highway of rapidly changing weather patterns, and the clouds, the most spectacular manifestation of the changes, formed the palette of her daydreams. She was not a nerdy kid, not exactly; she just lacked the self-protection skills for middle school. Was Ferret also awkward back then, one of the skinny boys trying to melt back into the fence at recess, or was he one of the bullies?

"Nothing in particular," she says. "I have always been intrigued by clouds."

The second slap comes out of nowhere, a backhand smack across her left cheek. His college ring, the same generic design as the one in her jewelry box at home, slices a track through the skin. She brings her hand to her face, looks down at the blood on her finger. Being hit hurts more than she ever imagined watching film actors.

Tobias leans forward, and his eyes drill into hers. "Don't fuck with me. Our country is at war. If you don't help us, that makes you a traitor."

Norah did not warn her about being hit; maybe Norah is not trustworthy. Jess teases her about being naïve; she might advise believing no one in this place. The thought of Jess brings a quick surge of warmth and she tries to prolong the moment. She pictures Jess wandering through the rooms of their apartment, straightening piles of mail and journals, making sure the windows are locked tight against the wind pummeling the windowpane. Jess must be fighting off an invading army of tormenting images but never could she imagine this frigid cell, this ferret of a man.

Ferret tosses a towel onto her lap. It takes long seconds before her hands can move to hold it briefly against the sting on her cheek. She lets it slide to the floor, and he watches it fall. He unsnaps the waist restraint and motions Gandalf to rise but her leg muscles are frozen and will not respond right away. Ferret motions to Austin, who steps forward and helps her stand up and then returns to her position against the wall, equidistant from the two of them. Gandalf must grip the back of her chair and even so, she wobbles.

Without dropping his gaze, Ferret snaps open a hunting knife. Slipping the blade under the waist elastic of her underpants, he slices downward to the leg opening. The cotton slides to the floor along her other leg. He cuts one bra shoulder strap, then the other. Finally he slits the fabric between her breasts.

Her bra swings open and the prosthesis falls from its pocket. It hits the floor with a small bounce. Gandalf watches Ferret's sneer dissolve for an instant before he pulls his mouth back into control. She refuses to cross her arms over her chest, just lets them hang by her side, so he can fully appreciate the scar, the way it curves slightly across the left side of her chest and disappears into her armpit. She does not have to look down to know how the wound blooms purple in the cold air.

# 21. AUSTIN, 6:40 P.M.

By the time Austin stumbles down the hill to the ferry, the sky is already purple-gray. Rain beats a steady rhythm on her slicker hood. Her presence on the dock triggers the sensor, and the floodlight reflection multiplies in the puddles.

Bert steps out of the guard post. "You're late. Ready for a bumpy ride?"

Austin nods. She wishes she could pilot herself across the narrow sound instead of being transported like a tourist. Pops agreed to let her use his old outboard for the commute, but Henry Ames shot down that idea. Something about security, controlling all access to the facility. Makes sense, but tonight she can't bear the thought of Bert's amiable chitchat.

Bert peers ahead at the black water. "You okay? You seem spooked."

She nods but doesn't answer. Spooked is a good word for it. Bert probably has no clue about the business of the employees he ferries back and forth. Would he care if he knew? Grow up, she tells herself. What did she expect they'd do at the facility? Serve the prisoners tea and crumpets? Whatever crumpets are.

By the time they reach her grandparents' dock, the rain is relentless. Fat drops batter the slippery wood. Austin climbs out of the boat, waves to Bert, and shouts over the wind. "Thanks. See you at 6:00 am."

"If we're not all blown out to sea." Bert doesn't sound worried. "Give my howdy to your folks."

Gran is waiting at the back door with a towel. "I worried you'd be stuck out there all night. You're late." She peers into Austin's face. "And you look awful."

"Sorry," Austin says. "I couldn't call. We were in the middle of an . . . something."

"Are you okay?"

Is she? She wants to fall deeply asleep and not dream. She wants to sob until the ache of not being able to cry dissolves. She wants to burrow under a pile of quilts and comforters until she is so warm that Gandalf can feel it too. She wants to call Gandalf's girlfriend and tell her what's happening. She wants never to return to Hurricane Island. Either that or take Pops's boat over there right now and rescue Gandalf from that place, even if it turns out the woman has been doing math equations with a terrorist.

No one should be hit like that. No one deserves that, especially an old lady who has clearly suffered enough already. Austin knows what it feels like. Slapped and punched and lying on a gurney in the health services emergency room the time she needed stitches. Her boyfriend all pale and concerned, explaining to the campus cops how she slipped and landed hard, striking her shoulder and her cheek on the sharp edge of the TV table. Then—as soon as the nurse left the room—the jerk slipped his hand under her shirt and murmured how much he wanted her. Assaulted and humiliated, aroused and shamed, all at once.

She can't erase the image of the purple line curving across the woman's lopsided chest. She has never seen that before, what it looks like after a cancer operation. She crosses her arms against the reassuring symmetry of her breasts.

But she can't share any of this with Gran. "I'm just tired," she says. "The storm is getting bad."

"Tell me about it." Gran laughs. "Your grandfather is in hurricane heaven, glued to the Weather Channel. If the cable goes out, he'll drive us stark raving. You hungry?"

That too. She wants to eat until all the hollows inside are filled up. "Starving," she says, circling her arms around Gran and resting her chin on her gray hair, almost the same color as Gandalf's.

When Pops walks into the kitchen, they're still standing like that.

"Mushy stuff," he says, wrapping his arms around both of them.

Austin breaks away first. "I'm starving and exhausted and I have to be back early tomorrow." She looks at Pops. "You think Bert'll be able to get over?"

"Funny you should ask," he says. "This is a magnificent storm. Come watch the radar with me."

"Go ahead," Gran says. "I kept your plate warm."

Next to her on the sofa, Pops points at the screen. "See that red arrow? Gena is just cruising right along, aiming right up the coast at us."

"Where is it now?"

"*She*, not it. Still down south, off Cape Hatteras. She's a big girl."

"How big? Like Edna?"

Gran hands her a steaming plate of spaghetti and a glass of milk, like she's still six years old. She wishes that she was still a kid, had never heard of detention centers or enhanced interrogation techniques.

"Really big. We're already getting the rain even though the eye is twenty-four hours out. But this is nothing yet. It was so bad with Edna that Navy bases all along the east coast ordered their warships out to sea. Safer than the harbor." Pops stops talking and looks at her. "How come you're so interested all of a sudden? Yesterday you wouldn't listen to a word about this stuff."

Austin shrugs. "Someone at work. She studies hurricanes, was all excited that you lived through Edna out here. She had a lot of questions. That's all."

Pops smiles. "Tell her to give me a ring. This storm brings back all the details."

"That's not going to happen." Austin spears a meatball. "You tell me, and I'll pass it on. How bad was it here?"

"Bad enough. You got to remember Edna came just a week after Carol, so double whammy. Rivers flooded, trapping folks on top of their houses watching their cars washed downstream. Trees down and power out. That storm killed twenty-nine people, eight of them right here in Maine. Afterwards they retired the name Edna. They do that for the brutal storms, in respect for the lives lost."

"Where were you?"

Pops glances towards the kitchen. The water is running, so Gran must be washing dishes. She doesn't hear so well these days, but he lowers his voice anyway. "That's part of why your grandmother hates your little island. I was out there during the storm. Wasn't supposed to be, and I could've died. I spent two days in a quarry cave."

"Why?"

"A dare. My family was frantic."

"And Gran?"

"She thought I was dead." Pops smiles. "We were sweethearts."

Austin is silent for a few moments. "Gabe used to talk about the cave. Where is it, exactly?"

"There are a series of them along the north and west quarry walls, but they're pretty shallow and small. The secret one, where I hid, is at the south end of the east rim."

"Where, exactly? How do I find it? Come on. I'm not a little kid anymore."

He whispers. "It's well hidden. But you know where the lovers' initials are, right? The ones you and Gabe found?"

She nods.

"That's the cave, right there. The entrance is narrow, with a sharp turn so it looks blind." He shakes his head. "I'd feel better if you didn't mention this to your Gran."

"What's her beef with the place?"

"It's her story and it's complicated, all mixed up with her family and the quarry company out there."

"But that was a hundred years ago."

"People may forget some kinds of history, but not family pain. Betrayal and shame don't go away. What happened to her family on Hurricane Island shaped your grandmother. I hope she'll tell you about it someday, or maybe you'll figure it out on your own, but I can't say any more." His voice changes back to normal. "How was work?"

"My turn to be stubborn." Austin stands and picks up her dishes. "You know I can't talk about that."

But really, she wishes she could tell him all of it. About the awful cold and stripping prisoners naked. About how she felt when Tobias interrogated Gandalf—and hit her—like the bones in her own arms and legs were melting into mush. Lots of men on the islands smack their wives around. They wouldn't think twice about Tobias's actions. But Pops made it clear what he thinks about men hitting women after Austin loaded her duffle bags into the Greyhound bus and came home in the middle of spring semester, her bruises murmuring the shame of her boyfriend's idea of foreplay.

Pops speaks softly, doesn't take his eyes off the television screen. "You don't have to keep the job if you hate it so much."

"Did I say I hate it?"

"Don't have to. Anyway, what's so important to save money for? You still want to go to Texas? I guess the good news is after this job experience you can always join the Texas Rangers."

Austin can't help smiling at him. "Do they still exist?"

"Sure. Chuck Norris didn't die." Pops flutters his hand in her direction. "Go to sleep. You're interrupting the hurricane coverage."

## 22. RAY, 9:02 P.M.

"Okay, Pops. I'll leave you to your storm." Austin leans down to kiss the bald spot on the top of his head. "Goodnight."

"Sleep tight. Don't let the bedbugs bite."

It's an automatic response, but every time Ray says those words he remembers the morning Austin came to live with Nettie and him. Their daughter Abby marched into their kitchen with four-year-old Austin draped over her shoulder. She dropped the duffle bag on the floor with a dull thud and slid her sleeping child onto a chair. Arranging the girl's limp arms on the table and easing her head down on her grungy stuffed giraffe, Abby tossed her keys onto the Formica.

"I'm leaving. Taking the noon ferry," she said. "My apartment is paid up until next week. Throw out whatever crap you don't want."

Ray had a hard time finding his voice. "What do you mean? Where are you going?"

"Probably Boston. When I find a place to live and a job, I'll come back for her."

Nettie shook her head. "You can't just leave. You have responsibilities."

"If I stay one more hour, I'll die." Abby smoothed the snarls in Austin's dark hair and walked out of the house.

Ray had often wondered if they should have stopped her. Simply refused. Would she have dragged the child with her, into whatever foolish life she was looking for and would that have been better? But they didn't argue. Instead, they took the Bob Marley posters off the walls and made Abby's old room into a bedroom for Austin. Every morning Nettie took the girl to school with her. Every evening Austin sat at the Formica table and did puzzles or colored pictures or homework while Nettie cleaned up after supper and packed everyone's lunches for the next day. Every night, after two stories and a glass of water, Ray tucked her in with her giraffe and kissed her forehead and recited, "Goodnight. Sleep tight. Don't let the bedbugs bite."

For years after Abby left, he and Nettie asked themselves what they did wrong. How could they have raised a daughter who could abandon her child like that? Abby had always pushed the limits, broken every family rule, but Ray tried not to dwell on how strict Nettie had been in response. Sometimes when she tried to teach their daughter the importance of honesty and telling the truth, she could be, well, harsh.

There was one time, Abby must have been five or six, when she took a dollar from Nettie's purse to buy candy, and Nettie caught her with the half-eaten evidence. Abby lied about taking the money—what kid wouldn't—and that infuriated Nettie more. "If you can't follow the family's rules, you can't be part of the family," Nettie said. She locked the child in the hall closet, banished there with the winter jackets and rubber boots, broken skates and single mittens. Ray didn't know how long Nettie would have continued the punishment, but after fifteen minutes he couldn't stand listening to Abby's choking sobs and opened the door.

Was that bad parenting, what Nettie did? What he did? He didn't know. They loved their daughter and never spanked her, but still. He wondered if Abby remembered that day and the closet as clearly as he did.

He also remembered the way his wife's tears seeped into Abby's hair as she read Margaret's letters, shards of pain that caught the lamplight. What was Nettie thinking that night? He wondered if she learned something important from the letters. When Abby left Austin with them, Nettie was a much gentler mother the second time around. Hopefully they did a better job.

But maybe not. Because here's their girl, looking spooked out of her skin with this new job and yearning to go off on some futile search for her no-good father.

"Why so serious?" Nettie sits on the sofa and picks up the canvas bag she once carried to and from school, now stuffed with promotional leaflets for the Three Sisters Land Trust. "You worried about that storm?"

He shifts over and burrows his face into her neck, where the faint aroma of rosemary lingers. Nettie never wears perfume. "My scent is Eau de Garden Herbs," she chided him the year he bought cologne for her birthday.

She takes his face in both hands. "Tell me."

He shakes his head free. He can't explain his premonition, but something is very wrong. The rumors don't help. All that gossip about something nasty happening on Hurricane Island, something involving Homeland Security and the military. His Austin doesn't belong mixed up in that crap. And Austin's curiosity about the initials and the bad old days, that doesn't help his worries.

It's probably nothing. Or maybe he's simply responding to the atmospheric changes ahead of the storm. All animals feel the danger by instinct.

Even as a fourteen-year-old, he knew that Edna was deadly. And yup, it had been crazy to take the dare and doubly crazy to row over to the island, with the hurricane almost upon him. He will never forget those two days, huddling in the cave with the howling of the storm outside, knowing that Nettie would kill him if the storm didn't. Because even back then, long before cell phones and texting and Facebook, there was no such thing on the island as private business. Everyone knew he'd taken the dare and gone to Hurricane. Nettie was there when his cousin dared him. "You'd better not go," she warned Ray. "Please don't go." But he did it anyway.

He pats Nettie's hand. "Nothing to tell. It's just when she gets home from that job every night, she looks half empty. It scares me."

Nettie leans her head on his shoulder. They listen together to the surges of rain and wind ramming against the window.

"I know," she says. "Me too."

## 23. HENRY, 11:14 P.M.

He is locked in his home office with the computer off, the green-shaded desk lamp the only illumination. Cat's footsteps upstairs are almost obliterated by the wind-blasted surges of rainstorm outside. He stares at Dr. Cohen's cell phone in the center of his desk blotter. An ordinary device that is absolutely where it shouldn't be, making it extraordinary, and dangerous. He has never before broken the chain of evidence, never willfully broken Bureau rules and protocols. And the action he is contemplating could be considered a possibly worse violation: abuse of power.

He wishes he understood more clearly why he is jeopardizing his career for a math professor. The only explanation he can come up with is that something smells wrong, and he joined the Bureau to do the *right* thing. He can't imagine proceeding with the interrogation of Dr. Cohen. Tomorrow he'll have Tobias take over and he'll monitor the man closely. A compromise, he reassures himself; that's what being an adult is all about.

Compromise and *compassion*, which is not a concept he has ever thought much about. But maybe that's what it is, the thing that's eating him up: knowing that his prisoner's friend, or partner, or whatever they call her, is waiting in fear.

He reaches for Dr. Cohen's phone, turns it on, and presses the photo icon labeled Jess.

A female voice answers on the second ring. "Gee?"

"No," he says.

"Who's there? Is Gandalf there?"

This is crazy. What can he possibly say to her?

"Is Gandalf alright? Who are you?"

He can't speak. How can he reassure her, without getting himself deeper in trouble? What was he thinking?

"Please. Whoever you are. Can you at least tell me if she's alive or dead?"

Panic flails in his chest. Panic and pain. He has to hang up. Someone might trace the call back to him. But still, he owes this woman something, doesn't he? He clears his throat.

"She's alive." The words come out as a croak.

Immediately, he disconnects and powers down the phone, slipping it into his jacket pocket. He collapses forward onto his desk blotter, letting his head fall into the cradle of his folded arms. Compassion or not, that was a stupid, stupid thing to do. His brain is unraveling. He's letting his emotions hijack his judgment, just like Tobias says. His thoughts spiral wildly, careening from Dr. Cohen's blue-tinged skin to the frantic voice of her friend on the phone, from the unsatisfactory interrogation to the approaching hurricane. Not to mention his worries about Tobias.

Things are falling apart, his dreams eroding under his feet. All he ever wanted to do was keep the world safe and prove to his father that he can make a difference working for the Bureau. Instead, he's losing control of his staff. His leadership is weakening. He can tell by the way people look at him. Not only Tobias, the other guys too. Do other men feel this way? Useless and empty? Do they ever worry about the ethics of it all?

To be fair, it's not entirely his fault. It's a complicated constellation of events and reactions. The place itself doesn't help, so isolated and dilapidated, with its history of conflict and betrayal and violence. He warned the Bureau bigwigs about Hurricane Island, but they never listen.

He stands up and stretches. His muscles feel stiff and old. He knows he should exercise more, maybe lug that stationary bike up from the basement. Not that his being in shape would have any effect on the Bureau or on his job. Because bottom line, after all the excuses are said and done, he is in charge and he will be defined by the failure.

He walks towards the window, listens to the onslaught of rain, turns back again. It really isn't fair. He gets no logistical support from the Regional Chief. His only experienced field agent is Tobias, who is getting more and more out of hand. The guy almost killed the math professor today and who knows what he'll do tomorrow in search of information the woman almost certainly doesn't have. In the morning, he'll talk to Tobias, take him off the Cohen case entirely. Yes, that makes sense. Maybe he was wrong earlier. Maybe he *will* finish the interrogation himself and do it right.

He paces faster. Twenty years and he understands Tobias less and less. They worked well together and moved together up the ladder, always first and second in command, until Tobias started requesting advanced counterterrorist training. He even did three months at Bagram with the CIA during the short window when the military intelligence agencies shared information and technical know-how. It will be difficult to reprimand the guy, but it has to be done. That's what leadership is all about, isn't it? Doing the difficult tasks. Taking responsibility.

The red message light on the computer starts blinking on and off, on and off. Probably the Regional Chief again, demanding results from the interrogation. The familiar ache starts up in his chest, the pesky rodent burrowing in there, gnawing on the inside of his breastbone and trying to chew its way free. No way can he take the Chief's arrogance tonight, or his contempt. He turns his back on the computer, locks the office behind him, and feels his way upstairs in the dark. He'll deal with the message in the morning. Maybe he'll be lucky; maybe the storm will cut off the power, and he'll have a few days' respite.

Tonight, right now, he needs to cast off this catastrophe of a day, to shed his work skin and forget he made that inexplicable telephone call. He slips into bed next to Catherine, kisses the flannel sleep mask across her eyes. He moves his pillow closer and tries matching his respirations to her soft snoring.

It doesn't work. He isn't sleepy. His arms and legs feel squirrelly and charged. He thinks about the tabs of chewable Benadryl in the bedside table, but he can't afford to be dopey at work in the morning.

He touches Cat's shoulder. Maybe he can wake her up with the feather light touches she calls fern-kisses and just maybe, she will be in the mood. Or he can go to his other love, to his beautiful things. Why can't he have both? For months he's been aching to share his true self with his wife.

He swings both feet to the floor, and feels around for the leather slippers Melissa gave him one birthday, back when she still spoke to him. In the bathroom, he plugs in the lamp made from the bumpy round shell of a sea urchin. The lavender light is luminous, otherworldly. Cat gave it to him for their fifth wedding anniversary. "When one of us turns it on," she instructed, "it's an invitation to seduction." He feels a flash of guilt using their special lamp for himself, but pushes the thought away. There is nothing wrong about this.

He stands in front of the linen closet. Years of marriage have defined their separate spaces, but he still worries that in a fit of menopausal energy Cat will decide to rearrange the old beach towels and sleeping bags stored on his shelf and discover his hidden things. He digs under the camping tarp for the wooden box that once held his father's fishing gear. He retrieves the key from the bottom of his cracked leather dopp kit, turns it slowly and jiggles. The lock is rusty; it requires babying, but he takes his time and jiggles it just right and it clicks. He sits naked on the fluffy pink toilet lid cover and opens the box.

The new underwear mail-ordered from California has curvy padding over the buttocks and a gaff to flatten his dick. Garter belt attachments dangle front and back. Then, silk stockings. Real silk. Carefully, he brings the sheer stocking to the toes of his left foot and eases it over the nails and along the instep, careful not to snag it on the callus on his heel. The fabric caresses his calf. Some guys shave their legs to enhance the smooth feeling, but Henry loves the soft crackle of silk on hair. Loves the coming together of opposites, how a few square yards of French silk and lace transforms his body from awkward and clumsy to graceful and elegant. Eloquent, even. Draped in jade satin, his body speaks its hidden sweetness. Whispers it with the rustle of fine fabrics.

The stockings pull up smooth over his thighs. He attaches them to the hooks and stands with his back to the mirror on the bathroom door, looking over his shoulder. Bending down, he straightens the dark seams to bisect the back of each leg, admiring the way the stockings swell over his calves. He loves the smooth slither of a stockinged foot slipping into high heels, his newest pair, gold sequins sparkling in the soft light. Then the black lace brassiere.

Finally, he shivers into the sleek satin dress. The deep teal color vibrates in the low light. He urges up the back zipper. His chest expands and opens, and the last tendrils of ache dissolve. He regards himself in the bathroom mirror, shoulders to toes, ignoring his face with his five-o'clock shadow. He turns again to admire the low scoop neckline in back and smiles at his reflection. He looks good, like a person who is fully himself, even if himself is dressed like a herself. He does not fully understand, but it is obviously right.

Admiring himself in the mirror isn't quite enough. He loves himself like this and he loves Cat. She's a good person, and they have a strong marriage. She will be okay with this.

Leaving the sea urchin light on, he cracks open the bathroom door and listens to her breathing. At the threshold to the bedroom, he steps out of the gold shoes and walks to the bed, relishing the slight crunching sound of stockings on carpet. He stands by the bed, inches from Catherine's right arm.

He wants to touch her. To say, Look at me. Open your eyes and see me. Like the blog he read online last week, written by a man who finally shared his secret with his wife, and she embraced it. That couple wasn't any younger than Cat and him, or any hipper.

He can picture it perfectly. A romantic dinner on the good china in the dining room, not melamine plates at the kitchen table. Candles and soft music. After dessert they will dance, draped together with a shared velvet stole. They will sway to the music, satin rustling against silk. He will unwrap their shawl, and she'll slowly unzip the long back closure of his dress. Then he'll unbutton her satin blouse, kissing her breasts. One by one, four spike heels will slither off silk-stockinged feet, teeter, and drop onto the rug.

He hesitates. Once Cat knows, there's no going back to this perfect, untarnished moment. A wormy feeling in his chest cautions him that maybe this isn't the right time. Maybe he should tell her when they are walking together, comfortably dressed as man and woman, on the rocky beach they both love. But he can't wait, not when he feels so lonely in his beautiful clothes. He pushes the cautions away and reaches down to take off her sleep mask. The elastic strap gets tangled in her hair.

She opens her eyes, blinks. Her face is unfocused, sleepy.

"Honey," Henry says.

"Hmmmm?" She closes her eyes and starts to turn over.

"Cat." He makes his voice serious. "Look at me."

She blinks. "What's wrong? Is it Lissa?"

"Nothing's wrong. Everything is fine. I'm fine. Please, look at me." He takes her hand and places it on his chest. The satin is glossy in the dim light spilling from the bathroom.

She looks and this time her eyes stay open. She touches the fabric, pushing her fingertips into the silicone falsies, and jerks her hand back. "What's going on? Why are you dressed like that?"

"I want to share this with you. I like to dress up. Like you do."

She cradles her hand, the one that touched him, against her neck, cupping it with her other hand as if it's an injured bird. "I don't understand."

"It's good." He strokes her inner arm, the soft sleeve of extra flesh. "Trust me. It's not creepy. I promise." His chest swells with love for her. It *is* good. Cat is good and she loves him. She will understand and accept. She will be one of the good wives. He leans down to kiss her.

She turns her face away and reaches for the lamp on the bedside table. When she switches it on, Henry leans back slightly, and Cat's eyes widen.

"I don't understand. Are you gay? Or one of those men who wants to be a woman?"

"No, nothing like that. I'm your same old Henry. It's all okay."

She puts both hands on his chest. At first, he thinks her touch is tender, an embrace, but she shoves him away, hard. He falls against the wall.

"It's *not* okay," she cries. "It's sick."

He scrambles to stand up. "It's still me."

"No." She throws off the quilt and stands facing him in her worn flannel nightgown with rosebuds. "My Henry is a man. He wears button-down shirts and trousers. *This* is not the person I fell in love with."

Uh-oh. It's not going well. He reaches for her again. "I promise you. Nothing is different."

Cat is wide awake now. He knows that look. "So," she says, her voice getting icy, "has it all been a lie? Our marriage and Melissa and everything?"

He grabs her shoulders. He has to stop her saying these things. She tries to shake him off, but he grips her harder. "No lies," he pleads. "This is me."

The sob starts deep in her throat, gathers volume, and explodes into a howl. Startled, he drops his hold on her shoulder. She runs into the bathroom and slams the door behind her. He hears the lock click.

He stands alone in their bedroom. His arms hang stiffly by his side, hands not touching the teal satin.

Outside, the wind groans.

# 24. AUSTIN, 11:58 P.M.

Outside her bedroom window, the wind drums a loose shutter against the shingles in a fierce staccato beat. Austin can't sleep. Images of Gandalf haunt her, blue-tinged skin and fake boob bouncing on the cement floor.

She tries to summon her usual nighttime dreamscape—her dad. Because it isn't fair. Everyone has a father even if he joined the Marines or never sends a penny to help out and always forgets their birthdays. Even Tobias has a father who toured the facility her first week on the job. Austin was already suspicious that beneath Tobias's sexy camouflage lurked a true slime ball, but his dad kept touching his shoulder saying, "Good work, Son. Your country thanks you."

It's not that she doesn't appreciate her grandparents. They raised her and she loves them. But they are old, and old-fashioned. Sometimes she builds fantasies—she knows they're childish but she can't stop—about what her life would be like if her parents stayed together. Not on the island, someplace more exciting, Portland or Bangor or even Boston. She and her mom would shop together for cool clothes. Her dad would declare Sunday father-daughter day, and they'd go to the aquarium one week, roller-skating the next. No, the three of them would do that together, her mom spinning circles in the inner ring where the really good skaters dance and twirl, while she and her dad hug the outer rail and gawk. On school vacations her dad would take her backpacking, maybe they'd even do the Knife's Edge trail on Katahdin.

Austin switches on the light. Her only photo of her dad, handsome in his lobster garb, leans against the lamp on her bedside table. Listening to the wind wail, Austin looks at his open face and pictures him warm and dry in Texas. She has daydreamed the scene so many times—ringing his doorbell, leaning her backpack against the wall of his apartment. Or he could have a ranch in Texas, where she can learn to ride horses and brand cattle. First, she has to save some money. She made the mistake of sharing her Texas travel plans with her college boyfriend. He said that her dad might be angry if she showed up at his ranch, that he probably left because he didn't want to be her father. But what did the boyfriend know? He turned out to be a grade-A jerk. He'll probably grow up to be like Tobias.

Spinning fantasies about her dad isn't working tonight. Instead, other images keep butting in—the purple line across Gandalf's chest and Tobias's crude comments, the initials on the quarry wall and romance and mystery, plus whatever it is that makes Gran hate the place. It's too much of a coincidence—there's got to be a connection between the people with the initials and whatever happened to them in 1914, and the awfulness on Hurricane Island now.

Grabbing her quilt, Austin walks into the living room. She has looked at Gran's family photo albums many times, but always haphazardly. And she has never searched specifically for people with the initials MEC and AF. She might as well try, because there's no way she's going to sleep much tonight.

She settles on the sofa with Gran's albums stacked on the coffee table. This time she'll start at the beginning and look at every single photo, even the fuzzy old ones from before her mom was born. Thorough and systematic, that's what Henry claims leads to success in life and work. Tobias rolled his eyes when Henry said that, standing on the side of the training classroom where his boss couldn't see his expression. Of course, maybe there's no connection between finding clues about people long dead and getting sensitive information from a criminal. Not that Gandalf—she just *can't* think of her as #524—seems at all like a criminal, not after the interrogation session. But what does Austin know about that stuff? Nothing, that's what.

Austin has never wasted much time on the oldest album. The photos are faded brownish and way old—even Gran can't identify everyone, and they're probably all dead anyway. But tonight she's determined to be thorough and look at every single picture. She turns the fragile pages. The black triangles holding the corners of the photos on the page are coming unstuck, the glue dried out and worthless.

Halfway through, she stops to study a photograph of five stair-step children posed left to right, tallest to smallest. The two freckled boys in the middle make a wider step, identical twins it looks like. The children are slim and fair with big eyes, except the sixth, the smallest—an infant curled up in the arms of the oldest girl. The baby has the same saucer eyes, but her skin is olive-toned, and the hair caught up in a ribbon is jet-black.

Austin eases the photo from the three remaining black corners and turns it over. Under the date, 1915, six names are scrawled in a round, girlish script, in the same configuration as the people in the photograph. From left to right are Margaret Elizabeth, Carrie Ann, John Edward, Joseph, Thomas, and Angelina. Angelina's name is written on the far right, in the appropriate position for her size, but an arrow loops back to under Margaret's name, as if someone wanted to be absolutely certain that everyone was correctly identified.

Margaret Elizabeth? Gran's maiden name was Carter. Could Margaret be MEC?

That's probably nuts, but Austin can't shake the feeling of familiarity. Then she remembers the framed photo on the mantel and fetches it to compare—both have the same old-timey coloring and the same stair-step children. But the one on the mantel is taken in front of the potbelly stove in the living room where she stands in her pajamas. Judging from the age of the people, the one on the mantel was taken about five years later. The littlest girl, dark-haired Angelina, stands in her rightful place in the hierarchy of birth order. And the big sister—Margaret Elizabeth—is missing.

Austin looks back at the photo in the album, the one with the baby. She may not recognize the faces, but she knows those cliffs in the background. She sees them every day at work. Austin makes a mental note to nag Gran again in the morning about the two photos. MEC has got to be Margaret, and she's got to be related to Gran. Why else would Gran have gotten so upset when Austin asked about the initials? So, whatever happened out on Hurricane that was such a big deal—that shaped her, Pops said—it must have something to do with Margaret and AF.

A strong gust of wind rattles the windows. How nice it would be to forget about Hurricane Island and Tobias. To sleep late in the morning, cocooned in her warm bed while the hurricane rages. To erase the image of Gandalf alone in that interrogation room. Naked, with the lights on and music blaring, air conditioning blasting, and the ocean damp seeping in through flimsy wooden walls, the woman might not survive the night.

Austin shivers and draws the quilt tighter around her shoulders. She closes her eyes to squeeze the tears back. She should have done something—anything—to help. Not just left her alone to freeze.

# SATURDAY

SEPTEMBER 10

# 25. RAY, 12:47 A.M.

Something loud wakes Ray. A loose shutter, or maybe a tree banging against the roof. He better check. It's blowing hard out there, and even a small gash in the shingles in this downpour could mean disaster.

Downstairs, Austin sits on the sofa in a warm circle of light from the lamp, surrounded by the family photo albums. Ray watches her for a moment before she looks up.

"Did I wake you?" she asks.

"No. The storm did. What's wrong?"

She wipes her eyes. "I can't sleep."

"It's blowing something fierce. Did you hear a bang out there?" He adds a log to the stove and sits next to her on the sofa. "You might not be able to get over to work tomorrow. Today."

Austin buries her head in her hands.

Ray pats her shoulder. "I wish you wouldn't go back. Nettie's right. That place is still causing trouble a hundred years later."

"What happened out there anyway?"

"Lives were ruined."

"Ruined how?"

"You know the story. When the granite industry was booming, the company brought stone workers over from Europe. They settled here, had families. Then the quarry business went sour."

"Why?"

"Someone invented reinforced concrete, and it was cheaper to build with. Granite orders stopped coming, and there was no work. People here were furious."

"At the owners?" Austin asked.

"Some. But the owners blamed the Italians, because their union demanded safer working conditions. Increased expenses for safety made it even harder to compete with the concrete. The union threatened to strike."

"Did they?"

"They didn't get the chance. In the middle of one night the foreigners were rounded up, loaded onto boats, and sent back to Europe. That was in 1914, at the beginning of the war. People say the German submarines torpedoed them, sunk a couple of the boats. But the Italians didn't go easily. The night they were sent away, that's when the bomb destroyed the quarry office. The company claimed the union was all socialists and anarchists."

Austin hands him the faded photograph with the quarry cliffs. "This was taken over there. Who are they?"

"The baby is Angelina, Nettie's mother."

"Gran's family *lived* on Hurricane?"

"Until the quarry closed, after the bombing. Then everyone left."

"That makes Angelina my great-grandmother, right? She's so exotic-looking. If these are her brothers and sisters, why isn't Margaret in that photo?" Austin points to the framed picture from the mantel.

"What do you know about Margaret?" Ray asks.

Austin turns over the photo and points to the writing on the back. "Just her name. And that she's missing in the photo Gran keeps on the mantel."

Ray lowers his voice. "Nettie doesn't talk about Margaret. Folks say she was an odd girl, stormy and mysterious and totally obsessed about the little island. Apparently she used to row over there and wander for hours around the quarry. One day she disappeared."

"Disappeared how?"

"A dingy was missing. The family figured she . . . well, they thought she might've taken her own life. She had never been happy." Ray hesitates. He doesn't want to lie to Austin, but it's not his story to tell.

Austin touches Margaret's face in the photo, then looks at Ray. "Do you think Margaret is MEC?"

Ray doesn't know what to say. Austin should be having this discussion with her grandmother. But even four generations later, Nettie is still hurt, or ashamed, or whatever those feelings are.

"Yes," he says. "I have suspected that."

"Who is AF?"

Ray shakes his head. He has no idea about that. "Some boy she loved, who didn't love her back maybe, or went off to war and never returned?"

"When Margaret disappeared, she didn't leave a note or anything?"

"Just a small chunk of carved granite on her little sister's pillow."

"A rock? Why would she do that?"

"Don't know. But Margaret was obsessed with Hurricane Island, so it probably has something to do with that place."

"Where is that rock now?" Austin asks. "Can I see it?"

Ray is surprised at her request. He knows the exact location of the piece of rock: on the top shelf of the closet in the sewing room, stitched away in the cloth envelope Nettie sewed for the packet of blue airmail envelopes that his usually sensible wife refuses to talk about. Or throw away.

"Your Gran has it." He hesitates and then adds, "And there are some letters her mother left her. Letters sent airmail from Italy with no return address. I've always figured they were from Margaret."

"So she didn't die?"

"Guess not."

"What's in the letters?"

"All I know is that they made Nettie cry."

"Why won't she talk about them?"

He shakes his head. He has no answer for that one either.

"Does this have anything to do with why my mom left?"

"No," he whispers. I don't know, he thinks.

"I want to read the letters," Austin says.

He stands up. "I wish I could give them to you, but they're not mine to give. Ask your Gran." Or find them, he thought. "I wish you *would* read them. Nettie has always blamed Hurricane Island for Margaret's troubles. The little island spooks her, whether it's reasonable or not. And now the place is spooking you too, isn't it?"

"No." Austin shakes her head. "The place isn't the problem. It's the people running it who scare me."

## 26. GANDALF, 1:15 A.M.

Cold. Dark. Dank. She has been left alone for hours, at least six or eight and maybe more, tied to her chair and blindfolded. First, the sensation in her hands and feet diminished, then it disappeared entirely, and the feeling in her face too. Her body was cold before, when Ferret came, but now it is different. Now, the icy fingers reach into her brain and attempt to erase her memories. She holds tight onto thoughts of Jess, so the grabbing snow hands cannot take her away. Her mind slips from the grip of the ice and grabs onto the thick fur of Sundance instead.

The cat was already middle-aged when he and Gandalf moved into Jess's apartment; he was set in his ways and used to her solitary academic life. Those first years Sundance simply ignored Jess, accepting food but disdaining her overtures of friendship.

It wasn't until Gandalf was sick that Sundance finally acknowledged Jess as family.

During the weeks of chemo nausea, the two women and the cat spent hours in the bathroom; Mozart helped a little and Sundance rubbing against Gandalf as she sat on the black and white tile floor. After her surgery, Gandalf's chest was always cold, even in summer; only the vibrating heat of the cat draped over her shoulder could warm her. Later, Sundance sometimes curled up against Jess's feet at night, occasionally crept into her lap as they sat on the sofa before dinner, drinking pinot noir and watching the BBC News. "So this is why people love cats," Jess said one night, rubbing the tender place under his chin.

Gandalf's mind skis away, frozen and fast and gliding out of this place. She embraces them in her mind: Jess is on the sofa, the old cat on Gandalf's lap. His head rests against the empty place, the gone breast. Her numb fingers circle Jess's braid and Sundance's tail. She will not let go.

# 27. AUSTIN, 2:34 A.M.

After Pops goes upstairs, Austin waits until the creaking of his footsteps and the bedsprings fade into the wild storm music outside. Then she tiptoes upstairs to the sewing room. Gran is pretty predictable—she probably hid the letters in the same spot she always used for birthday presents. Austin hesitates a moment before taking the fabric envelope from the top shelf of the closet. But Pops wouldn't have told her about this if he didn't want her to find it and read the letters, would he?

Sitting up in bed, the wind and rain against her window are louder, more raucous and insistent. Austin draws the covers around her shoulders and studies the fabric packet. The faded blue trumpet flowers are delicate, fragile, against a profusion of fernlike greens, as if the cloth holds beloved family treasures rather than hidden artifacts of—what did Pops call it—of shame. Austin can feel the thin letters, just a few of them, and the hard lump that must be the chunk of rock. A long line of stitches weaves through the washed-out blue blooms, sending a strong message of keeping the unwanted past safely tucked away. Message received, Austin thinks. Received and about to be disregarded.

She rummages in the top drawer of the bedside table for her nail scissors. Snipping the running stitch at both ends, she pulls out the thread and a walnut-sized chunk of granite tumbles onto her lap. She holds it closer to the lamplight. Silvery-pink stars sparkle on the leaf shape carved into the light gray stone. Tucking the rock back in its fabric home, she removes the bundle of letters—just a half dozen of them—the blue paper crinkly with age.

There is no return address, but the postmarks are from Italy, and the envelopes are arranged by posted date. The narrow flaps have been sliced open. Austin takes the onionskin pages from the top envelope—May 15, 1931—and smooths the paper flat against her knees. She holds the first page closer to the light. The ink is faded, and the tiny handwriting is hard to read.

*Carissima Angelina,*

*Happy Birthday, little sister. It's hard to believe you're sixteen!*

*Actually, it is not hard at all, because I have thought of you every day of the eleven years since I left you and Storm Harbor. I have only one photograph of you, as an infant in my arms. Every single day, I kiss your face and pray that you don't hate me. All these years, I promised myself that when you turn sixteen, I would write you a letter and tell you the truth.*

*Today I'm keeping that promise. I will start at the beginning, so that you'll understand the choices I made. Perhaps you will never be able to forgive me, but now that you are a woman, perhaps you can imagine things like this happening. I pray that you can.*

*If this letter is to be about truth-telling, I must begin by correcting the lie in the first paragraph: You are not my sister. You are my daughter.*

Huh? Austin looks up from the page. She tries to recall the details of the photographs in the living room, the ages of the children. Is that Nettie's big deal, the shameful secret that lasted a century? Teenaged Margaret got knocked up and had a baby? Easily a quarter of the girls in Austin's school had kids before graduation, or else got married and had premature babies weighing eight pounds and change. None of them pretended the kid was her sister. But then, maybe things were different back then.

*Your papa is Angelo. When we met, he was an Italian stone carver working at the quarry. He played the mandolin in the dance band at our Saturday night socials. It was his hands I noticed first, all the way across the room of spinning, whirling dancers. His fingers blazed along the strings, and his eyes never left my face. That first night we walked together in the moonlight. We took the path to the quarry and sat on a stone slab. I was careful to keep a foot of space between our*

*bodies on the rock, but nothing—not even our different languages—
separated our feelings.*

*Before I met Angelo, I avoided the quarry as much as possible. If
I had no choice, if Mother sent me to deliver a message to father or
his forgotten lunch pail, I turned my eyes away from that vast open
hole. I covered my ears to the blasting, thumping, banging noises that
filled it and boiled up into the sky. I held my handkerchief over my
face against the light-colored dust that covered everything and clogged
my throat.*

*But the quarry was a different place with Angelo. We lay with
each other in a hidden cave on the eastern border of the pit, where the
men had finished carving out the giant pieces of granite. Sometimes
we explored the wild parts of Hurricane Island, had picnics in won-
derfully private and romantic places. His favorite was the tiny cove at
the base of the cliff near our cave. No one ever came there. It was our
secret place. With Angelo Fabrizio, everything was secret and special
and different.*

Austin's breath catches in her throat. MEC and AF: Margaret Elizabeth
Carter and Angelo Fabrizio. She brings the page closer to the light.

*Angelina darling, I remember every detail about the morning he
showed me the initials. We had been seeing each other for about a
month. Four weeks of slipping away from my chores at home, from
school. The hardest part was lying to Carrie. We were the closest of
sisters. But Angelo was worth every single, worrying second.*

*How fresh and clean the world looked that day! I skipped along
the dirt path to the quarry, hopping over tree roots and shadows. I
wore my favorite yellow skirt, embroidered with black-eyed Susans
around the hem. The flower centers were the same color as his eyes,
deep brown with honey-colored flecks.*

*Angelo stood waiting at the cave entrance. He put one hand over
my eyes. He placed my hand on the rock face just inside the gap. Feel
it, he said.*

*My fingers read the letters and numbers growing from granite,
with maple branches entwined in a circle and studded with leaves
like a crown of nature. My heart swelled open to breaking.*

*MEC + AF. 1914. Our initials. Our year.*
*La pietra è per sempre, he told me. Stone is forever.*

Austin wipes her cheeks. What's wrong with her, getting soppy over a silly letter written from one long-dead woman to another? And what does any of it have to do with the mess her own life is in? She glances at the clock. Her alarm will ring in three hours and she'll have to face Gandalf again, face Tobias.

She'll just finish this one letter and read the rest in the morning.

*I wanted to tell Carrie about Angelo, but I was scared she would tell our parents. So I put everything out of my mind except my lover. When I wrapped my arms around him and breathed in the smell of his arms and chest and mouth, worries of my mother's pursed lips and my father's union troubles and the disapproval of the neat row of white houses along the road below all disappeared.*

Austin closes her eyes. She feels the touch of Angelo's rough hands on Margaret's face and her shoulders and her breasts. The world outside their little cave is gone, and so is hers—the battery of wind and rain, images of Gandalf and the freezing room on Hurricane Island. There is only skin and tongues and arms and legs entwined like the circle of carved branches keeping watch on the stone wall outside. Austin closes her eyes, and imagines.

# 28. HENRY, 5:00 A.M.

Henry is already awake when the alarm rings. He folds the blanket over the back of the sofa and props the throw pillows perfectly in the corners the way Cat likes them. The bedroom door is unlocked, and she's sleeping way on her side of their bed. The quilt, the one he bought her on their honeymoon in Amish country, is pulled up to her chin. The pattern is called Forever Love. The irony makes his throat ache.

He slides between the cool sheets and turns towards her, across a queen-sized chasm. She opens her eyes but doesn't look at him.

"Cat." He doesn't know how to continue. He follows her gaze across the room, to the window plastered with dark leaves. He tries to imagine what she is thinking.

He tries again. "Listen."

She bites her lower lip, and his lip hurts. He wants to touch her but he understands that would be a mistake.

"Just because I like to dress up," he says, his voice breaking a little on the word dress, "doesn't mean I'm . . . sick." He doesn't use the word *pervert*, but he knows that's what she's thinking. Is it sick for a man to like the caress of raw silk, the rustle of taffeta and the electric charge of satin against skin? "I know I should have told you years ago. I shouldn't have just . . ."

Just what? Just showed up in his marriage bed wearing his best teal gown? So. Damn. Stupid. He leans back on the pillow.

"I'm so sorry," he whispers.

She sniffles, and he offers her a tissue, but she doesn't take it. He says her name, but she won't look at him. He gets out of bed and goes to the bathroom to shower.

It's a short walk from their house to the harbor, but he gets drenched. His rubber boots skid like a tourist's on the rocky path. He slips twice, and falls onto his knees. The rain slices horizontally into his slicker, driven by wind gusts stronger than any force he has ever felt. The earth is unfamiliar, transformed into a foreign country rather than the landscape his feet have known for decades.

Bert idles his boat at the dock, rocking furiously with the windy swells. Henry raises his hand in greeting and climbs into the cabin. Gripping the metal railing, he sits next to the window, resting his forehead against the glass. His body feels battered. His bruised knees sting under his rain pants and trousers.

He looks around the steamy cabin; only two of the usual dozen employees have shown up for the ride to work. Cat's cousin Cyrus, the one with all the freckles, and a woman who works in the kitchen. Where are the rest of them? Come to think of it, where's Tobias? He usually comes over on the early boat.

"How bad is it?" he asks when Bert comes inside.

The boatman shrugs. "Not awful, yet."

"But you're sure this is safe?"

"Should be. Protected waters, less than half a mile."

"What are we waiting for?" Henry asks.

"Austin Coombs." With the heel of his hand, Bert rubs a clear spot in the condensation on the window. "I think that's her coming now."

Henry peers out. "Have you seen Tobias this morning?"

Bert shakes his head.

Henry opens his mouth to ask more, then changes his mind.

Bert helps Austin into the swaying boat and on the bench next to Henry. "Hold tight, everyone," Bert says as he engages the gears and maneuvers the boat away from the dock.

"Chances are we won't be able to get home tonight," Henry says to Austin. "Did you bring a change of clothes and a toothbrush?"

Austin toes the small duffle at her feet. "Gran packed me a bag. Even my flannel PJs." She crosses her arms across her chest and shivers. She turns her face away from him. Henry wonders if she's thinking how much a pair of flannel pajamas would mean to the Cohen woman.

The boat lurches roughly to the side, throwing Henry off balance and against Austin.

"Sorry." He feels himself blushing and turns back to the window. "It looks bad out there."

"My Pops says it's going to get worse all day today. Do we have back-up power? Like a generator?"

"Of course. We'll be fine." Tobias is the one who oversees the physical plant, who knows the details of the emergency systems. Suddenly that makes Henry nervous. Where is Tobias, anyway? He has never missed a day's work.

"I'm surprised Tobias isn't here," he says. "He usually takes the early boat."

Austin rubs her eyes, which are red and swollen. "After he questioned the new detainee last night he said he was staying overnight, to keep an eye on things."

Damn. Henry rubs his sternum and considers her statement. Double damn. Tobias knows better than questioning a detainee without his supervisor's knowledge. Would he really disobey a direct order like that? Henry really has to talk seriously to the guy, first thing this morning when he gets to work. If he ever gets there, he amends, as another wave slams into the small boat.

Austin is still looking at him. Staring, actually.

"What?" he asks her.

"You okay? Your face is green, and you're rubbing your chest."

"I'm fine." He shoves his hand in his pocket. "You don't look so good yourself."

"Not much sleep last night." Austin looks down at her lap. She hesitates and then asks, "You wouldn't really use the guys with the new detainee, would you?"

"How do you know about them?"

"The staff talks. You know."

"And why is this your concern?"

"Because with Gandalf? I mean, because of her . . . You know, the operation she had?"

Gandalf? Geez, since when has this green-as-grass guard developed a first-name relationship with a high-interest detainee? That is not a good thing; it stinks of fraternization and who knows what else. He presses the heel of his hand into the center of his chest, remembers that she's watching, and drops it to his lap. Right, like *he* should lecture anyone about breaking protocol. And what surgery? Why is he out of the loop on this?

"Dr. Cohen is not your concern," he says sternly.

Austin tosses him a look that's not exactly subordinate, the kind of disdainful expression Melissa wore when she thinks he was being particularly dense or offensive. Then Austin grabs her duffle bag and slides down to the other end of the bench. A few moments later she pulls some blue pages from her pocket and begins to read, ignoring him entirely.

That's not his problem now; he's got plenty of his own. When this damn boat gets to the island, first he will take something for his heartburn. Then it's time to have a major talk with Tobias and set him straight. This insubordination must stop. Right now.

# 29. AUSTIN, 6:20 A.M.

He says that Dr. Cohen isn't her concern? What bullshit. Guarding Gandalf is her job. Austin glances at Henry Ames and wonders if he worries about what happens to the woman, to Norah, to the other people he's supposed to extract information from. He seemed to care yesterday, but maybe he was just worried Gandalf would die before he got his precious intelligence. Does he mind if they're harmed because of the actions his staff takes, carrying out his orders? What kind of man could he be? She looks down at her uniform. What kind of person does that make her, being part of this place?

She can't think about that, not now, on her way to work. Instead, she pulls the folded envelopes from her pocket. Tucking the granite chunk in the palm of her hand, she finds the second letter. This one is thicker, dated two weeks after the first.

*Angelina, I so wish you could know your papa. I believe that I was looking for someone like Angelo long before I met him. Carrie teased me that I thought I was too good for the local boys. And it was true that they bored me, wanting nothing more from life than a seaworthy boat and a shot of whiskey on Saturday nights. Angelo was a few years older, with muscles strong from cutting stone, but also a tender heart.*

*He is an artist, trained in the tradition of Carrera, his home city in Italy. That's where we live now, and where I hope you will come someday to visit us. Carrera is in Tuscany and is a place with a long tradition of both fine stone art and union organizing in the quarries and the carving sheds. I love his carving and I love to kiss the bumpy calluses along his palm, the healing cuts on his fingers. I marvel that carving graceful images in granite leaves the artist's hands so scarred.*

*Another thing that set him apart all those years ago was how much he tried to make the world more equitable. At lunch every day he'd sit with the other Italian union men, reading aloud to each other from the foreign newspapers, making large gestures with their arms, and arguing about the coming war and their union. Angelo taught me that breathing the granite dust made workers sick in their lungs, and they needed special machines to clear the air. He told me their plans, how they negotiated with the company in good faith, but if the owners refused, they would strike.*

*Angelo asked me questions about the company too—how they operated and where they kept their books and when they made bank deposits and withdrawals. At the time I wondered why he cared, but I would have told him anything. I knew these things because my father (your grandfather, my dear Angelina) was a manager for the company. So at home I heard a different story. Father said that the Italian workers were anarchists, that a strike would destroy the company.*

*One rainy day in late August, it all fell apart. At breakfast Carrie repeated the gossip from the well: the quarry company was bankrupt, and the foreign workers would soon be deported. Some of them, she told me, had already been sent away. Luckily not Angelo, I thought. We were to meet during church. I planned to fake being sick, but I didn't need to pretend. My stomach was bilious, and I couldn't eat breakfast.*

*After my family left for church, I put on my rain cloak and took the water pail to stop at the well on my way home. The white clapboard houses of the village appeared balanced on a cloud, their foundations and front stoops shrouded in rain and mist. Just beyond the quarry office, I turned onto the forest path and a downpour pummeled the earth into mud, carving deep gullies at my feet.*

*Maybe I was walking too fast on an empty stomach, because everything got dark and my head spun, pulling my insides along. My stomach clenched and lurched. I leaned over a fireweed bush and vomited. Afterwards, I washed my mouth with rainwater, but I worried that my kisses would smell like sick.*

Austin doesn't feel so good either. She feels nauseous and her thumb hurts, where she has pushed it hard against the broken edge of the carved leaf rock. The boat is tossed by wind and waves and the words on the page will not stay in line. She looks out the window—they're pulling up at the small dock. Carefully folding the fragile pages, she arranges the letters deep in her pocket, nestled around the granite chunk.

# 30. TOBIAS, 7:21 A.M.

Tobias keeps an eye on the monitors while he drives the electric shaver over the bump of his jaw and down his neck. These days, the monitors are the only things he trusts. Unlike some people, the monitors can be counted on for the truth.

Like now. He watches the wharf monitor, where Bert brings his boat around for a third try and finally manages to dock. Henry gets off first, struggling with his backpack and the girl's duffle, then offers a hand to Austin as another wave slams the boat into the wooden pier. Now that the storm is here in full-force, Henry is apparently prepared to stay at camp. Apparently Tobias is the only one with the smarts to really plan ahead. Not that he'll get any credit.

The boss is still playing the gentleman, trying to keep himself and Austin from being blown off the dock and pitched into the bay. The girl looks miserable, and Henry looks pissed off. So he probably knows about yesterday's interrogation.

Tobias runs his hand across his face. Good enough. He minimizes the view of the dock and returns the camera positions to the default positions before opening the staffing file. *Some* people might be tardy, but he's at work and on task even though it won't be easy to make a staffing plan with half the men not showing up. He struggles to rearrange the expression on his face before the boss comes in. He's been told often enough that he can look surly, even outright defiant. That won't do today.

The instant the door opens, Tobias feels the force of Henry's fury. Really, the boss's face would benefit from some readjustment. The guy looks frantic.

"Damn you, Tobias. What's going on with the Cohen detainee?"

Henry sounds like a lunatic too, his voice high pitched and hyper-controlled. He pulls his slicker off and steps out of his rain pants, draping them over a chair. Water rivulets run down the yellow oilcloth and drip onto the floor.

Tobias keeps his tone calm. "Nothing's going on, boss."

"Nothing? You almost killed an important suspect yesterday. And then you continued the interrogation after I specifically told you not to? Is she okay this morning?"

"I haven't checked yet." Tobias tries to look relaxed and unflustered. The three raincoat puddles swell and spread across the floor.

"Well, then. Let's do that now." Henry snaps the switch for the interrogation room monitor. Ms. Cohen sits curled up on the chair, blindfolded, nude except for the waist strap. Motionless. He turns to Tobias. "Damn! I can't believe you left her like that all night. Are you insane?"

"Definitely not. The SLIC protocol stipulates that . . ."

Henry slams his hand on the desk. "I don't give a rat's ass about your SLIC protocol. That's not how our Bureau operates. We use our brains to get information, our powers of persuasion. Maybe a little humiliation or prevarication." He readjusts the temperature control. "But we do not cause significant physical distress or harm. We do not endanger our citizens."

Tobias watches the three puddles converge. Let the boss vent his anger, and then they'll move on to the work at hand. Fingers of rainwater edge along the cracks between the pine boards towards the outside wall. The floor isn't even level. Construction was rushed and inexcusably sloppy, like so many things at this place.

"Are you just going to ignore me?" Henry's face is pale, instead of red with anger.

Tobias feels a wave of pity for Henry. The guy looks sick. He's a dinosaur and he doesn't have a clue. Tobias tries to speak gently. "Time to join the 21st century, boss."

"Yes, I'm the boss. And you're reassigned to the Men's Barrack duty, effective immediately. I'm going to check the outbuildings to make sure the generator is gassed up and ready." Henry reaches for his drenched slicker, then seems to change his mind and leaves it hanging on the chair.

Tobias opens his mouth to object but is stopped by Henry's expression.

"Do you understand me?" Henry says. "You're off the Cohen case. I don't want you anywhere near the woman." Henry slams the door behind him.

Off the case? When he is so close to a breakthrough? Can the boss really be so naïve that when he looks at the Cohen bitch, he sees only an old lady, a professor? How can he not understand that terrorists come in all sorts of ordinary packages, that sometimes the innocent-appearing ones are the most dangerous.

Tobias slams his fist against the desk. Maybe he isn't like Henry, full of grandiose ideas about saving the world. But he has always expected that if he works hard, he'll do well for himself and move ahead in his career. And that was happening, maybe more slowly than he liked, always climbing the next rung on the ladder one step behind his mentor. But Henry isn't going to be much use any more.

Pushing his chair back from the desk, Tobias stands up and kicks at the rivulet, splashing the water across the dusty floor. He switches to the perimeter camera view. After a few moments, Henry comes into sight wearing a one-piece rain coverall with a lobsterman's headgear. He shuffles along the building, bent against the storm, with one hand holding onto the thick ropes strung between buildings. Can the wind really be that bad? Looks like he's aiming for the plant building. As if the guy knows the first thing about generators.

A small beep snags his attention back into the room. He checks his phone, but there's no message. He glances at the monitors, at the desktop, and opens the drawers. Nothing. Another beep. He follows the sound to Henry's jacket.

He finds the phone in the inside pocket and turns it over in his hands. The screen flashes the low battery warning. But this isn't Henry's cell. Henry uses the same standard issue phone the Bureau provides to all staff, probably with a built-in bug so they can monitor every fart.

Tobias turns the phone on and studies the photo icons under contacts. Holy shit. It's the Cohen woman's missing phone. He checks the phone log and discovers that two calls were made to the prisoner's girlfriend, Jess.

This is dynamite. At the very least it's a violation of the chain of evidence, maybe even treason. Grounds for dismissal. Grounds to bump Henry out of the Bureau and out of his way. Logically, the Regional Chief will name Tobias as interim Special Agent-in-Charge. No question that would be the best thing for the detention center and for the Bureau. But is the presence of a detainee's missing effects on Henry's person enough to make that happen?

Maybe it's time to collect evidence of Henry's other vulnerability, the kinky stuff. Tobias switches the monitors back to the default camera positions, slips the Cohen phone into his pocket, and climbs the two flights to Henry's office.

Long ago he programmed his own retinal image as an override into the security system and Henry's office door yields without difficulty. He glances quickly around the small room. Henry is a predictable guy. If he has anything to hide, it will be in his desk. Tobias doesn't know exactly what he's searching for, but he'll know when he sees it. He locates the master desk key on his keychain.

He rummages through Henry's things: linty rubber bands and old phone chargers, outdated email printouts and assorted binder clips. In the middle drawer on the left, carelessly hidden under a stack of building requisitions, bingo. A lady's silky black slip wrapped in fancy tissue paper. Tobias wonders for a moment what Henry does with it.

Shoving the slinky fabric into the pocket of his fleece jacket, Tobias grins and salutes the empty room. He doesn't bother closing the drawer or locking the door behind him. Henry is finished and he'll find out soon enough. Henry Ames messed with the wrong guy. Walking down the hall, wind wailing through cracks in the walls, Tobias struts a little. He has earned this.

Back in the monitor room, Tobias presses his forehead against the window, cupping his hands around his face to peer outside. The familiar landscape is obscured by rain and blowing, swirling debris. An ancient spruce has cracked and fallen across a birch trunk that looks too frail to hold the weight. Amazing that they still have electricity.

The storm's strength is immense, and so is his. The hurricane's power surges through his own veins. He feels magnificent, and Henry can't hold him back any longer. Not now, when he is getting close to winning. He has so much to do.

First, the interrogation. He'll keep Austin involved. She's young, not yet contaminated by the boss's attitudes. If the girl plays her cards right, she can climb up the ladder of success with him. She has potential, not to mention a great ass. He feels jazzed, wound up, with energy to spare. He sits on the edge of the desk and touches her photo icon on his phone.

"This is Austin."

"Tobias here. I need you in the monitor room. Right now." He disconnects without waiting for her answer.

The girl arrives within minutes.

"Where were you?" He points to the chair across from his desk.

"I'm assigned to the Women's Barracks today."

"Not any more. You're with me."

He slips off the desk and walks behind her chair. He rests his hands on her shoulders, and she shudders. She must feel it too—the chemistry between them. He won't make her wait, like the others, to hear about the change in leadership.

"I've got news," he says. "Henry's going down. I have the proof I need to call the Regional Chief." With his left hand, he takes the phone from his pocket and holds it out, like a precious jewel, on his outstretched palm. "The poor bastard took the detainee's phone. He called her girlfriend. He compromised the evidence, jeopardized the entire investigation. He's out." He smiles at the confusion on her face. "I'll explain more later. Now, we have another session with #524." He lets his right hand slide from her shoulder onto her breast.

Austin stiffens, then jumps up from the chair. She looks terrified. And exhausted. Whoa. Okay, maybe he's moving too fast. She's young, needs wooing. That will have to wait until later, after the interrogation.

"Sorry." He opens his arms, palms up in surrender. "I couldn't help myself."

"Sir," she says. "I'd like to be excused from the interrogation."

Excused? Does she think this is high school? Besides, he needs her. There is some kind of bond between her and the detainee. He's seen it. Maybe the bitch feels maternal towards the girl, since she can't be a mother the normal way. He can use those emotions to his advantage. If #524 doesn't want to cooperate, maybe watching him screw her surrogate daughter will convince her. He'll even enjoy the work.

"No excuses. Meet me in ten minutes in the interrogation room. 0900. Bring tea and a blanket."

The girl nods and backs out of the office. He checks his watch. Ten minutes isn't enough time to gather some of the guys, to make up the peanut gallery. That's what he likes to call it, the peanut gallery. Silly name, from some old-time kids' show Lois used to reminisce about. Hah. Lois will regret walking out when she hears about his promotion. Serves her right. Still, maybe it's better to forget about the guys this time. Out of respect for the woman's . . . deformity. Her half-empty chest makes sexual humiliation seem, well, in bad taste or something. Yes, that's the right decision. He can be as sensitive as the next guy, even though Lois claimed he has the morals of a banana slug in heat. He returns the detainee's phone to his pocket.

This next call will be tricky. He's got to sound reluctant as he offers the Regional Chief the information about the compromised phone. The Chief already knows about Henry's kinky propensities, but he won't be happy to learn that the Special Agent's extracurricular activities are out of the closet. That unfortunately a lady's black silk undergarment has been discovered in his office at the detention center, suggesting an alarming lack of discretion on Henry's part. No, the Bureau won't tolerate that. It's bad for morale, not to mention the possibility of a leak to the press. He smiles to himself, and dials the Regional Chief's direct line.

# 31. GANDALF, 9:02 A.M.

Gandalf opens her eyes to the tight grip of the blindfold. The air feels hideously damp but not quite as cold. Possibly Ferret was scared he would get in trouble with his boss if he killed her, so he turned the temperature up a couple of degrees.

Whatever the reason, the numbness is faded and instead everything hurts again. The cold clamminess seeps in until the damp coalesces with flesh, merges into bone. The worst pain is in her buttocks, where the fragile cell membranes of her bare skin feel fused to the metal chair. The waist strap is so tight she cannot change her position, and the blade of immobility stabs into her muscles. No, it is worst on the left side of her chest, her not-breast, her scar. Without the protection of their flesh coat, her ribs burn. The pain radiates out from her breastbone, squeezing her heart and lungs with crystalline bone. Ice bone. The cavernous ache hovers on the wrong side of numb, piercing her flesh in unpredictable patterns, an incomprehensible and atonal cadence.

The icy knives stab her brain too, skewing thoughts and slowing them down. Images slog along, each one trying to catch onto the tail of the one before, grabbing at it but feeling it slipping away. She must hang on to those thoughts or she will lose herself.

The door opens, finally. When the blindfold is removed, she blinks, squinting in the fluorescent light. It is Ferret again, with Austin, who carries blankets and tea, but Ferret points to the chair in the corner of the room and tells the guard to leave them there.

He does not loosen the waist strap. He starts right in, asking again about the conference and her work with Ahmed, who and what and when and how, the same questions from last night. Was it last night? His right foot taps against the floor. She tries not to stare at his foot and will not let her fingers reach for her wizard charm either. She refuses to look at the blankets and tea, refuses to let her exasperation with the repetition show, tries just to answer each silly question. But the whole time she has just one question in mind: what does she have to say to get the blankets and tea? She glances at Austin standing against the wall, but the young woman seems to be staring at the back of Ferret's head, probably so she will not have to look at Gandalf's chest.

Ferret leans forward in his chair and the foot-tapping tempo increases. "So how would you characterize your friend Ahmed's practice of his Muslim religion? Was he devout? Did he ever discuss jihad?"

"He never discussed his religion with me, period. We only talked about our work." She feels the annoyance creeping into her voice and must banish it, so he will not hit her again.

Ferret rubs the back of his head, as if it hurts. Maybe he can feel the intensity of Austin's gaze. Stop being silly, Gandalf tells herself; concentrate on saving your life.

"Hard to believe he didn't mention his uncle's death. Weren't you two in contact about the paper for the Ann Arbor conference?" His voice sounds stiff with frustration too.

She can't stand this anymore. Over and over the same questions. The aching cold. She feels the sobs building in her belly, her empty, shriveled belly. She will not give in to it; she refuses to cry. She doesn't want to die here, in this awful room. If only she had opened her heart more to Jess, if only she had agreed to marriage, maybe she would not now feel so profoundly alone. She stares at Ferret and uncrosses her arms, leaving her chest exposed. It is possible he has a heart, or a conscience, despite evidence so far to the contrary. It is possible she can access something human in the man; that is what Jess would advise.

"Please," she says. "I have told you everything I know. Or do not know, to be more accurate. How else can I help you?"

"Good. I'm glad you asked that. Finally, a little cooperation." He smiles and Gandalf flinches. His smile might not be a good thing.

But it is. He waves his hand in Austin's direction. "Give her the blanket and tea." Austin removes the waist restraint, and Gandalf leans forward, ripping the skin of her buttocks from its metal bond, so that Austin can wrap the blanket around her. Sitting on the scratchy wool is heavenly. She holds the warm mug in both hands, close to her chest.

Ferret opens the briefcase at his feet and pulls out a laptop computer. *Her* laptop.

"There's still time for you to help us. If we know what the terrorists are planning, we can stop them, even at the last moment."

The lukewarm liquid caresses her mouth, her tongue. She swishes it against the inside of her cheeks, then swallows and lets it slide into her throat, down her esophagus, into her stomach. Oh, warm, and sweet. Sugar. She could weep for the sugar. Caffeine and sugar will jump-start her brain. She will be able to think more clearly, figure out what to do. She takes a second gulp before looking at Ferret.

"What would I have to do?"

"Just email Ahmed Makhdoom."

"But what do I say?"

"The truth. That you're being interrogated by the U.S. government. That you're in grave danger because of your friendship with him. That if he doesn't help us identify and stop the attack planned on your country, you will be held responsible. Bad things will happen to you, and to Sandra too. Beg him. Say, 'Please, Ahmed. Help me.'"

This doesn't make sense. Even if Ahmed were a terrorist, which she doesn't believe for an instant, pleas from an academic colleague certainly would not deter his plans. And why do they need her for this plan, when they have her computer?

"I don't understand. Why don't you just send the email?"

Ferret's mouth tightens. "We may not be fancy professors, but we're not stupid. Ahmed will suspect we have taken your computer. He won't trust the message unless it contains some secret fact, a nugget of past history that only you and he could know. To prove that it's you. Like a place you once ate raw oysters when you were in grad school. The nickname you gave some dumb shit who flunked out of your grad school class."

"I despise raw oysters," Gandalf says half under her breath. Ferret has been watching too many Cold War spy movies. She drains the cup of tea and rolls the slightly warm mug against her neck. It is humiliating to be so tempted by his words. She wishes Norah were here to help her figure this out, to identify the flaw in his plan, to argue with whatever twisted logic she is missing.

But perhaps she is approaching this all wrong. She is a scientist, trained to keep an open mind and investigate all possibilities. Maybe she should try to see things from the government's point of view, because Ferret seems to believe Ahmed is a plausible suspect. How well does she really know Ahmed; he *could* be a terrorist. Ferret's people must have some credible evidence against him, to go to these lengths to contact the guy.

"And if I do this, if I email Ahmed?"

"Then you can go home to Jess." He pulls her phone from his pocket and holds it up. "I'll even let you call her after you send the email. But you must do it now."

Jess! She touches the wizard charm against her chest. Why not? What harm can a begging email from an old friend do? All right, briefly more than a friend but that is buried in history and totally irrelevant to Ferret's questions. Ahmed probably will be suspicious and ignore such a message, like those Nigerian prince scams with their bank accounts. He certainly won't do something drastic just because a colleague, an old friend, asks him to save her. Would he? How can she balance that slim possibility against her need to talk to Jess, to hear her voice and tell her she is okay?

"Did you hear me? This must happen right now."

"I don't know," Gandalf says. "I am considering it."

Something makes her look at Austin. A small noise, perhaps just an intake of breath. Austin is backed up against the wall, her expression surprised, shocked even. As if she is appalled that Gandalf would think about cooperating. Ferret follows her glance.

"What's wrong with you?" Ferret jabs his finger at the girl. "You got a problem? Your job is to watch and learn something. I'm the only one in this place who can teach you interrogation skills. Don't bother waiting for Henry because I told you about him. He's finished here. Kaput. I'm the boss now, in charge of the whole operation. Things are going to be done right in the future, the very near future. If you know what's good for you, sweetheart, you'll stick with me."

Gandalf trembles. There is something ugly, something rancid, in the way he looks at Austin. Gandalf wants to put her own miserable body between the two of them, to protect the girl. How weird is that? Austin is a guard, not a friend. The girl has made that perfectly clear.

Ferret turns back to Gandalf. "Am I making you nervous? Perhaps you feel maternal towards this young woman. Maybe she's the daughter you never had? Never could have, really, because you're a lezzie."

Gandalf looks away. The guy is revolting but he is good at his job, the way he rummages around her brain and ferrets out secrets that only she and Jess know. Those have been their fiercest quarrels, really the only angry fights they ever have. Gandalf wants a daughter, and she wants to name her Penelope. She and Jess have discussed the various options for years: adopting, foreign kids, fostering. "We're too old," Jess says. "We are not," Gandalf insists. "You just don't care as much as me, because you have David, you've had a child." Then Jess: "That's how I know we're too old."

Gandalf glances at Austin. She and Jess would never let their daughter take a job like this, no matter how much she needed the money. She blinks back tears, because if they had a daughter, this situation would be that much worse.

Ferret intertwines his fingers behind his neck, leans way back in his chair, and looks back and forth from Gandalf to Austin. His smirk grows into a wide grin.

"Now I get it. So that's how it is. Come here," he orders Austin.

Austin doesn't move.

"I said, come here." He unclasps his hands and points to the ground at his feet.

Gandalf tries to catch Austin's eyes, but the young woman will not look at her. Instead, Austin pushes away from the wall and walks slowly to Ferret's side. Seated, his eyes are at the level of Austin's chest; he stares at the buttons on her uniform shirt, at her nametag pinned slightly crooked over her left breast pocket.

Without warning, he grabs both of Austin's wrists. With one hand he pins them behind her back. With his other hand he begins unbuttoning her uniform shirt. Slowly, one button and then another, down the row.

He looks at Gandalf. "Guess you don't like it when I touch your new girlfriend, do you?"

He has Austin's shirt totally unbuttoned now. He unhooks the front closure of her bra and cups her right breast in his hand. Gandalf bites her lip. The man is unhinged and this is *her* fault; he must still be reeling from the fright of her own lopsided bosom. He buries his face between Austin's breasts, then takes her left nipple in his teeth, all the while smiling at Gandalf. Then he stands up, reaches for Austin's belt and unbuckles it.

Austin thrashes, whipping her shoulders back and forth to free her hands. She lifts her knee towards his groin, but he blocks the move and swings the back of his hand across her mouth. Austin gasps and stops struggling. Ferret grins, then slowly unzips her trousers.

Gandalf is responsible for this and cannot allow it to go any further. "Stop," she says. "I'll do it."

# 32. AUSTIN, 9:49 A.M.

"I'll do it," Gandalf says. "I'll send the email."

Austin's tongue explores the gash inside her lip and recoils from the metal taste of blood. She isn't sure if she's relieved or disappointed at Gandalf's surrender. Mostly she's still scared and still furious, because even when Gandalf caves in, agrees to his demands, Tobias doesn't let go of her wrists.

She ignores the throbbing of her mouth and stares at the brass doorknob. It's important to have a small thing to concentrate on, especially operating on almost no sleep. Her friend who got pregnant in high school swears she got through thirty-six hours of labor by focusing on a photograph of two pears and a pineapple on the hospital wall. It's the mental discipline that does it, that makes you feel strong in a situation where you have no power. The night her college boyfriend came to her dorm room stinking of beer and itching to fight, she stared at the framed garden print hung over her desk. Stared until she felt the warm Italian sun on her arms and smelled the lilac bloom. Until he smashed her face.

Finally, Tobias lets go and pushes her away. Heart pounding, she faces the wall to button her uniform shirt and tuck it in, and fasten her trousers. When she resumes her position leaning against the wall, she watches Gandalf's face and the back of Tobias's head. He points at something on the laptop, then gives it back to Gandalf and begins dictating the wording of the email message.

Gandalf glances up, and meets her gaze. How can the woman justify contacting her old friend? Doesn't she get it that she might be putting him in danger, whether or not he has any ties to terrorists? Suddenly Austin understands why Gandalf agreed to contact Ahmed—she's doing it to make Tobias stop assaulting *her.* To protect *her.* How astounding that the professor would do that, for a stranger, for a prison guard she hardly knows.

Her anger smolders, then flares. It changes directions and turns towards Tobias. Austin feels herself moving, being pushed—no, pushing herself—over a line, a chasm really, a deep dividing place in her life. Because she doesn't believe any more that doing the job is important, not if it feels this wrong. She doesn't want to be on Tobias's side any longer.

She stares at the back of Tobias's head where a cowlick forms a spiraling bulls-eye. She wishes she had her gun, but it's only issued to her for certain assignments. Besides, who's she fooling? She could never shoot someone, not even Tobias. Before the training for this job, she never even held a gun. Pops wouldn't have one in the house, not after 'Nam. Nettie argued with him, said her brothers all hunted, and nothing bad ever happened, but Pops was adamant.

The room is quiet as Gandalf types, but outside the storm sounds brutal. The thunder is so frequent it blends into an endless explosion of sound. Austin imagines the accompanying lightning. Maybe it will hit them, and end this mess.

"Done," Gandalf says. She hands Tobias the computer.

Tobias reads the screen. "Who's Cassidy?"

"His cat," Gandalf says. "In graduate school, Ahmed and I adopted kittens from the same litter. We named them Butch Cassidy & the Sundance Kid. Ahmed loved that film. He spent the two months before graduation researching international pet travel restrictions and quarantine policies in Pakistan so that he could bring Cassidy home with him." She paused. "I do not think many people know about Cassidy."

Tobias nods. "Perfect." He pushes Send, watches the screen, and then looks up. "On its way."

What will he do to them now? Austin must act, and soon. In spite of exhaustion, in spite of not knowing exactly what to do, in spite of all the reasons to do nothing, she must stop this man. Now. She looks around for something to hit him with, but the room is bare of potential weapons.

Except for Tobias's holstered handgun. He isn't expecting any reaction from her, any fighting, but he'll be charged up and quick to respond. First, she has to get his gun. There's only one way she can think of to distract him, and that might not even work. But she bets Tobias thinks so highly of himself that it wouldn't occur to him to question a woman's motives, not when she's coming on to him. Like her jerk of an ex-boyfriend, Tobias probably thinks a smack is foreplay.

The thought of touching him makes her gag. I'm crossing the line, she thinks. Once I break these rules, I can never go back.

She looks again at Gandalf, shivering and blue-lipped despite the blanket. She thinks of Margaret, breaking the rules about who to love and then leaving her family, her daughter. She thinks about the packet of letters in her trouser pocket. Letters she can't wait to finish reading.

She steps forward and puts her arms around Tobias.

"You did it," she whispers. "That was so cool."

She nibbles his neck. Licks his ear. She reaches for his pistol, and her hand freezes. She can't do it! There's no way she can shoot him, but maybe the butt of the gun will do the job. How much force does it take to knock out a man?

He turns to find her mouth and kisses her hard. She wants to bite off his tongue, but instead forces herself to move one hand to his waist, slide it under his belt and his shirt. Her other hand touches the pistol and slips it from the holster. For a split-second, she is undone by the bumps on the grip—so much like the rough bumps on the chunk of granite in her pocket—and a blast of doubt makes her hesitate. This is something she can never undo. Then Tobias grabs her breast and squeezes, hard.

Austin grabs onto the barrel end of the pistol and pulls away from his embrace. She brings her arm back and swings with all her strength, aiming for the cowlick.

# 33. HENRY, 12:10 P.M.

Returning from checking the generator, about which he knows next to nothing, Henry feels lucky to make it back to his office. He can't remember ever feeling this dismal. Between the malevolent power of the storm, the disgust on Cat's face last night when she pushed him away, and the withering dismissal in Tobias's voice when he made that comment about joining the 21st century, he can't imagine a good outcome to any of this. So his unlocked office door is puzzling, but it hardly registers on the wretchedness scale as he towels off his wet face and hair.

The urgent alert light is still winking on his computer and now there are two red priority messages from the Regional Chief. The first is just what he expected: JR demands results. Henry sends off a quick reply that interrogation is progressing but significant yield is unlikely. He doesn't bother adding his opinion that the Cohen woman almost certainly knows nothing about terrorism.

The Chief's second message was sent just a few minutes ago. Henry has to read the first paragraph twice. *We have been concerned about your leadership for some time. We now have a major crisis under your command. You are relieved of your duties. Do not leave the facility.*

Crisis? What crisis is that? Does the Bureau have him under surveillance? And not leave the facility: does that mean he's under arrest? Calm down, he tells himself. It isn't as if he can go anywhere right now. He rubs his sternum and returns to the message.

*Until further notification, Tobias Sampson is in charge of the facility.*

Ah. So that's it. Tobias. He must have contacted the Regional Chief. Henry glances down at his bottom desk drawer. It gapes open. He doesn't have to look to know the black slip will be missing. And he did remember to lock his office door, but Tobias has been here.

It isn't ordinary defiance then. And after everything Henry has done for the man's career, even signing off on those nut-case classes Tobias keeps taking, courses titled Advanced Surveillance Systems and The Psychology of Counter-Terrorism. But really, deep down Tobias isn't an evil person. In their early years together at the Bangor field office, they both wanted to protect citizens from the bad guys, and neither one of them believed that the ends justified the means.

Where is Tobias, anyway? That's another thing to worry about. Or maybe not: *You are relieved of your duties.* That means it isn't his problem anymore.

The ache in his chest deepens. It spreads outward from his breastbone, creeps along his ribs and around to meet at his spine, squeezing and gnawing, somehow rumbling in tune with the constant thunder shaking the building. Henry rummages in the top desk drawer for the antacid bottle. He tosses six tablets into his mouth and chews. Returning the bottle to the drawer, he notices his gun box and holster. He hates the thing and rarely wears it, but these events might demand a drastic response. He fumbles putting on the shoulder holster, zips his sweatshirt over the bulge.

It might not officially be his problem now, but he still feels responsible. He needs to find out what's going on with Dr. Cohen, and he doesn't have the stomach to check it out in person. He scoots his desk chair to the metal cupboard next to the window. The view is totally obscured by wind-driven rain. It probably isn't so smart to be standing next to the window with trees crashing down outside, or even using electricity for that matter.

Just for a minute.

He spins the dial to unlock the heavy-duty padlock on the cabinet and turns on the closed-circuit surveillance of the interrogation rooms he had installed four months earlier, because who knows, given the way the cowboys in Washington are acting, he might need to defend himself at the Hague some day. This old-fashioned, off-the-grid system is definitely a Luddite solution, but it's the only way he could think of to circumvent Tobias's retinal scan scrutiny. He rewinds, then presses Play.

The interrogation room image is distorted by static and the sound even more so. Interference from the storm, or maybe Tobias has installed some kind of jamming software. Dr. Cohen is strapped into the metal chair, with a line across her face that looks like blood. The woman's left breast is missing. Damn. Tobias can't have—no, that's a healed surgical scar. That must be what Austin meant on the boat, about the woman's operation. Even Tobias wouldn't use sexual humiliation techniques with a woman who had a mastectomy. Would he?

Has Tobias always been this sadistic? Over the years Henry has known a handful of agents who lost it, in one way or another. There was that Polish guy from Chicopee, Massachusetts, whose textbook psychotic break came complete with little green men who pointed their unicorn antenna at his living room sofa and spoke in a frequency only he could hear. There've been others too, but no one talks about them once their desks are cleared and the bronze nameplates unscrewed from the office door.

On the screen Tobias jabs his finger at her face and yells, but Henry can't hear the words. He turns up the volume, but only the racket gets louder. Static snow on the storm-crackled monitor intermittently obscures the interrogation room but Tobias's smirk is visible as he leans back in his chair. The screen flickers off, and when the picture returns Tobias holds a phone in his hand. It looks like Dr. Cohen's phone, but how can that be? Henry pats his pocket. Did he leave it in his fleece, or maybe his raincoat?

Tobias must have searched all his things.

Tobias yells at Austin and points to his side. The girl walks towards him, looking reluctant. What's he doing with her shirt? Her breasts, her pants? The guy *is* psychotic. How can he have missed the signs? He has to stop this now.

He checks his watch. It's almost 12:30, and the time stamp on the screen reads 11:45. Damn. The events on the tape are over. Whatever Tobias did to the girl, it's done. He can't stop anything. He might as well finish watching the show, a rerun of MI-5 on steroids. He puts two more antacid tablets in his mouth and chews.

A flash of lightning ignites the semi-darkness outside the window. At the same moment, the room shakes with thunder. The lights flicker twice, then dim. The background crackle on the monitor grows more intense. Henry can barely follow the action on the screen, but he can't stop watching either, especially when Austin swings something at Tobias's head, and the man collapses. The monitor explodes with static for thirty seconds and when the screen finally clears, only one person remains in the interrogation room. Tobias, strapped to the metal chair, handcuffed and gagged.

Henry stares at the screen, his brain a scramble of relief and glee and worry. He can't think clearly. The wind screams, and his ears hurt, and his chest aches, and his thoughts are gerbils racing in circles, repeating and spiraling and he can't follow his own mental sequences. Does he want the prisoners to escape, after more than three decades of fighting on the side of the guys with the white hats? Does that make him some kind of traitor?

At least, he better try to minimize the damage. He ejects the mini-disk, shuts down and locks the system, then calls the guard station at the dock. It takes seven rings before Bert finally answers.

"How's it going down there?" Henry yells over the static on the line.

"Pretty wild. Big spruce down across the road. No major structural damage. Yet."

"Listen. We may have a situation here." Henry chooses his words carefully. How loyal is Bert, and is he loyal to the job or to Henry? "Two people are, well, unaccounted for. Don't mention this to anybody, but if you see them, let me know. And don't take them off-island, okay?"

Bert laughs. "Ain't nobody going off-island for a while, boss. Who's gone missing?"

"A female detainee named Cohen. And the new guard."

"Austin?"

Too late, Henry remembers that Bert waited the boat for her that morning. He must know her. Not just know her; they are probably related like the whole screwy island.

"Yes," he says. "Remember, not a word about this to *anyone*, Bert. Just let me know if you see them, okay?"

"You bet."

Still holding the phone, Henry stands at the window. How long can the bedlam continue? The eye of the hurricane can't be too far away, and then things should calm down. He better go outside and check with his staff. Former staff.

But first, one more call. He touches Catherine's photo on his phone screen. He listens to the rings, then to her voice message. Which is probably good, because what can he possibly say to her after last night? He can't apologize for who he is, and he isn't sorry about that, not really.

"It's me, Cat. I need to talk with you. Please call me." He hesitates. Should he say more? No, no use worrying her about the job stuff. She'll learn about that soon enough.

He ends the call. What should he do now? Dr. Cohen and Austin are out there somewhere. Officially they are no longer his responsibility, but can he just let them escape? Maybe he can persuade them not to run. Honestly, he'd like to join them, get off this damned island and never return, but that's not a viable option. Is it? The only thing he knows for certain is that he can't just sit here and wait for whatever is coming at him next.

He grabs his rain jacket from the hook and snaps the flashlight from its wall charger. Patting his gun for courage, he slips into the dark hallway.

# 34. RAY, 1:06 P.M.

Without taking his eyes off the Weather Channel, Ray mutes the volume and reaches for the ringing phone. Rain drips off the reporter's dimpled chin, on location somewhere on Long Island. Severe storms fascinate Ray as much as—okay, more than—the next guy, but he can't be the only person disturbed by the way these Weather Channel fellows get so excited by natural disaster, so thrilled by catastrophe.

"Yeah?" He watches as the footage switches to the flooding in Portland's harbor.

"Pops? It's me."

Austin's voice sounds thin, even a little teary. Not likely. That girl never cries, not even the time she dislocated her elbow playing Red Rover in fourth grade, not even when she came limping home from college with a broken face.

"What's wrong?"

"I need your help."

"You got it. What's going on?"

"I'm not sure. Seems like Henry Ames has been—I don't know what— like there's a mutiny or something. I think he made a mistake with some evidence, and now Tobias Sampson claims that he's in charge. And the guy is nuts. Like totally out of control. Like *torturing* people."

Ray glances towards the stairs. Should he fetch Nettie from her sewing room upstairs? If something bad happens to their girl, she'll never forgive him. "You sure you're okay?"

"Yeah, but I've done something bad, Pops. I had to. This place is some sort of FBI prison, and Tobias was hitting this woman I'm assigned to guard. And then he was, trying to attack me. Like, you know . . ."

He does know. Austin never talks about what happened at college, with her so-called boyfriend. But he saw how she looked when she came home, and later the local sheriff got him a copy of the report from the Emergency Room.

"Did he do anything to you?"

"I told you, I'm fine. But I hit him, and I'm in big trouble. Can you get us out of here? Off the island?"

"Of course." His eyes swim. Assaulting a federal agent sounds like very big trouble. "Where are you now?"

"Still in the building, but I'm heading for the secret cave at the quarry. The one where you hid during that other hurricane, with the initials."

Ray walks to the window and gazes out towards the Hurricane Sound. The wind is churning the waves in a fury. The currents will be treacherous. "Okay. I'll talk to Bert and we'll meet you at the cave."

"They'll be monitoring the dock. And the storm is horrible. How will you get to us, get us off the island?"

"We'll figure that out. Bert knows every inlet, every cove. You get yourself safely to the cave and wait for us, okay?"

"Cove," Austin says. "That reminds me. Don't be mad, Pops, but I found the letters you told me about, from Margaret to Angelina. I took them and I've been reading them. Don't say anything yet. Just listen. The letters are from Margaret and she had a lover, an Italian stone carver. They used to meet in the cave—in your cave, with the initials. I can't wait to tell you all about it. And Margaret mentions a hidden cove, not far from the cave."

He thinks about the rocky island coast and the treacherous tides. About the endless persistence of torrents and currents and undertows, both natural and human. "We'll find it," he tells Austin. "Like I said, Bert knows every inch of that coastline. We'll get to you."

"There are three of us, Pops. Write this name down: Gandalf Cohen, she's a professor from New York. There's a lawyer too. Norah Levinsky. She works for the Human Rights Litigation Center, also in New York. These women were, like, kidnapped. Their families don't know they're here."

He writes it all down, the names and phone number for the professor, on the inside cover of Nettie's *Readers' Digest*.

"Will you call Gandalf's girlfriend, Jess? Let her know Gandalf is alive. Ask Jess to contact Norah's people."

"Yup. Anything else?"

Austin is silent for a moment. "I think Henry Ames is in trouble. He looks awful. Maybe you'd better let his wife know."

The storm obscures Hurricane Island from his view, but Ray stares in that direction. "Is that a good idea? You sure Henry isn't part of the problem out there?"

"I'm not sure of anything, except that Tobias is going to come after us. I've got to get moving."

He places the receiver in the cradle and stares at his scribbled notes. He better do this before he thinks about it too much. He dials the New York area code and a woman answers the phone. Jess.

"My name is Coombs. Ray Coombs." He speaks slowly, not sure what to say. "I'm calling from Maine. I have some information about your friend. Gandalf?"

"Omigod! Is she okay? I've been frantic."

"She seems to have gotten herself into some trouble with the feds up here." He pauses. "Homeland Security and the FBI and what-all."

"What kind of trouble? No, that doesn't matter. Is she all right? Can I talk to her?"

Who does this woman think he is, anyway? "Far as I know, she's fine. As to coming home, well, that's a bit complicated, ma'am. She's no longer in the detention center, but she is still out on the small island."

"Detention center? I don't understand."

"Me neither, to be honest with you. But my girl Austin, my granddaughter who works over there, says your friend was being treated badly. Austin helped her escape. They're hiding now. There's another prisoner, too. Some New York lawyer. I need you to call her people."

"Treated badly how? Is she hurt? And where exactly are you? What small island? My son and I will come immediately."

A son. So she must've been normal, straight, whatever, at some point. "We're in Maine. Your friend is on Hurricane Island, in a place like a prison. It's hard to get here right now, probably impossible. The storm's still blowing hard, and there's flooding to come."

"That doesn't matter, Mr. Coombs. Tell me where it is, and how we can meet up with you."

He hesitates again, wondering why this woman would trust him. He could be part of the group who took her girlfriend. He's not sure he'd have such faith in a stranger. Not that she has a whole lot of options. "From Rockland you take the state ferry to Storm Harbor. When the ferries are running again, that is. Let me know which boat, and I'll meet you."

"I'll be there. What about the other woman?" Jess asks.

Ray reads off the names and numbers, everything Austin told him, while the woman writes it down. "You'll try to reach her people?"

"Yes, yes of course. But if Gandalf is in prison, how're we going to get her out?"

"You let me handle that part. I have some folks who can help."

"I'll call you back when I've made travel plans." She pauses. "One more thing. Are you the man who called me last night?"

Last night? Must've been someone from Hurricane. "No ma'am. Not me."

After they say goodbye, Ray pushes the disconnect button and holds it down. He can admit it to himself; he was a bit bothered about calling her. There aren't any lesbians living on the islands, leastways not that he knows of. But Jess sounded worried and relieved, just like any girlfriend would, if that was the right word.

Catherine is next. "You'd better come over here," he says. "It's about Henry."

There's a long silence on the other end. As if she already knows something is wrong.

"Tell me," she says.

"Not on the phone. Just come. Bring rain gear. We've got to get over to Hurricane."

After they hang up, he walks upstairs to Nettie's sewing room and peeks in. Nettie is asleep in the soft upholstered rocker. No reason to disturb her, not until he has a plan. While he waits for Catherine, he'll figure out what to do. Bert will help, but how can two ordinary guys fight the feds?

He looks again at his sleeping wife. Nettie would suggest calling Evelina. She's their link to the government, their voice in Washington. That's why they elected her, isn't it?

"Thanks," he whispers and tiptoes back down to the kitchen. He watches the wind hurl broken branches of rain-soaked leaves against the kitchen window.

# 35. AUSTIN, 1:15 P.M.

Austin peers up and down the first floor corridor, then slips back into the supply storeroom. Gandalf has dressed in fleece pants and jacket. She stands in front of the tall metal shelves, arms loaded with extra shirts and wool socks, boots and rain gear.

"Pack light," Austin says. "It's a long walk."

"Where did you go?" Gandalf asks.

"To make a phone call." Austin unzips a small duffle bag and hands it to Gandalf.

Gandalf stares at her for a moment—like maybe she doesn't believe her—before dumping her selections into the duffle. She pulls a yellow slicker, crackled with wear, from the top shelf. "This fabric is ancient. I thought the Army developed new high-tech lightweight materials for combat use."

"Maybe so. But this is what they sent us."

"Perhaps this prison is not high priority?"

"It's new, not yet fully operational," Austin says. "And these are oilcloth, like the lobstermen wear. They last forever and keep the rain out." She reaches for an orange box on the top shelf. "Here's a first aid kit. You might want to clean that cut on your face."

"What about your mouth?" Gandalf asks. "Where he hit you?"

Austin tongues the cut place. "It's not bad."

As Gandalf takes the orange box, the building shakes with an explosion of light and noise. Sparks burst from the overhead fixture. They fan out in rainbow arcs and dance against the floor. The thunderclap is simultaneous—

the boom bounces against the walls and reverberates inside her skull. When the embers fade away, the darkness is complete and shocking.

Austin blinks several times, as if the problem might be in her eyes. The darkness feels like deep underwater, thick and heavy. It's hard to catch her breath. She stretches both arms out to find something solid. Her left hand feels a fleece shoulder, grabs it.

"I guess that's it for electricity," Gandalf says.

"I'm surprised it lasted this long." Austin slows her respirations. She holds onto Gandalf's shoulder and the panic recedes a little. She remembers Tobias's gun in her pocket.

"Is there no back-up generator?"

"There is, but I don't know if it's automatic or needs to be turned on. And our priority is to get out of here."

Still gripping Gandalf's sleeve, Austin turns in the remembered direction of the door. According to the orientation materials, every room has an emergency flashlight in a wall charger. She shuffles along the wire shelving until her outstretched hand finds the wall, the door, and then the flashlight. Smart planning on someone's part. She switches on the light and props it on a stack of sweatpants, pointing the beam at the ceiling.

"Just take the basics—warm stuff and waterproof." She adds a universal phone charger and set of cables to her backpack. "We have to get away from this place right away and we can't carry much in this wind."

"I need supplies for Norah too." Gandalf crams her foot into a second pair of socks, then pulls on a rubber boot.

"Norah?" Austin stops packing water bottles and energy bars into a small back pack. The creepy flashlight beam shadows on the wall stop too. How does Gandalf know Norah? Isolation of the detainees is a strict rule, crucial to the mission. Tobias is a stickler about that.

Tobias! The memory is a kick to her chest. She has never reacted like that before, like a fighter and a schemer—putting her arms around Tobias and kissing his neck and then slipping the gun from his holster and hitting him. She wishes her college boyfriend had been there, so she could have clobbered his head with the gun butt too, while her anger was raw and adrenalin surging.

Gandalf is staring at her. "You know Norah. The prisoner in the room next to mine?"

"Yeah, but how do *you* know her?" Austin zips the duffle bag, hefts it to feel the weight. She wills herself not to look at their deformed silhouettes against the storeroom wall. Even with the storm raging, she'll feel safer when they're outside these walls.

"Is that really important now?" Gandalf asks.

It isn't.

"No. Let's get out of this place before someone organizes a search." Austin's mind races ahead, planning how they will turn off the flashlight, hug the wall and creep down the murky corridor of the administration wing, every step taking them farther away from Tobias. Hopefully he's still bound and gagged in the basement interrogation room, but he'll soon figure out a way to get free. They will make their way around the corner to the locked doors of the women's section. Hopefully the locks will respond to her thumbprint, or be entirely nonfunctional with no electricity. Somehow, they'll get in, rescue Norah, and get out.

Still, she can't help wondering how the two female prisoners connected and what else might be going on right under her nose. Could this be some sort of test Tobias set up? Or are the two women playing her for a fool? They're older, smarter. It's possible they planned the escape, bringing her along for her knowledge of the area.

No, hitting Tobias was her idea and escaping is the logical and only possible consequence of that action. And if she's honest with herself, it wasn't totally spontaneous, not really. The whole time she watched Tobias interrogate—torment—torture—Gandalf in that freezing-cold room, the seed of the action was forming in her mind. The whole time she stared at that cowlick on the back of his head, her eyes were boring into bone and willing his skull to split open. She imagined his brains exploding, oozing their wicked contents onto the cold cement floor.

"Do we have a plan?" Gandalf asks.

Austin swallows hard and thinks about the cave and the hidden cove, about how Margaret's letters might help save three lives. "I know a place we can hide for a while until the storm lets up."

"Is it very far?"

Austin shakes her head. This woman might be a professor, but she doesn't have a clue about Maine weather or surviving outdoors. About how narrow and slippery the ledge will be in the storm. She'll learn soon enough.

"How do we get off the island without a boat?" Gandalf asks.

Even *with* a boat. Austin grew up with Pop's stories about hurricane storm surges and riptides, how a watery vortex can appear without warning.

But, one thing at a time. "My Pops will get us out of here. Now stop asking questions and pack."

Gandalf nods, and her elongated shadow on the far wall bobbles like a dashboard doll. Austin wants to laugh because the woman looks so absurd in her oversized yellow slicker, so totally un-professorial. Or maybe she wants to cry, because someone has to be in charge of keeping the three of them alive, and given the available choices, that someone seems to be her.

# 36. RAY, 1:48 P.M.

He isn't sure why his landline is working or how long service will last. Better take advantage of it and make the last call. He stirs the spaghetti sauce simmering on the stove and sniffs. Too bad he won't be home for dinner. Maybe Nettie will call her sister to come over.

Checking the phone list thumb-tacked to the bulletin board, he dials Evelina's office on Capitol Hill. He wraps the phone cord around his body and turns his back to the staircase. Nettie's hearing isn't so hot, except when he doesn't want her to hear something. He expects Evelina to be at work on a Saturday afternoon, but is surprised when a girl sounding about fifteen answers the phone. He wastes precious minutes convincing the receptionist that he is Evelina's kin, that his business involves the Congresswoman's father Bert, and she will want to speak with him. Finally the girl agrees to put him through and the canned music clicks on to make him suffer while he waits.

Before Evelina, no one from these islands ever served in Congress. Course she doesn't live on Storm Harbor any more, but her father worked at the lobster coop until Henry offered him the job ferrying employees back and forth to Hurricane. When Evelina comes home during their recess, she talks with people and she listens. Most folks think she's a pretty good advocate for the fishermen, even though they're split on her vote against sending good money after bad in Iraq and Afghanistan. And Bert is so proud of her you'd think she was elected President.

After a bit, Evelina's familiar voice comes on. "Is my Dad okay?"

"He's fine."

"How's the storm up there?"

"Eye's still a couple of hours away. Pretty wild up here and getting worse." He pauses. "How're you doing, cousin?"

She laughs. "What do you want? You only admit to our family ties when you need a favor."

He tries to figure how to put it. His fear for Austin is getting in the way of his thinking. How much does Evelina know about the Hurricane Island facility? Did she support it or fight its placement in her backyard? Since it's all supposed to be secret, the newspapers haven't reported anything.

"Well?"

Might as well just jump in. "There's a problem at the detention center on Hurricane."

It's Evelina's turn to hesitate. She's probably trying to guess how much *he* knows. "What kind of problem?"

"You know that our granddaughter Austin works out there, right? As a guard?" That's good, he tells himself. Remind her that it's her cousin's kid involved here.

"I didn't know that."

"Only been there a few weeks. She hasn't said much, but Nettie and I can tell she's been bothered. Torn up."

"Has she told you why?"

Austin hasn't said anything, not really. He respects that in the girl. She's loyal, even if the loyalty is misplaced when the people in charge are rotten.

"Not until today," Ray says. "She called me from work a little while ago, all upset. Mutiny is the word she used, but I think she means a takeover. She said something about torture and uh, sexual assault, and an out-of-control FBI agent."

"That's just what we need. Abu Ghraib on home soil."

Is public relations her only concern? "There's more, Evelina. Apparently my girl defended herself and two female prisoners against an attack by this rogue agent. She helped the two women escape."

"And you're sure my dad is okay?"

"No one's hurt that I know of. Not yet."

"Well, that's something." She pauses. "Are you sure about your facts? A rogue agent sounds like a TV show."

Sounds pretty much like Washington politics to him, but insulting the woman won't get Austin any help. "I've just got my girl's word."

"Of course," Evelina says. "Have you checked in with Henry Ames?"

Shoot. He was hoping not to bring Henry into the conversation. He isn't supposed to know Henry even works over there, though of course everyone does. Course, he's also heard that Henry's daughter Melissa now works in Evelina's office. Too many cousins, just like Austin says.

"No." He draws the long vowel out for three beats to cover his hesitation. "Not directly. But sounds like Henry might be in some sort of trouble too, so I called his wife. And another thing, one of the detained women is a lawyer. With some outfit called the Human Rights Litigation Center."

"That certainly complicates things."

There is silence on the line. Ray waits. Where does the Congresswoman stand on locking up U.S. citizens? She might be deeply implicated in the bad stuff. That doesn't sound like Evelina, but power can change people. And maybe kinship only gets you so far if reelection is coming up in just over a year.

"The anti-terrorism services think they can get away with anything," she finally says. "I have a friend, a mentor really, on the House subcommittee on Homeland Security. He's been looking into human rights violations during interrogation. Frankly, I didn't believe the things he told me. Maybe I should have." Anger percolates in her voice. "What can I do to help?"

That's a relief, though he wishes he knew what to tell her. "I'm not exactly sure. Talk to your friend about it, I guess, and see what he thinks. I'm heading over to Hurricane soon. Your dad will help me get these ladies off the island. But we'll need your help with the feds."

"What about Reuben?"

Ray hasn't thought to contact the sheriff, but Evelina is probably right about that. If things go well, they'll need his help to secure the place. And, if things go bad, well, Reuben will know what to do.

There's a soft knock on the kitchen door. Ray stretches the phone cord across the room and opens it, waving Catherine in.

"Would you call Reuben?" Ray asks. "Catherine's here and we'd better get to Hurricane before it's too late."

"Sure. And I'll nose around and talk with my friend from the New York delegation." Evelina pauses. "But I can tell you one thing, there's no keeping something like this quiet. News will get out; it always does. I'll also call the Human Rights Center. That's better than waiting for them to contact us. We're talking press conferences, congressional inquiries, the whole shebang."

"I just want to get my girl out of there."

"It doesn't work like that, not in government."

Ray hesitates. "Well then. One more thing you should know."

"What's that?"

"I gave your name and phone number to the family of the other woman, the one who was . . . mistreated over there."

"Do you mean tortured?"

"Something like that."

Evelina doesn't answer. Maybe this mess was too politically loaded for a sophomore Congresswoman from Maine.

"Cohen is her name," he continues. "Her friend, her *girl*friend, Jess Somebody, might get in touch with you."

"This gets better and better, cousin. I'll get back to you."

"Thanks," he says. "Try me at your dad's work phone. I'm heading over there."

He hangs up and turns to greet Catherine. She's Nettie's cousin too, by marriage. A second cousin or maybe twice-removed but still, she's family. Course that doesn't mean they have to like each other. Ever since she married Henry Ames, Catherine became part of the better-than-the-rest-of-you branch of the family tree. He looks at her red-rimmed eyes and again considers waking Nettie. She's so much better at comforting folks. No, smarter to let her sleep. That way, she can't try to stop him.

"You okay?" he asks.

"What's going on?"

Ray takes his slicker from the hook by the door and grabs the box of Fig Newtons on the counter. "Austin called me just now. Said Henry's second in command— "

"Tobias."

"Yup, Tobias staged some kind of coup. He attacked my girl. She fought back and escaped with two female prisoners."

"I never liked that man." Catherine shivers and pulls her raincoat tighter about her chest. "What did Austin say about Henry?"

"Just that he's in trouble. And that he's sick."

Her face crumples.

"Does he have some kind of medical problem?"

"His doctor suspects a heart condition. Something that can mimic a heart attack. Henry refuses to have the tests, insists it's just heartburn."

"Bert and I are going to get Austin off the island, along with the two women they've been holding. We'll get Henry too." What else can he do? The guy is family.

"I'm coming with you."

Ray nods. That's what he expected.

Tiptoeing to the bottom of the stairs, he listens for Nettie. Better not to wake her. She'll argue that taking the boat out in the storm is too risky, but of course she would want him to help their girl. He blows her a kiss, real soft, and leaves a note on the kitchen table. He turns off the flame under the spaghetti sauce and closes the kitchen door softly behind them.

# 37. GANDALF, 2:01 P.M.

Curled up on her cot in the storm-darkened room, Norah looks nothing at all like Gandalf imagines. For one thing, she is much smaller; suddenly the child-sized finger squeezed through the hole in the baseboard makes sense. In the circle of Austin's flashlight, Norah's face is dark against the white wall, but also pale, as if the skin is coated with a fine dust of despair. How long has Norah been in this place? Two weeks, maybe three, she said. Anyone would lose hope.

Norah's expression is perplexed, suspicious. "What's going on?" she asks Austin, then points at Gandalf. "Who's she?"

"That's Gandalf." Austin tosses a pile of clothes onto the cot. "I thought you two knew each other."

"We have never actually met," Gandalf says.

"We've spoken through a hole in the wall." Norah interrupts and turns to Austin, anger twisting her face. "A hole you guys *cut* in the wall to spy on us."

"Austin is helping us escape," Gandalf says. "Put on some extra layers so we can get out of here."

"But . . ." Norah begins. She hesitates, then pulls a pair of fleece pants from the pile. She holds them against her body. The bottom six inches spill onto the floor.

Gandalf leans against the outside wall, which groans with the unrelenting battering of the wind. She cannot wait to escape the building, even though it means exposure to the storm. She grabs another fleece hoodie and a pair of thermal long johns from the pile of clothing and shoves them into the duffle.

Austin shakes her head. "Too much."

"I am already cold to my bones, and we're still inside."

Norah looks up from stuffing socks into the toes of a large boot. "It takes weeks to get warm after that room."

"Why didn't you warn me," Gandalf asks, "about Ferret's violence?"

"Ferret?"

"The guard. I don't know his name, but he looks like a ferret."

Norah snorts. "He *does*."

"His name is Tobias." Austin stands by the door and adjusts her backpack. "And speaking of the bastard, let's get out of here before someone finds him."

"Finds him?" Norah asks.

"We'll explain later." Austin braces her thumbs against her temples and digs eight fingers into her forehead.

Gandalf's brain races. Austin looks distraught; what if she is having second thoughts about helping them? She is taking an enormous risk for two women she barely knows. What will her supervisors do if they catch her? Charge her with treason? Court-martial? Is she military? She does not act like a soldier.

"Are you in the Army?" Gandalf asks.

"No, I'm a civilian, not that it matters. I'm royally screwed when they catch us. Let's get out of here. Now."

Gandalf snaps her slicker closed. Austin said *when*, not *if*.

Norah finishes rolling up the cuffs of her rain pants and grabs the duffle strap. "I'm ready." She stops. "What about the male prisoners? Shouldn't we get them out too?"

Gandalf shakes her head; that is really not a good idea. "They might really be terrorists from Pakistan or Afghanistan or someplace."

"Relax," Austin says. "This place is only for U.S. citizens."

"Besides, what makes you think they're any more dangerous than we are?" Norah turns to Austin. "How many men are here?"

Austin flashes her a suspicious glance, then shrugs. "I don't know. Maybe twenty or so."

Norah stands up straight, hands on hips. "Are any of them actually guilty of something? Or were they picked up for no good reason, like us?"

"How would I know?" Austin pushes past Norah and grasps the door handle. "You two can debate all night, or we can try to get out of here."

"Tell us the plan," Norah says. "In case we get separated or something."

"I'll show you." Austin hands Gandalf the flashlight and digs into her pocket. She pulls out a folded package of blue papers, a crumpled duty roster, and a pencil stub. As she shoves the blue papers back into her pocket, something small bounces onto the bed. Austin snatches it up quickly, but in the flashlight beam Gandalf catches a glimpse of a ragged chunk of rock.

Austin pushes the rock back in her pocket and slaps the roster face down on the bed. She aims the light at the blank page and draws a square in the upper left corner. "We're here." She makes an X on the right hand wall. "We'll leave by this door, at the end of the corridor." She draws a vertical line south that intersects a thicker horizontal line and then bumps into a large circle filling the bottom third of the paper. "Once we cross the road, we'll be in woods until we reach the quarry."

"But that door faces east," Gandalf says. "That's where the worst wind will be coming from, because of the counter-clockwise hurricane pattern."

"No time for a science lesson," Norah interrupts. "What's at the quarry?"

"I didn't know that, about the wind direction." Austin looks at Gandalf. "You have a better plan?"

"It depends on the exact path of the eye, and how big it is. People think that everything is easier once the eye passes, but it is rarely that simple. I wish I had my computer. Even my phone weather app could help us."

Austin reaches into her pocket for Gandalf's phone, then pulls the universal charger from the backpack and plugs in the phone. When she turns it on, there's a weak signal. "Quickly," she says. "I can't believe we still have cell service and it won't last long."

The three women stare at the small flickering screen. Gandalf studies the sweep of red and orange splotches across the map. Finally she turns off the phone and looks up.

Austin switches on the flashlight. "Tell us."

"I think the eye will be here in a couple of hours, though it is tracking to our west, over the mainland. That will slow the storm down some and reduce the wind speeds, but also makes it harder to predict."

"So we should wait for the eye," Norah says. "When it's easier walking, right?"

"No." Gandalf shakes her head. "The opposite. Once the eye passes, the eye wall that follows can be extremely powerful. We should leave immediately and try to get to your hiding place quickly. Hopefully our pursuers will wait for the eye and be stopped by the wall. Also, leaving by a south-facing door would be best."

"Great. So then the storm surge and riptides can get us," Austin mutters. "Still, I like the idea of leaving right away. I want to get away from here now, before Tobias finds us. We can pick up the ropes at the mess hall door."

"What ropes?" Gandalf asks.

"Blizzard ropes. They're strung from building to building, so people don't get lost in a bad storm. I can't remember how far the network goes, but I think it takes us to the road." She points at the thick horizontal line on the map. "The road connects the dock down here with the airfield at the top of the hill."

"Then what?" Norah's voice is thin.

"Across the road we follow the path through the woods to the old quarry." She points at the lopsided circle. "We hide here. And wait." She takes the phone from Gandalf and stuffs it into her pocket with the map. "Let's get going."

Hide where, Gandalf wants to ask, and why don't you trust me to keep my own phone? But she changes her mind. They must get away from the building quickly; once the eye brings relative calm, people will come looking.

Austin opens the door. Peering out into the dark, she stands motionless for a moment before waving Norah and Gandalf into the dim hallway.

"Take a good look and orient yourselves," Austin whispers, aiming the flashlight down the corridor. "We're going to have to do this in the dark."

Adjusting her backpack, Gandalf follows the flashlight beam and memorizes the corridor. She counts the doors on both sides and notes the stairwell on the left. When Austin switches off the light, the three women huddle together while their eyes readjust. Then Austin takes a step forward and the others follow, shuffling as silently as their oversized boots and crackling oilcloth allow. They aim for the small barred window in the door at the far end of the corridor, a square foot of murky light.

Gandalf links her elbow through Norah's. Her right hand skims the cement block wall. She counts a doorway each time her hand bumps over the molding, slides across the heavy wooden door, then climbs back up over the ledge of the doorjamb onto the rough wall again. One, then two, finally five doors, moving towards the cloudy square beacon.

Ahead on the left, in the shadowy alcove at the bottom of the stairs, a dark shape protrudes from the wall. As they approach, the shape becomes the figure of a person, a man. He steps into the corridor and blocks their way. Norah squeezes Gandalf's elbow. Austin switches on the flashlight.

Henry Ames looks awful, his skin a bruised gray. He half-smiles at them. "Going someplace, ladies?"

## 38. HENRY, 2:39 P.M.

He isn't sure what he expected to accomplish by confronting the women or what he thought he'd feel. A charge of adrenalin, or maybe he even half-hoped to redeem himself as a functioning agent? But when he steps into the hallway, the action evokes more dread than thrill. It might be exhaustion or whatever's going on in his chest, but looking at the panic on Austin's face, at Ms. Levinsky's resignation, at the Cohen woman's barely suppressed fury, he's had enough.

And since he's being honest with himself, he can admit that he has no desire to stop their escape. In fact, the Coombs girl probably had the right idea about dealing with Tobias.

"It's not what it looks like," Austin stammers.

Henry waves her words away. He doesn't want her explanations.

"The other officer," Gandalf begins.

Norah interrupts her. "Tobias—"

"Is out of control," Henry says. "I know."

"He said he's in charge now." Austin's voice seems to beg for his contradiction.

"That's true." Henry puts out his hand to steady himself against the wall. "I've been relieved of my command."

The three women exchange glances.

"He assaulted me," Austin whispers.

Henry nods. "I taped his interrogation and watched it. You did what you had to."

"So what happens now?" Austin asks.

"Are you going to make us go back?" Norah adds.

His career is over. Let Tobias deal with it. Besides, he has bigger worries than his job. Cat hating him, for one thing, and Melissa feeling pretty much the same, even without knowing the worst thing. It makes him nauseous to imagine what his daughter will say when Cat tells her. In any case, it's almost impossible to concentrate. The pain under his breastbone is constant now, and he's run out of antacids.

"No," he says. "I'm not going to do anything."

"Are you letting us go?" Gandalf asks.

Henry nods. "This is the first decision I've made in a very long time that feels right. Get out of here while you can." He leans against the wall. He isn't actually making a decision; it's more that his cells have given up, have divested themselves of any residual loyalty to this place.

"You look awful," Austin says. "Are you sick?"

"Just heartburn. You'd better move quickly, before someone finds you."

Austin glances at Norah, then Gandalf, raising her eyebrows in a silent question. Both women look puzzled. Austin touches his arm. "You can come with us, if you want."

"Thank you." He shakes his head. "Go."

He watches the women take the stairs down towards the mess hall, towards the rage of the storm. Maybe he should go help them. Alone they won't get far in this storm. He hopes they get away. He probably shouldn't feel that way, but he does. He'd better check in with Bert again. And much as he hates the idea, he should also go untie Tobias because no one should be left like that, not even him. Tobias isn't really an evil man, down deep. His actions are misguided, certainly, but he and Tobias want the same thing for their country, don't they? Pushing away from the wall, he turns on his flashlight. Before anything else, he needs antacids.

The infirmary door opens easily. After this is over, he'll have to convince the DC guys that installing locks with keys makes much more sense in this storm-magnet place. Or not, because he'll never have to try to convince those turkeys about anything, ever again. They never listen, anyway. After this is over, he'll most likely be out of a job, and probably brought up on charges. In the very best scenario, he'll be pushing papers around the support desk of a podunk local office somewhere. No thank you.

Sitting on the edge of the sickbay bed, he rummages through the medication box and shoves a handful of antacid tablets into one pocket. He unscrews the top of the bright pink bottle and chugs the disgusting stuff.

Dismal Bismol, Melissa called it when she was little. He shoves the box under the bed. Can't have drugs sitting out in plain sight.

He checks his cell phone, but service is out. He wishes he still had Dr. Cohen's phone, wishes he had really talked to her girlfriend, but that chance is gone. He lets his head fall forward into his hands. He should call Bert, who'll be keeping track of the hurricane, if the dock guardhouse is still standing. It takes two tries to push himself up from the sagging infirmary cot, then a minute to catch his breath. Luckily, the ship-to-shore phone is just down the hall and has battery backup.

In the duty room, two Army sergeants, Cyrus and the tall guy with the gravelly voice, stand smoking in front of the window, staring out at the spiraling eddy of wind and rain, tree branches and leaves. Henry can never remember the tall guy's name.

"Everything okay here, men?" He squints at his nametag. Stanley Mason.

"You bet," Mason says, "if you don't mind this. It's like being inside my mom's blender do-hickey."

"All our visuals are out, sir," Cyrus says. "Communications and surveillance."

"What about the generator?"

"Flickering in and out. Could be water in the line."

Damn. Henry steps closer to the sergeant. "Hasn't anyone gone to fix it? The phones and lights are optional, but perimeter security system isn't." It's odd that he still worries about security, but it's just habit.

"Tobias said he'd take care of it. We haven't heard from him in . . ." He looks at Mason, who shrugs. "Must be over an hour, sir."

Henry points to Cyrus. "Gear up and take a look at the generator. And you," he turns to Mason, "do walking rounds in the Men's Section."

The two sergeants look at each other. Maybe they've already heard that he has no authority to give them orders. But no, that's worry on their faces, not insubordination.

"Is the staff meeting still on for 1700 hours, sir?" Cyrus asks.

"Yes," Henry says. Maybe there'll be a miracle before then.

After they leave, Henry opens the ship-to-shore closet, grateful that some areas are considered too marginal in importance to warrant high-tech security.

"The dock's still standing," Bert reports. "You find your people?"

Henry catches his breath. What does Bert know? "My people?"

"You said you were looking for two women?"

"Oh. Yes. Taken care of." Why lie to Bert? Soon everyone will know he's been fired. When he walks by, people will snicker, or look away. He shakes those thoughts away; he has work to do now. "What's the update on the storm?"

"Last I heard, looked like the eye was heading right for us. That puts us in the quadrant to get the worst of it, right now, over the next hour or two. It'll let up some when the eye gets here. Then, heavy rain." Bert pauses. "And flooding."

"Thanks. We'll sit tight," Henry disconnects. Flooding? He can't focus on one more potential problem. His heart is still thrashing about the women. It was stupid to mention them to Bert.

One more call to make. He dials his home number, but Cat doesn't pick up. Why isn't she home? Where can she be in the middle of a hurricane? He wants to sob into the answering machine. Instead he controls his voice, forcing steady syllables from his throat. "We need to talk. I love you."

He hangs up and surveys the room. Everything looks ordinary, except the whirling, howling mess outside the window. Will he ever return to this room?

Closing the duty room door behind him, Henry stands in the dark corridor, letting his flashlight beam drift uselessly to the wood plank floor. What should he be doing? For the first time in decades, he doesn't have orders, doesn't know what is expected of him. Or what he expects of himself.

Right now, there's no choice. He has to deal with Tobias.

# 39. RAY, 2:43 P.M.

The carport offers no protection against the rain and wind.

"We could wait for the eye," he says to Catherine. "We'll get a calmer period then. An hour if we're lucky before the eye wall hits."

"Wait how long?"

He shrugs. "At least an hour, maybe more. Course the sea won't be any calmer."

Catherine shakes her head. "Let's just go."

Those are her last words, though he wouldn't be able to hear anything else anyway. "Hang on tight," he says, maneuvering the boat away from the dock into the narrow sound.

She grips the rail with both hands, but he can't pay much mind to her. Furious waves slap the hull, jerking the wheel from his hands. The swells are as big as he's ever seen in the protected sound, tossing their boat like an angry animal trying to dislodge a predator clawing his back. An angry sea, he thinks, fighting for its life. Like his girl, fighting to get away from the trouble on Hurricane. He remembers something Austin said about seeing the island from a plane on some work-related trip she couldn't talk about. From above, she said that Hurricane Island looked like a woman pursued and heading furiously out to sea. Austin always did have a good imagination.

Almost two hours later, his arms shaking with exhaustion, Ray manages to dock the boat next to Bert's ferry. The rain and wind have calmed, leaving an odd quiet and an ochre glow in the sky. Catherine holds the rope tight while Ray climbs onto the pitching wharf. With several boards missing, the dock has a sad look, like the half-toothless man who sells tickets at the ferry office. Bert sticks his head out the door, gestures Catherine inside, and helps Ray tow the boat around back, out of sight. When the boat is secure, Bert steps aside so Ray can enter the small room.

"I got a staff meeting up the hill soon," Bert says, standing in the guard post doorway with his odd head tilt and one-eye squint. "If I don't go, Tobias will come down here looking for me. Stay inside. Don't let anyone know you're here."

"What about Henry?" Catherine asks.

"I'll try to find out," Bert says.

Catherine sits at Bert's desk, her mouth grim. She crosses her legs and swings her lime-green rainboot back and forth. Ray turns to the window, giving her the only privacy available in the tiny space.

Using the sleeve of his flannel shirt to wipe a clean circle in the grime, Ray presses his forehead against the thick-smudged glass. The sky has mellowed the metallic yellow glow to pearl and a pencil of sunlight shines through an amoeba-shaped break in the clouds. No matter what your trouble, Nettie always tells him, you've got to enjoy the moment. He knows she's right, but it's pretty much impossible to concentrate on the storm's palette at a time like this.

## 40. AUSTIN, 2:51 P.M.

The three women huddle at the door between the empty mess hall and the storm. Water and splintered branches pummel the wire-fortified window.

"Once we're outside," Austin tries to make her voice strong and confident, "it'll be hard to talk—impossible maybe—so let's go over the plan again." Such as it is.

"Grab onto the guide rope outside this door and follow it due south towards the road." She tries to remember how far the rope network extends. It was covered in orientation, along with other useless details about the camp layout. Who knew she would ever need that information. She closes her eyes and tries to picture the map—she's pretty sure the ropes will lead them to the road.

"Across the road are woods. We'll be safer there."

Of course the east rim cave wasn't on the orientation map because the Washington suits don't know it exists. Locals know about it, but probably many of them don't know exactly where it is and have never seen it. Just like in Margaret and Angelo's time. The three of them should be safe there, for a while. Tobias is the wild card.

"Then what?" Norah asks.

"Then we'll hide out. Ready?"

Is she? She wishes Pops were here, to tell her what to expect from this storm. Or maybe not, because if he said to wait inside, she would not—could not—follow his advice. They've got to get away from this building, and fast, just like Gandalf says.

It takes the weight and strength of the three of them—leaning and shoving against the door—to overpower the wind and push themselves outside. The door slams shut behind them. Austin gasps. She grabs the rope and Gandalf. She has been in gale force wind before, but this one knocks her breath from her chest. It slams into both ears and forces its way into her brain, banishing all other sound. It tears at her skin, wraps itself around her throat, kicks against the backs of her knees.

Stunned by the racket, they huddle close for a moment, sheltering their faces in the flapping tents of their raincoat hoods. Then—gripping the rope with both hands—Austin steps out into the dreadful spiraling air and starts across the yard. Gandalf and Norah follow. Austin leads, but she can't see more than a foot of rope in front of her hands. The air spins around her, swirling a vortex of leaves. Rain slashes sideways against her body, explodes craters into the gravel path. Branches—splintered and ripped apart—fly through the sky, bounce along the ground, crash into her legs.

Despite the chaos of the storm, she quickly falls into a rhythm with the rope. Gripping it with her left hand, reaching forward with her right as far as she can, then pulling herself two steps forward. She feels the tug of Gandalf's hand on her shoulder, then gripping her elbow. Within minutes, her hands are raw. The rain carries the salt of the sea and it stings the broken skin. It burns her eyes too, but she keeps walking, wrapped in the blast of the wind. How long can they do this? How long have they been going? There's something timeless about the cadence of it: Reach. Pull. Step. Step. Breathe.

Good thing the rope network is there, even if it was built for rich brats whose parents paid thousands of dollars so their troubled kids could straighten out under the supervision of Mother Nature. Austin used to scorn the outdoor adventure program. She joined in scoffing at the long-haired and multiply-pierced teenagers who occasionally came into town looking for beer or joints. She is briefly contrite for her part in the ridicule. Your ropes might just save our butts, she sends silent thanks to the kids she once mocked.

She reaches, steps, and stumbles on a split-trunk tree, falling hard against it. Stooping down to rub her shin, squinting into the dark current of rain and leaves and chunks of tree, she catches a glimpse of the edge of a building. White paint, so they're almost at the guard tower. If she remembers correctly, the rope will end soon and they'll be at the gravel road that bisects the island from the wharf uphill to the airstrip.

Grip. Reach. Pull. Step. Five more times until Austin clutches the thick eye-ring screwed into the white wall and tries to catch her breath. She wipes her eyes with her sleeve, but the oilcloth smears the wet across her face.

Turning back to Norah and Gandalf, she shouts above the fierce sibilance of the storm. "The rope ends here. We'll cross the road and head into the woods."

The wind whips the words from her mouth and flings them into the roar, a faint harmony to the deep rumble of thunder. By the confused expressions on their faces, Gandalf and Norah don't understand her. The wind will consume the three of them too if they aren't careful, will hurl them into the fury, leaving behind no trace except the assault of rain on storm hats. She pantomimes her hands holding tight, hoping Gandalf and Norah understand the importance of holding onto each other. It would be so easy to get separated out here.

Once they get into the woods, walking will be easier. But first there's the road and if the tower guards have any visibility at all, that's where they'll be searching. There's no other way to get to the quarry. Austin peers up at the tower, but she can't see any evidence of the observation windows. With any luck, the guard up there—if anyone is on duty in this mess—can't see them either. Except they've got all this specialized equipment, high tech surveillance scopes that can see in the dark and who knows what else. She pushes the image of Tobias in infrared goggles from her mind.

Stepping away from the wall, she tightens her grip on Norah and Gandalf's hands, and pulls them forward. Holding their hands high, she shouts—one, two, three, go. They clamber over a split tree trunk, lightning gashed and charred, then push against the wind into the debris-strewn road.

Halfway across, Norah trips and falls hard onto the spiky end of a shattered branch of a downed tree. She cries out and grabs her thigh.

Austin tries not to look at the bloodied wood, instead puts her arm around Norah and half-carries her across the road. In the dark of the spruce forest, they burrow into a thicket of branches.

"How bad is it?" Austin hunkers down to examine Norah's ripped pants.

"It's bleeding."

Gandalf points to her duffle. "We can make bandages from clothes."

"Okay," Austin says. "You're the Girl Scout in charge of first aid. But first we have to get to safety. We're almost there," she adds, although honestly they aren't almost anywhere, except in big trouble.

"And where's *there*?" Norah asks. Again.

"A cave in the cliffs," Austin says. "The last part of the trail involves walking along the quarry. That'll be tricky but we can do it."

"Can you find it in this mess?" Norah asks.

"Sure." Austin peers up into the murky dimness. The wind and rain are less fierce. Could the hurricane eye be approaching?

Gandalf reads her mind. "Not the eye yet. Some hurricanes are structured like giant pinwheels. Imagine that the arms are swirling bands of energy. This is most likely a break between arms. In addition, here we are protected by the forest canopy."

"Okay," Austin says. "So let's hurry. We want to be snug in our cave when the eye gets here. That's when they'll come looking for us."

"And then?" Norah asks.

"More storm," Gandalf says. "The eye wall."

"I mean, after we're in the cave."

"We rest," Austin says. "And wait."

And maybe—even exhausted—she'll have a moment to read more of the letters, in the very place Margaret and Angelo used to meet.

"I don't know how far I can walk with this." Norah looks worried, her gaze jumping back and forth between Gandalf and Austin. "You won't leave me out here, will you, if I can't keep going?"

"Of course not." Gandalf turns to Austin. "How far is it?"

"Normally? Ten minutes. In this weather it could take an hour." Austin helps Norah to her feet. She grasps both women's hands.

"We'll carry you if we have to," Austin says. Lucky she's so small.

"We are in this together," Gandalf adds, though her voice doesn't sound so sure.

Sticking together is their best shot. But what chance do they really have, their band of outsiders? A dyke, a commie, and a drop-out abandoned by her mother. No chance at all.

## 41. TOBIAS, 3:11 P.M.

By the time he hears footsteps in the hallway, Tobias has given up struggling against his restraints. He has also stopped feeling grateful that the power loss means no air conditioning. In the dark room, the air has congealed, grown humid and stifling. The gag tight across his mouth makes him want to puke. Finally, the doorknob rattles and turns. At last, someone in this place is doing his job. Heads are going to roll over the abandonment of the routine campus-wide surveillance rounds, and they won't be his.

The door opens to Henry's stooped silhouette in the doorway. Not the person Tobias wants to find him like this.

Henry stands in the doorway, immobile and mute.

Tobias grunts through the gag and stomps against the floor for emphasis.

"So," Henry says quietly. "How do you like it?"

Whoa. Tobias stares at his former boss, his mentor. The guy really is losing it. And he looks god-awful, as if all the blood has drained from his body along with his gumption and his manhood, not to mention all the training the Bureau has given him. So maybe this is better than being found in this condition by one of his men. Henry is out of here in any case.

Tobias tries talking again and gags. Hopefully Henry will get around to unfastening the cuffs before he keels over or totally freaks out.

Finally, Henry moves. He slices off the plastic cuffs with a pocket knife, then steps back.

Tobias springs from the chair, ripping off the gag. He rubs his wrists and stamps his stiff legs. "What's wrong with you, man? What took you so long?"

Henry just stands there staring at him, as if Tobias is a piece of dog crap in his wife's precious daylily garden. Not that Catherine invited him to even one of her garden parties after Lois jumped ship. Not even one. The bitch must've said something to Catherine. Some damn lie.

"This is all your fault." Tobias points his finger, pistol-style, at Henry, then swivels away. He paces a circle around the small room, his voice boiling over with all the things he hasn't been able to say. Not only while he was gagged, but over the past few months. About surveillance and technology, the mirror frames and camera angles, and all the times Henry ignored him, overlooked him, disrespected him. About watching Henry's leadership falter and Tobias had to keep saying Yes Sir anyway. Well, those days are over. Finished.

Henry interrupts his list of grievances. "You found Ms. Cohen's phone, didn't you? Called the Regional Chief."

"Damn straight," Tobias shouts. "You screwed up big time with that phone, buddy. Remember a little detail called the chain of evidence?"

"You complained about my leadership?"

"*What* leadership? You think I'm going to let your incompetence destroy this place? Let my country miss out on crucial information because you've become a wussy wimp? No way. I'm in charge now, and the staff will be informed of that fact at the staff meeting." He points his finger at Henry's face. "Your career is finished."

Henry stands up straighter. "I saw what you did in the interrogation room. I watched the tape. If I'm a wimp, you're a monster. That kind of abuse is not what the Bureau stands for."

Whoa, Tobias thinks, what tape? He will certainly have to deal with that.

"You betrayed me personally, as well as the Bureau," Henry continues. "You broke into my office. My desk."

"Yes, your little secret is out." Tobias says in a high-pitched voice, "Hen."

A week ago Tobias wouldn't have thought it possible, but Henry looks feeble. He seems to wobble on his legs, as if he is standing up in an unstable boat on a choppy sea. Henry lines up the fingers of both hands along his breastbone, one fingertip next to the other, and pushes. Like his chest is about to burst open, and he has to hold his runaway heart inside. But Tobias doesn't feel sorry for him, not one bit.

"You look like shit, Henry. But you deserve it. If those women escape, it's on your head."

Henry doesn't answer. Damn the guy, won't he even defend himself verbally?

"Hen," Tobias says again. A whisper at first and then the words grow into shouting and it feels fantastic. "Hen, Hen, Hen. HEN."

Henry sits down in the chair, collapses into it. He places his left hand over his right, clutching at his shirt. He opens his mouth as if to say something, but doesn't. He closes his eyes and slumps forward.

Holy shit. Tobias catches him, breaking his fall. He lowers Henry's dead weight slowly. It's just a reflex. Honestly, he doesn't care if the guy's face smashes on the cement floor.

"Can you hear me?" He turns Henry onto his back and digs his knuckle into his sternum, like they did on *ER*.

Henry opens his eyes. "Get help."

Must be his heart. Henry isn't that old, only eight or nine years older than Tobias himself, which makes him just short of fifty.

"Help me," Henry says again.

Tobias grabs a towel from a hook on the back of the door. Dingy but not filthy, the best he can do. Folding it, slipping it under Henry's head, he remembers another towel, bright red and gold stripes. And another Henry, younger and stronger, lying on a towel on a white sand beach. What was it, fifteen years ago? A junket paid for by a surveillance equipment company. Henry rarely took advantage of opportunities, but that one time he went with Tobias, and they had a great time.

For just a moment, staring down at Henry's face so slack and pale, Tobias has a moment of doubt. Henry was good to him. Mentored him. Can he leave the guy to die alone in an interrogation room?

He shakes his head. Sure, he feels loyalty to Henry, but his country is more important than any individual. This pathetic guy lying on the floor is what happens when a person doesn't change with the times. Caribbean junkets are finished now. And so is Henry.

There's one more thing to take care of. Tobias opens Henry's jacket and eases his gun from the holster. When he tries to stick it in the pocket of his fleece jacket, it catches on the silk of Henry's stupid slip. He waves the black fabric over Henry's body and tosses it onto his chest. A fair trade for the pistol, and a fitting shroud, he thinks as he closes the door behind him.

Alone in the hallway, Tobias tries to strategize. Leaving nature to run its course might be the best solution all around. If Henry dies from a heart attack, the Bureau will avoid potential charges of incompetence, the potential scandal, reporters and all that. It makes no difference to him, personally, *how* the top job becomes available. Who cares if it's by firing or death, as long as the job is his. Too bad to miss the opportunity to say "I told you so" to the old pervert. Tranny. He still doesn't get what is so exciting about the black slip without a girl in it, but no matter.

He secures Henry's gun in his own empty holster and walks slowly down the hall, trying to figure out how much time he has until someone discovers the body. The surveillance system isn't fully operational on the emergency generator. But when the power grid is back, the monitors will show the contents of Interrogation Room D. By then, he has to have a watertight story and his ship in order. He isn't quite sure how to go about organizing that. Henry usually does the squishy-soft work, wording the reports just so, making nice to the higher-ups. No problem though. Tobias can do all that.

But the first item of business is to catch those two bitches.

## 42. GANDALF, 3:45 P.M.

Gandalf teeters on the ledge, pounded by wind and rain and dreadfully aware of the invisible water below. She shuffles sideways along the cliff face, hugging the wall so closely her cheek scrapes rock. Her body shakes with chill and wet. The rain splatters against her raincoat, down her neck, into her boots. The eye, the calm, should be here by now. And the sky; how can the sky be both dark and yellow at the same time? She wonders how Norah and Austin are doing. They are shadows known only by the grasp of their hands. No one has spoken in eons. Gandalf has no sense of time or distance; the dark is profound and all around them, stretching some unknown distance into forever.

She stumbles, catches herself, and moans. She must rest. She slumps, leaning the full length of her body against the stone, forehead to boot tips.

"You okay?" Austin shouts into her ear. "We're getting close."

Gandalf nods even though no one can see the gesture. She cannot remember ever feeling so totally spent, so almost gone. It is obvious that Austin is lying so that they will not give up, will not let the hurricane win, will not let themselves be tossed into the wild green depths of the quarry. They will never get to the cave, if it even exists. She closes her eyes and listens to the rain slam against her hood and against the water surface below, whipping it into ocean waves. She is intensely alone, separated from the world by mist and rain and exhaustion and the eerie yellow darkness of the storm. Still, better to die out here than in that awful room.

There's something satisfying, although in a perverted sort of way, about experiencing this phenomenon she has spent her life studying. Living inside the raw and real power of it after knowing its abstraction and its equations. And it is possible, unlikely but conceivable, that her knowledge of wind circulation and storm patterns will help them survive.

A hand touches her face, and she opens her eyes. Norah leans close. Rain drips off her nose, and her breath is warm on Gandalf's cheek. "We'll make it," she shouts above the screaming of the wind and the rapid-fire assault of rain on stone. "Don't give up."

If Norah can walk with a gouged thigh, Gandalf can keep going too. She nods again, and they inch forward along the ledge. They move together, almost blindly, squeezing each other's hands every few steps for comfort.

Just as Gandalf starts to notice a slowing of the rhythm and the muscle of the rain, just as she begins to hope that the storm is losing power, Austin yells something and stops, throwing her arm out to halt their progress. The wind steals the words but Gandalf catches the excitement in her voice. The women crowd close together as Austin points to a shadow in the vertical cliff wall. Twisting her body sideways, Austin disappears into the impossibly thin slash in the rock face.

"We're here." Austin's shout from inside is barely audible. She sticks her head out and grabs Norah's hand, and Gandalf's. "Look at this," Austin says, guiding their finger to shapes on the wet granite wall.

Gandalf rubs the mix of tears and rainwater from her eyes. She tries to decipher the stone characters, which stand out as if the rock around them has been chipped away. They feel like letters, Gandalf thinks, or possibly numbers, inside some kind of circle.

"I can't see them," she tells Austin.

"Just for a minute." Austin shines the flashlight onto the crevasse wall. "Tobias could be watching for lights."

MEC + AF. 1914. The initials and date are handsomely carved inside a circle of intertwined branches and leaves, intact except for a small broken area in the leaves. But why is Austin wasting their time with artwork when they are fighting for their lives?

"Let's get out of the rain. I don't care about an old carving." Norah takes the flashlight from Austin. "I've got to sit down."

After the ferocious howl of the wind, the silence in the cave pulsates in her ears. Gandalf drops the duffle, dark with rain, and helps Norah sit. While Norah holds the flashlight, Gandalf peels the wet fabric of Norah's pants and examines her thigh.

"How bad does it look?" Norah asks, biting her lip.

Gandalf wishes she knew more about first aid. The cut gapes open, moderately deep and oozing. But worrying will not help the situation.

"Not terrible," Gandalf says. She pulls a cotton tee shirt from the duffle and wraps it snugly around Norah's leg, fastening the makeshift bandage with a knot.

"Austin," Norah calls. "What are you doing out there?"

"Just making sure we weren't followed." Austin joins them and sits cross-legged on the ground. She leans over to look at Norah's leg. "You okay?"

Norah nods. "It doesn't hurt much. Mostly, I'm exhausted." She looks at Gandalf. "You?"

"I cannot get warm," Gandalf says, "Or oriented. How long have I been here? What is today?"

"Saturday," Austin says. "You came on Thursday."

Is that possible? Could that horror in the airport have been just two days ago?

Austin rummages in the backpack, brings out two thick candles and a matchbook. "We'd better save our batteries." She lights the candles and drips wax onto the rock floor, then holds the candles upright while the wax hardens.

"Speaking of batteries," Gandalf says, "May I have my phone back?"

Austin digs her hand in her trouser pocket and hands the phone to Gandalf with the power pack.

Gandalf presses the device to her chest, then to her lips. She can call Jess and let her know she is alive. Jess will have a plan. Jess can organize anything, a truly amazing quality for an English professor. Gandalf lets herself relax for a moment. She imagines herself wrapped in Jess's arms in their queen-sized bed with matching reading pillows, denim ones with pockets for their books and reading glasses. Don't go there, she warns herself. You are not home free yet. She turns on the phone.

No service. Nothing. She lets her head thud back against the cave wall. They are marginally better off away from the detention center, but without communication or transportation, the whole island is a prison.

The candle flames flicker against the stone.

"So tell me." Norah breaks the silence. "What happened with Tobias?"

"Austin was a hero," Gandalf says. "She grabbed his gun and slugged him with it. Then she tied him up and stuffed a gag in his mouth."

"You did that?" Norah holds out her hand to Austin for a high-five.

Austin keeps her hands rooted in her lap. "Tobias had to be stopped," she says after a moment. "Call it self-defense."

Gandalf studies Austin's face; she is young to hide so much. She pictures Ferret's hand shoved down Austin's trousers, his tongue against her breast. "It was more than self-defense." She shivers. "Group defense, maybe. Who knows what he would have done to any of us."

Austin's gaze is heavy on her face. "What did you write in that email? To Ahmed?" She turns to Norah. "That's Gandalf's friend, who they think is a terrorist."

Why must she keep explaining? "Ahmed is not exactly a friend, more of a long-distance colleague," Gandalf says. "We work together. I haven't actually seen him in years." Thirteen years, to be precise.

"Tobias *made* you email him?" Norah takes three power bars from the backpack, hands one each to Gandalf and Austin. She tears the wrapping open with her teeth.

Gandalf nods. "By threatening to rape Austin. And he insisted I include something personal in the email, so Ahmed would know it was me writing." She unwraps the bar and takes a bite. "In grad school, Ahmed and I adopted kittens from the same litter, named them Butch Cassidy & the Sundance Kid." She pauses to swallow. "So I asked how Cassidy was doing."

Austin nods. "We saw the photos of Sundance on your laptop. Weren't you nervous that Ahmed would know it was you and give them information?"

"Not at all." Gandalf half-smiles. "Cassidy was run over the day after graduation."

"Smart," Norah says. She changes her position and grimaces.

"Don't take this wrong," Austin says. "But just between us, is it possible your friend is a terrorist?"

"How can you ask me that?" Gandalf hugs her knees to her chest and buries her face in the sodden fabric. Actually, maybe it is a fair question; at least if anyone has a right to ask, Austin does. She looks up. "I doubt very much that Ahmed is a terrorist. I would be totally shocked if he has any information at all that these guys would want. But how can I know for certain? I really have not seen him in years."

"That's what I thought." Austin turns to Norah. "By the way, I may need a good lawyer."

"You got it. The Center will go after these pricks."

"They are Homeland Security, aren't they?" Gandalf asks.

"And the Army," Austin says. "And FBI."

Norah makes a face. "So then we'll probably lose. We usually lose. They've bought Congress and made it legal to do what they do."

"What does that mean for your lawsuit?" Gandalf asks. "And for us, if we get out of here?"

"*Posse comitatus* was intended to keep the military out of domestic affairs. But over the years various Presidents and Congresses weakened the safeguards, claiming that new challenges make it necessary to give the armed forces more power. Now troops are brought in to handle crises ranging from urban drug wars to the Olympics."

"Is that necessarily bad?" Gandalf asks.

"They're also used to gather intelligence on citizens and to track down terrorists," Norah says, "like you. *You* were likely fingered by a computerized anti-terrorism fusion center, co-managed by the military and Homeland Security."

"Those were Army guys who cuffed and hooded you at JFK," Austin adds.

Norah leans forward, repositioning her thigh. "The first Bush established detention camps, ready to incarcerate dangerous citizens in the name of stopping terrorism."

Gandalf lets Norah's words dissolve into background noise. She asked the question, but cannot concentrate on the explanation. Maybe that was true when Bush was president, and that's why they elected Obama. Norah admits that she is a Communist, so she would not be happy with any administration. But all Gandalf cares about is getting home.

She rummages in the backpack for another sweater, then turns to Austin. "What happens now?"

"Now we wait." Austin points at Gandalf. "You're the hurricane expert. How much longer will this last?"

Gandalf bristles. "I study science, not mumbo-jumbo fortune telling. You think I turn around three times, toss sacred ashes over my shoulder, mutter magic words and the answer pops out from the ether? I can't even check the radar."

"Relax," Norah says. "You must have some idea."

"The eye is here now. That is why it's relatively calm. If we're lucky, our pursuers will be slowed down, or stopped, when the eye wall hits." She pauses. "Where is my computer, anyway?"

"Where do you think?" Austin snaps at her. "Getting you two out was hard enough. Sorry I didn't have time to gather up your precious belongings."

Gandalf touches her arm. "Sorry. I am just worried about my files."

"I know," Austin says. "Listen. Before we left the facility, I got Jess's number from your phone contacts."

"What good is that without service?"

"I called my Pops before we left this morning and explained what's happening here. I gave him Jess's number, and he promised to call her. I gave him your name too, Norah, and the name of your Center."

Gandalf tries to think about Austin's words, but the shaky exhaustion makes simple thoughts molasses heavy, sticky. And she is so cold. Still, it is good if Austin's grandfather calls Jess, who will somehow come and get her. "Thank you."

Austin looks down. "I also told him that Henry looks really sick. Won't be surprised if he calls Henry's wife, too."

"Damn it, Austin." Norah looks angry. "Henry is one of them. If his wife calls the feds, we're screwed."

"Henry's not that bad," Austin says. "He didn't stop us from leaving. I don't think Catherine would call anyone. Most islanders have no use for Washington."

Gandalf shivers to the cadence of their argument. "Please don't argue. It will not make things better. I'm glad your grandfather is involved, Austin, but what can he do against Homeland Security?"

"Not to mention the military and the FBI and FEMA," Norah adds.

"Pops knows everyone on the islands. He'll get us out of here."

Gandalf isn't so sure.

"I'll keep watch," Austin says. "Why don't you two rest, try to get some sleep? We'll have more walking and the boat trip later."

## 43. TOBIAS, 4:51 P.M.

His face burns. He holds the handset of the ship-to-shore telephone at arm's length, then mashes the earpiece into the flesh of his cheek, muffling the Regional Chief's scorching words.

"You want to be in charge? So prove yourself, Sampson. Take care of the problem. Find those women. Tomorrow's the goddamn anniversary, and your pathetic facility hasn't given me squat." In contrast to the heat of his message, the Regional Chief's voice is colder than the Cohen bitch's lonely boob. "I'm sending a team up there in the morning. You can bet Homeland Security isn't happy about this mess. Last thing we all need is another PR fiasco. Don't. Screw. Up."

After the click, the Regional Chief's words hang in the empty air.

"Yes, sir," Tobias says anyway. Fair enough, the Bureau has bigger problems. FEMA too, with the hurricane and the flooding and worrying about the anniversary in a few short hours. Maybe he shouldn't have said anything yet about the missing women. Now the brass thinks he's a worthless wuss.

He stands for an extra moment in the phone closet, willing his face to return to its normal color before returning to the duty room for the shift change meeting. Or what would be a shift change meeting if a new shift was arriving to relieve them.

His staff of six men sits in a row in front of the bank of windows. The rain flings itself against the glass, obscuring the world outside. He stands tall, shifting his weight slightly from leg to leg. This is where he belongs. In front of the room. In charge.

"Okay, men. Let's take stock of our situation. We're down five staff until the ferry is running again." He turns to the boatman. "When will that be?"

"Morning at the soonest," Bert says. "If the flooding on the mainland isn't too bad. And if the surge don't wreck the docks."

Tobias nods. That means the women can't sneak off island either. If he can't find them tonight, he'll get them in the morning when they are wet and tired from a night in the woods. "What about perimeter security?"

Stanley Mason stands. "The boss put me on perimeter duty, sir. I walked the ropes, saw nothing out of the ordinary." He looks at his feet. "Frankly, I couldn't see much, what with the wind and rain. Lots of trees down."

The boss, huh? Tobias tries to keep his face expressionless, to keep his glee from showing. Better say something now, let them know how it is. He draws himself up to his full five feet eleven.

"I have some bad news, men," Tobias says. "Henry Ames has been relieved of his duties. In the interim, the Regional Chief has asked me to step in. For now, your orders will come from me and only me." He locks eyes with each staff member, one by one, silently daring them to ask a question or make a comment. No one looks away. No one speaks.

"Okay," he continues. "What's up with the generator?"

Cyrus Carter stands. "I checked it at 1600, sir. Bled the line and recalibrated. To save fuel, I did not restart at that time. I set it to turn on at 1730." He glances at the wall clock. "Fifteen minutes from now."

Tobias nods. He can count on Cyrus. He's career Army, but the guy has potential. There's a role for him in this situation, maybe even a career move. "Good work, Cyrus. What about the men's section?"

One by one, staff members report on their stations. Tobias reviews the duty roster for the next twelve hours, assigning himself to the monitor room.

Bert raises his hand. "Sir?"

"What is it?"

"None of us has seen Austin Coombs in several hours. She was assigned to the women's section." He hesitates, then continues. "I'm worried, with the storm and all. She's kin to me. Cyrus too."

Tobias grabs a chair from the end of the row. He turns it backwards, straddles it, and regards his staff.

"I'm glad you brought that up. We have an unfortunate situation here, and I need your help. Our two female detainees, Cohen and Levinsky, have escaped from their rooms. We feel certain they are still somewhere on the island. At first light tomorrow, when the storm has passed through, and our staff is back to full force, we will begin searching for them." He allows himself a small smile. "They're not going anywhere tonight."

"How did that happen, sir?" Stanley Mason asks. "Did Ames screw up?"

"And what about Austin?" Bert adds.

Tobias looks away from the boatman and shakes his head. Time to end this meeting. "Need to know rule. But I can share this much with you. The detainees may have taken Ms. Coombs hostage. Cohen and Levinsky should be considered armed and dangerous. Keep your eyes open tonight and your weapons handy."

The men nod, grim looks plastered on their faces.

"Carter," Tobias says. "Stay back a minute. I want to talk to you."

Tobias and Cyrus don't speak as the other men file out of the staff room. Drumming his fingers on the top rung of the chair back, Tobias watches Cyrus's face, noticing the glance he exchanges with the boatman. How to best enlist the soldier's help? After all, he's asking him to think big, out of the box, not something the military encourages in its members. Asking him to put duty to country ahead of family loyalty, too. Bad luck that Cyrus is related to Austin, but there's no better option. He needs someone military, not one of the FEMA clowns, and the other soldier, Mason, has a well-known fondness for his beer.

After the duty room door closes, Tobias points to a chair.

"Take a load off," Tobias says, wondering what line of attack to use. What does Cyrus want? Probably what any man wants: a chance to impact the world, and look good doing it, to feel powerful. He has to exploit that desire, use it. "We have a sensitive situation here, and I need your help."

"Yes, sir."

Tobias crosses his arms on the chair back and leans forward, lowering his voice. "This is for your ears only, Carter. I didn't tell the other men the whole story. The detainees' escape is more complicated. It looks like Special Agent Ames helped them break out of the facility. He is AWOL. It's hard to accept, but the facts point to the conclusion that Ames has betrayed the Bureau and his country. He will face serious charges, maybe even treason. Our job is to capture him and re-secure the two women detainees. You with me so far?"

"Yes, sir."

"They've got to hide someplace until they can get off the island. I figure the most likely place is the old quarry. There are supposed to be caves there. Do you know anything about them?"

"Sure."

"Good man."

"What do you want me to do?"

"Help me capture Ames tonight, and the women. They're probably heading for those caves. They trust you. You're related, so you can get close. When you find them, signal me by flashlight beam. I'll be waiting on the cliff above."

Tobias searches Cyrus's face for clues. Is that disbelief in his blue eyes? Suspicion? He shakes his head.

"I know it's hard to believe. I've worked with Henry Ames for twenty years. He's a good man. He's my friend and mentor. But we've got to be realistic and face facts. Force may be necessary to neutralize the danger and bring him in. Hopefully, nobody gets hurt. Once the situation is under control, I swear Henry will get the help he needs."

Cyrus nods slowly. "What about Austin?"

Tobias hesitates. The wind smashes a tree limb against the window, over and over like a beating. "I'm concerned about her. She may be in grave danger."

Cyrus doesn't look entirely convinced. Tobias forces himself to wait a few moments, let the man think about it. He looks out the window. Daylight is gone. Tobias anticipated some reluctance. Time to sweeten the pot.

"When I take over this place," Tobias says, "I'll need a facilities manager, a second-in-command. Of course, that would mean joining the Bureau. If you're interested." He offers his hand to Cyrus and waits.

Cyrus hesitates only a moment before shaking it.

## 44. HENRY, 5:10 P.M.

Henry opens his eyes to utter darkness. His mouth tastes metallic, sour. His pulse hammers under his jaw, and he touches the place, comforted by the regular drumbeat of it. Tentatively, he inches his hand down towards his chest. The hot explosion from before has dwindled back to the familiar soreness. He rubs his breastbone, willing the habitual motion to trigger his memory. Where is he, and what happened?

He rolls his head back and forth, carefully, testing his neck. He's lying on something, not a pillow. More like cloth, with the terry feel of a towel. His hand reaches, finds a patch of something dried stiff, and jerks away. His fingers touch something soft lying across his belly, and he recognizes the silky fabric of his slip. He can picture Tobias stealing it from the desk drawer, later flinging it with a dramatic gesture onto what he assumes is Henry's dead body. Tobias would consider that the final insult. Henry weaves the silk in and out between his fingers and brings it to his face. He inhales through the thin material, imagining graceful families of worms spinning the fibers more delicate than air.

Calmer now, he strains to see through the thick darkness and begins to remember. There was Tobias pacing and bellowing, the pain in his chest mounting and spreading out and taking over. He must still be in the interrogation room; the floor is cement, damp under his body. Clammy. So, the dried stuff on the towel might be blood. His blood? Thick and clumsy, his fingers explore his scalp, but they find no sore or bruised areas, no wetness. He takes a deep breath and rolls onto his side and waits, but the white-hot pain does not return. So maybe it wasn't a heart attack, because then he would be dead. Maybe Doc Clemman is right about that Japanese heart disease. In either case, he better get up and out of here before the generator kicks in or the power comes back on. Before Tobias comes back to dispose of his body.

Damn Tobias. After all those years, the guy leaves him for dead. But there's no time to waste on regrets or sentiment.

Stuffing the silk slip into his pocket, he pushes himself up onto all fours. His arms tremble, but hold his weight. He can probably crawl if he has to. The thought of crawling makes his eyes fill. He hasn't crawled since Melissa was three or four, young enough to ride Daddy like a horsey. Twenty years ago, but it feels like last week. Every Friday evening, she would sit in her child-sized Adirondack chair on the back deck, waiting for Daddy to come home from work in Bangor. All week long, she kept a running list taped to the refrigerator of the things she wanted them to do together over the weekend, dictating the list to Cat until she was old enough to write it herself. They used to get along so well. Then she fell in love with Gabe and changed her name to Lissa. No, he couldn't blame Gabe. It was Gabe's *death* that changed her.

He rocks back and forth on his hands and knees, tentative, testing his balance. Melissa loved his bronco rides, even the time he got a little too exuberant, and she fell off, chipping a front tooth and staining Cat's light gray carpet with blood. But remembering the good times will not bring Melissa home.

Okay, enough of this. He stands on his knees and digs in his trouser pocket for the flashlight. It still works. Holding it in his left hand, he grabs the rungs of the metal chair and heaves himself upright. Dizzy. His chest complains again, squeezing, but not as bad as before. If he gets through this, he'll go to Portland for those cardiac tests. At least that will make Cat happy, if she is even speaking to him. Maybe it would have been better if he died of a heart attack. At least then she might feel sad and forgive him for the other thing.

The spinning in his brain begins to subside and he aims the flashlight beam around the room to locate the exit. Pushing the chair ahead of him like an old man's walker, he makes it across the room and puts his ear against the metal door to listen. Quiet. Luckily the power is still out and the electronic locks nonfunctional. Leaving the chair inside, he switches off the flashlight and slips into the hallway. He leans his shoulder against the cement block wall and wipes his forehead with his sleeve. How can he be sweating just from walking ten feet? Obviously, he won't get far, not like this, but he has to get out of the basement. His mind races through the options. The monitor room is just around the corner, but that's Tobias's hangout so he can't go there. The supply rooms, staff lounge, and general offices are one flight up. He might be able to find a safe hiding place there, but it's risky. He longs for his own office. It might not be the smartest place, but it's his place. He can hide there, if he can manage the two flights of stairs. He can rest a bit, then take a couple of No-Doze pills.

He steps along the corridor, still leaning against the wall. Not for support, he tells himself, just so he doesn't trip. It's slow going and he's moving blind, but a light might attract attention. He startles when he bumps up against the doorjamb of Interrogation Room C, but is ready for the next two doorways. He stretches his arm out to the side and feels the emptiness of the stairwell opening. A moment of panic, terrified he'll tip over into the opening, his heart will give out, and he will fall into eternity. So he allows himself a brief moment of flashlight illumination for orientation, for reassurance that the physical world is still ordered and intact. He sticks the flashlight back into his pocket and crawls up the first steps. He has to sit on the landing to catch his breath, but the next flight is easier.

Along the second floor corridor there are windows. Maybe the storm is winding down because there's a smudge of light in the sky. Not normal September evening light, more a splotch of yellowed gray, but enough to see that the hallway is empty. He makes his slow way to his office. He swears quietly as the door squeaks; nothing is immune to rust in this climate. He slips inside and closes the door.

The venetian blinds are closed, and the room is dark. Probably still not safe to turn on a light. Who knows what kinds of extra surveillance Tobias has going. Arms extended, he shuffles straight ahead until he bumps into his desk, knocking over the framed photo of Cat and Melissa eating lobster. He feels the glass for cracks, then sets the photo right. Even after their big fight, even after Melissa went to work for that damn Congresswoman, he keeps her picture right next to his computer where he can look at it every day.

"She voted against Iraq," he yelled at Melissa. "That woman voted to cut the budget for the intelligence agencies and the military in a time of war." Melissa gave him a look of such disgust, of utter loathing; he will never forget it. She left on the next ferry, and hasn't been home since. Cat visits her in DC every few months, staying in the Georgetown apartment Melissa shares with three other legislative aides. When Henry asks how their daughter is doing, Cat says "she's fine" and changes the subject.

He's too worn out to think about how he screwed things up with Melissa, and now with Cat too, but if he gets out of this mess alive, he will make it right with them both, no matter what it takes. Hands on the desktop, he circles around until he reaches his chair. Unhooking the gray cardigan sweater from the back of the chair, he pushes the chair away and crawls underneath, into the desk's kneehole. He sits cross-legged on the floor and pulls the chair back to form a gate. He folds the sweater, knit by Cat for a long-ago birthday, and places it on the chair seat for a pillow. The dizziness is a little better when he closes his eyes; he rests his head on the worn wool and slides his hand into his pocket for the comfort of silk.

He was ten the first time he wore his mother's slip. It was a Friday. He got home early that day; the note from school said something about a teachers' in-service program. His dad always worked late, and mom had a meeting she couldn't reschedule.

"Will you be okay alone?" she had asked the evening before. "Just until 5:30."

"Sure," Henry promised. "I can take care of myself."

The thing was, the house felt emptier, bigger and quieter than he expected. He dropped his book bag in the hallway and hesitated at the bottom of the stairs. No, he thought. I shouldn't. After his snack it was harder to not go upstairs, but he kicked off his shoes and spread his homework on the dining room table, a neat pile of notes and textbooks for each subject. At 4:30, he put his pencil down, perfectly parallel to the edge of the math paper and stood up. He only had an hour. Forty minutes, really, to be safe. He pushed the chair back from the table with a scraping, aching sound and walked upstairs to his parents' bedroom.

After that first time, he gave in to it whenever possible, learning to put his mother's things back exactly the way she had them. When he was thirteen, he bought a black silk camisole, telling the saleslady that it was a gift for his mother's birthday. She cooed at him, telling him what a devoted son he was. He felt bad, but only for a few minutes, because this was his own, and he could lock himself in the bathroom and put it on, wear it all day under his polo shirt. Occasionally, he wondered if other boys liked slinky fabric as much as he did.

Henry repositions his legs under the desk and the painful surge of circulation returns. Pulling the silk slip from his pocket, he tucks it under his cheek. This slip is so much finer than the one he found that afternoon in his mother's bureau or the one he bought himself as a boy. Between the embrace of the silk and the faint smell of wood-stove clinging to the wool sweater, he finally feels safe.

Wait a minute; did he lock the office door? He isn't sure. But he's too tired to dredge up the memory, can't even cling to the question in his head. No matter. He inhales the smoky wool and falls into sleep.

# 45. RAY, 5:42 P.M.

Just when Ray can't bear waiting one more second, Bert returns to the guard post.

"No sign of Henry up there," he tells Catherine. "I decided not to ask Tobias about him. The guy is paranoid enough without being questioned. He told us this yarn about the two escaped women holding Austin hostage."

"That's a damn lie," Ray says.

"There's more." Bert looks at the floor. "Tobias says that he's in charge now. Says that Henry has been relieved of his command."

Catherine squeezes her eyes closed.

"What are we waiting for?" Ray grabs his slicker. "Tobias is crazy. I don't want those women alone out here."

"We better find them tonight," Bert says. "I'm supposed to meet the day shift at Storm Harbor. Bring them out to begin an island-wide search at first light." He takes a rolled map from the shelf over his desk. He spreads it out, anchoring the corners with an ashtray, a paperweight shaped like a lighthouse, a stained coffee mug and his right elbow. "Do you know where the women are now?"

Ray examines the map. Once Austin points it out, darned if Hurricane doesn't kind of look like a lady running from the bigger islands, just like she says. He runs his index finger over the woman's backbone, the wooded spine of hills down the middle of the island that opens into the granite cliffs of the quarry. His finger stops at the southeast edge of the oval pit.

"Austin is heading for the east rim cave." He looks at Bert, who knows the waters around the Three Sisters Islands as well as any living man. "She says she heard something about a hidden cove near there. You know about that?"

Bert points south of Ray's finger to an indentation that's a mere squiggle on the island coast. "I've seen it. From the map, you'd swear there's nothing there. How'd she hear about that?"

Ray studies the map. "Who knows? Can you get a boat in and out?"

"The cove is tiny, and timing is tricky." Bert glances over to the chart tacked to the bulletin board. "We'll ride in on high tide, which isn't until after midnight." He looks hard at Ray. "We'll need the outgoing tide to get out. It'll take some luck too."

Ray nods. That trip will be much nastier than the ride across the sound from Storm Harbor. Following the rocky coast of Hurricane will take them around the woman's right leg right out into the open bay. Too risky?

Bert turns to Catherine. "What's your plan?"

"I don't really have one. I guess I'm going up there to look for Henry. And try to get him off the island before Tobias finds him."

Crazy woman. But then, Nettie would do the same thing if it were Ray up there in trouble, maybe real sick, with a crazy guy running the place.

"Well," Bert says. "We can't access the cove until high tide. So I'm going to walk Catherine up the hill, make sure she gets into the building. And I'll find Cyrus. He'll help us."

Ray isn't so sure about that. Maybe he will, maybe not. Family trumps pretty much everything else up here, but Cyrus is career Army. While Bert fiddles with his wet slicker, Ray asks Catherine, "Do you know how to get to the east rim cave?"

"I think so," she says.

"Meet us there, with Henry. We'll give you both a ride out."

Catherine studies the map for a minute. She reaches for her slicker, but Bert takes it and helps her on with it, just like it's a fur coat or something posh. As they move towards the guard post door, Bert hands Catherine a flashlight and slips something dark into her other hand.

Ray probably isn't supposed to see it, and he only gets a glimpse. But he's pretty sure it's a gun.

## 46. AUSTIN, 6:16 P.M.

The cave is quiet except for the breathing of the two sleeping prisoners. No, she shouldn't think of them that way anymore. Now it's the three of them together, and they are all fugitives. That word freaks her out, and she doesn't want to think about it.

She takes the packet of letters from her pocket. There's something romantic about reading them here, in this spot where Margaret and Angelo made love. Okay, maybe not romantic—given the bad things that happened to them—but still significant. Besides, maybe it will take her mind off the mess she's in now.

She blows out one candle. Better ration them. It could be hours before Pops gets here. Holding the letters close to the flame, Austin rummages through the pages, looking for the last paragraph she read on the ferry. Margaret vomiting on her way to meet Angelo, the day her world fell apart.

*I left my dripping cloak and bucket at the cave entrance and paused a moment, as always, to let my fingers trace our entwined initials before going inside. The cave was empty. Something bad must have happened. Angelo was never late. I felt faint again, those green-gold specks sparkling before my eyes, flittering like confused fireflies, and my stomach roiled.*

*Something must have delayed him. I was so worried, it's hard to remember how long I waited, or what I did. But I remember searching the cave, thinking he might have left me a message. I even looked*

*in the narrow back exit to the cave, even though it was full of spider*
*webs and I hated going there. The webs were undisturbed.*

Back exit? Austin thinks. She better check that out. After she finishes
reading.

*Finally I heard footsteps thud outside the cave. I scrambled to my*
*feet, but it was your Aunt Carrie inspecting our intaglio initials in*
*their leafy embrace. I figured this was the place, she said. She opened*
*her arms and hugged me. When I stopped crying, I apologized for not*
*telling her before. Why couldn't you fancy a local fellow, she asked.*
*Fabrizio is handsome but he's not like us. He's trouble.*

*No, I insisted. Once you get to know him, you'll love him too.*

*You still don't understand, Carrie said. He's gone. The Italians*
*were sent away last night.*

*All those men with their wives and mothers and babies herded*
*onto ships and sent out into the Atlantic Ocean filled with prowling*
*German U-boats? I stood with one hand resting on my belly, where*
*you were beginning to grow, Angelina. My monthly was over five*
*weeks late. How could I do this without him?*

*Carrie stared at my hand on my belly. Let's go home, she said.*

*I felt so confused and betrayed and angry. I swung the metal*
*bucket at his stupid carving. A small chunk of granite cracked off the*
*leafy circle and fell onto the ground. I started to follow Carrie but I*
*couldn't leave that piece of Angelo lying in the dirt. I slipped it into the*
*pocket of my black-eyed Susan skirt.*

Austin takes the granite leaf from her pocket and brings it closer her face.
Pink specks in the rock reflect the flickering light from the candle. Amazing
that this piece of rock has survived, even though all the people involved are
dead, and Margaret's story has been hidden and dormant too. Rubbing her
thumb over the carved ridges of the leaf, the bumpy texture, the rough place,
Austin returns to the letter.

*At home, Mother was waiting for me on the divan. She looked at*
*me hard—at my face, at my bosom, and finally at my hand resting on*
*my middle—and a hot river rushed over my burning cheeks. Until*
*that moment, I had never felt ashamed. I reached into my pocket for*

*Angelo's carving, and my fingers found courage. I returned Mother's gaze and nodded.*

*The Italian boy, she asked.*

*Yes.*

*That night the quarry office was bombed. The fire destroyed records and burned the payroll. The owners decided to cut their losses and close down. Everyone would be moving back to Storm Harbor. Except us. The next day, my father accepted the job as caretaker on the island. Our family would stay over the winter.*

*Mother told me that when we returned to Storm Harbor the next summer, my baby would be raised as her child. I objected, but Mother held up her hand. You have no choice, she said. We will never again speak of the Italian boy, of any of this.*

*I was forced to agree. But I insisted the baby be named after Angelo.*

*Every day I grieve for you, Angelina, for my family, for the people I grew up with. I grieve for my islands, for the granite cliffs of the quarry, even for that damp, smelly cave.*

*I live with the constant sorrow of leaving you. Abandoning you, some would say. Did I do the right thing? I still don't know.*

Austin sniffles and tries to picture Angelina waking up one morning with no beloved big sister Margaret. Abandoned by her mother, even if she didn't know Margaret was her mother, with just a chunk of granite left on her pillow. She reaches for the last letter. This one is short, just one page. Wait a minute—this one is dated 1945. What happened to all those years? Did Angelina ever forgive her mother and write back? Austin has a moment's pity for Margaret before hardening her heart again. The woman left her kid—how could anyone forgive that?

A noise makes Austin look up, but it's not from outside. Gandalf is moving around, probably trying to get comfortable. The last letter will have to wait.

## 47. HENRY, 6:42 P.M.

Henry jerks awake at the slow creak of his office door. He must not have locked it after all. Tobias could be right that he's losing his edge. Willing his terror quiet, he listens intently as footsteps shuffle across the pine floor. Is the power still out or does the intruder prefer the dark? No, he has a flashlight. The small disk of light sweeps across the floor. Henry stares at the floor just beyond the edge of the desk, his small slice of window into the room, while he considers his options: to continue hiding or wait for an opportunity to use the element of surprise and overpower the guy.

As if he could overpower anyone in this state. His head starts to spin again, just thinking about it. Breathe, he reminds himself, and he fills his lungs, slow and easy. He must feed the monster in his chest. The intruder's footsteps stop at the desk, inches from Henry's hiding place, and he can see the toes of the guy's shoes.

Lime-green boots.

"Cat?" he whispers. "Down here."

There's a rustle of oilcloth as she steps behind the desk and squats. "Henry?"

"What are you doing here?"

"What do you think? Looking for you."

That's good, right? He's so confused. "What time is it?"

"Almost seven. How do you feel?"

"You've got to leave. It's not safe. Why are you here?"

"Henry." She slowly pulls the desk chair out, revealing his burrow, then sits down next to him. "Listen to me. Austin Coombs told her grandfather that you were sick, and Ray called me. What happened? Are you okay?"

"The pain is gone now. But you've got to get away. Tobias is out of control."

Catherine brushes the hair from his forehead. "Bert will meet us at the quarry cave. He'll have boats to get us off-island."

"I've got to stop him."

"Stop Bert?"

"Tobias. It's my fault, Cat. I should've seen it coming. He's done awful things."

"We'll deal with that later. First let's get you to a doctor."

"I want to make things right. With my job, with you." He looks at her. "Does this mean you forgive me?"

"It doesn't mean anything, except we can't figure out anything if you're dead. We'll get off this island and get you medical care. Then we'll talk."

"You haven't told anyone, have you? Melissa?"

"No, of course not." After a long pause she adds, "I'm sorry."

"No, I'm sorry."

"I looked it up online, about what you do."

"No," he interrupts. "What I *am*."

"Yes." She stands and helps Henry up. "What you are. Like I said, we'll talk later. Now, let's get out of here."

He nods. "I've just got to grab a couple of things we're going to need."

## 48. TOBIAS, 6:59 P.M.

Tobias slams the door to the monitor room, throws the deadbolt, and punches the master switch. The power grid better be back on line soon, or someone's head will roll for sure, and it won't be his, no matter what the Regional Chief thinks. How long has it been since JR conducted an interrogation himself, even fired his weapon? Years probably. That's what happens with these guys, they get promoted up the food chain until they forget what it's like in the trenches. Until they lose any street smarts they might have once had. But this isn't about sucking up to the Regional Chief any more. This is about loving his country and doing the job right, even if every single person on duty in this place wimps out on him.

Speaking of everyone else, where's the rest of his staff? He jabs the extension for the dock guardhouse and listens to the ringing. Strictly speaking, Bert's shift ended, but doesn't he have a sense of duty? And what about the soldiers? He hasn't seen anyone since the meeting, going on three hours. He trusts that Cyrus is getting his ass out to the quarry caves as ordered. He's a soldier. He'll do the right thing.

One monitor screen hums and flickers, then brightens. Good, the generator feed to the emergency surveillance system is on board. At least something is going his way. He reaches to activate the feed from Interrogation Room D and then hesitates, his finger hovering millimeters above the button. In spite of Henry's deteriorating leadership, in spite of the ugliness of the past few days, Tobias feels reluctant to actually view Henry's body.

Not that the guy doesn't deserve what's coming. His actions are practically treason. But in the early days, Henry tried to be a friend and mentor.

He was clueless about it, like when he offered sympathy after Lois left. Clueless that Tobias was better off without the bitch, just like he's clueless now about how to fight terrorism.

Tobias rubs his eyes. He doesn't consider himself a cruel man, not like those guys who love inflicting pain. His older brother is like that, never the same after the First Gulf War and probably still causing global mayhem with the private security firm. Sometimes when the adrenalin rush is overwhelming and glorious during an interrogation, Tobias wonders if that's how his brother feels in the Sudan or Pakistan or wherever he is.

One time Tobias admitted that he envied his brother, and Lois went ballistic, calling him an animal. But then the next night at a club, after she flirted with a guy wearing a Che Guevara tee shirt with that simple-minded quote about being motivated by love, Tobias whispered that he too was motivated by big feelings of love for his country. He would never have gone squishy like that if he hadn't drunk so much, if Lois hadn't been acting like such a slut. She ridiculed him for that too. He got shit for being too macho and shit for being too soft. A guy can't win, can he?

So many people have turned out to be disappointments. Lois. Henry. His missing staff. Looks like he's going to have to do this alone. Him and Cyrus.

He resets the security options and reaches for the Room D monitor button, then freezes as he notices the digital readout on the screen: September 10, 2016. 7:07 p.m. In less than five hours, it will be the anniversary. And he has not obtained any intelligence to prevent another attack. Time to stop being soft, to clean up this mess. He pushes the button and Room D comes into focus.

It's empty.

The grungy towel lies on the floor, still holding the round indentation of a head, but Henry is gone. Tobias swivels the camera around, just to be sure, but there's no place to hide in the stripped-down room. Henry must just have been unconscious. Hard to believe the old guy got himself up and out of there.

Tobias punches the console button, and the screen goes dark. He has to find those women and bring them back into custody. Then he'll deal with Henry. If he's lucky, he'll find them together. But first, he'll need supplies.

Initially, he's shocked to find the storeroom so ransacked, discarded slickers and boots strewn around the floor. But on second thought, the mess is a good thing because now he is pretty sure where the women are heading.

There are really only three possibilities: The control tower at the airstrip offers shelter, but air rescue is impossible during the hurricane. The guard post at the dock is too obvious, because it's the easiest way off the island, and Bert is related to the girl. Sure, he'll check those places, but if the women took all that rain gear and warm clothes, they plan to be outdoors for a while, and that points towards the caves dotting the granite wall face along the quarry. Searching those will be a pain in the butt. There are supposed to be dozens of them, and he has no idea exactly where they are. But he has Cyrus and he has technology. They have nothing but desperation.

He chooses rain pants, rubber boots, and a dark slicker. Unlocking the safe, he removes a rifle with night scope, then packs extra ammunition for his .38 and the rifle, and a pair of heat-sensing goggles. He clips four sets of handcuffs to his belt and carefully chooses two thick coils of sturdy rope and an aluminum figure eight. He might have to rappel down that cliff. At the last minute, he slips a smoke grenade into the canvas bag. Those three ladies just might require a bit of persuasion to abandon their hideout. Once he finds it, that is.

## 49. GANDALF, 7:36 P.M.

Gandalf shudders awake, fleeing sleep-warped images of running through snow-covered forests, of Ferret's knife icy on her scar. She shifts her position against the cave wall. The candle has burned down halfway. The trembling light is both ghostly and oddly comforting. Next to her, Norah sleeps draped over the duffle. Austin sits opposite with legs extended; their feet almost touch in the middle of the small space.

"Hey," Austin says. "You okay?"

"Just cold. What's taking our rescuers so long?"

When Austin doesn't answer, Gandalf looks at her more closely. In the broken light of the candle, maybe she imagines the wetness on Austin's face.

"Are *you* okay?"

"Just worried. I feel responsible for getting you into this mess."

"No, you got us out of that mess." Gandalf runs her fingers through her hair. "Who knows what that creep had planned for me. And for you."

"Do you have to wear it short?"

"It?"

"Your hair."

"What do you mean, have to?" Gandalf asks.

"Because you're, you know, a lesbian."

Gandalf snorts, startling Norah awake. "Sorry, Norah." She turns back to Austin. "Why do you think that?"

"It's just that at my college they all had short hair." Austin shrugs. "So I wondered."

"There is no lesbian hair police, if that's what you mean. My partner has long hair." Picturing the braid hanging down Jess's back, Gandalf's sinuses fill with the coppery taste of unspilled sorrow. She might be out of that prison, but she doesn't feel free, or even much closer to getting home. She tries to imagine what Jess is doing right now, besides being worried out of her mind.

Austin stretches her foot in double wool socks across the empty inches to touch Gandalf's. "Sorry."

Norah looks from one woman to the other. "What's going on?"

Gandalf shakes her head.

"Nothing," says Austin.

"Okay," Norah says. "Here's a simpler question. What's the story with this island? You know, what used to be here before the prison?"

"A huge granite quarry, a hundred years ago. Italian workers were brought over as stoneworkers. When the industry collapsed, they were blamed and sent home."

"That's nothing new," Norah says. "Foreigners are easy to blame. Look at how Arabs are targeted."

Gandalf looks down. Norah's knee-jerk rhetoric drives her nuts, but at least an argument will help take her mind off Jess's silver braid. "Maybe there's a good reason the security services profile Arab men," she says. "Most terrorists are from that part of the world. The authorities have to do their job."

"You mean like picking you up and bringing you here?"

You cannot argue with someone like Norah, who always has the politically correct comeback on the tip of her tongue, but Gandalf cannot keep quiet either. "You don't think things got better with Obama?"

"Maybe some of the social issues are better. Like Don't Ask Don't Tell. And sure, it's huge to have a black president, even if he's only half-black like me. But in terms of civil liberties we've gone from bad to much worse."

"Like what?" Austin asks.

"Like this. They've broadened what the government can legally do if they claim they suspect us of terrorism. So fewer people fight back because they're scared this shit will happen to them."

"But there are real terrorists, aren't there?" Austin asks. "I mean, people flew those planes into the Twin Towers, right? So don't we have to find them?"

"Not this way," Norah insists. "Secret prisons and torture are wrong, and they don't work."

Gandalf shivers. It is an age-old moral question, always theoretically interesting. She draws another jacket around her shoulders, but suspects she will not be able to get warm no matter how many layers she uses. "So is there an ethical way to interrogate people, to get information that could save lives?"

"That's why we have the rule of law. Courts. Judges," Norah says. "It's a pretty flawed system these days, but better than kidnapping citizens and freezing them half to death."

Austin peers at her watch, then stands up and walks towards the cave mouth.

"What time is it?" Norah calls after her.

"Almost eight."

"So now what?"

"So nothing. We wait."

Gandalf touches Norah's forehead with the back of her hand, then lowers her face close to the leg bandage and sniffs.

Norah jerks back. "What are you doing?"

"Infection stinks," Gandalf says. "There's no smell yet, but I think you have a fever." She turns to Austin. "When do you think they'll get here?"

Austin pries the second candle from the mixture of dirt and dried wax and lights it. "You think it's easy to get us out of here? From right under the noses of the Army, Homeland Security, and the FBI? Well, trust me, it's not." Holding the candle in front of her, she walks towards the cave entrance.

Trust her? Gandalf wants to trust her, especially since there is no one else. Austin proved herself in the interrogation room, but she might be having second thoughts. Gandalf watches the younger woman making her way along the flickering wall.

"I want to know more about this place," Gandalf says. "About what we are up against here. Who is in charge? FEMA or Homeland Security or the FBI?"

"Or the military?" Norah adds. "Some of those guards wore Army uniforms."

Austin turns back and makes a face. "I'm not exactly sure. Henry is FBI, but apparently he's out. FEMA seems to provide the facilities management..."

Norah laughs. "That's a joke."

Austin spins around and points her finger at Norah. "None of this is funny. Homeland Security is pulling the strings, and there's nothing at all amusing about them. So go back to sleep and stop bugging me, okay?"

Norah rearranges herself over the duffle and closes her eyes as Austin stomps off towards the mouth of the cave. Back to those stupid initials. Gandalf wishes Austin would stop mooning over old carvings. She wishes Norah would stay awake, that they could have a private conversation without arguing about politics. For a brief moment, she even longs for the ignorant safety of their whispered exchanges through the hole in the baseboard, lying in the sawdust. Most of all, she wishes she was more optimistic that they would get out of this cave alive.

# 50. RAY, 8:40 P.M.

Ray paces back and forth across the eight feet of open floor space in the dark room, stomping to banish the worrisome images. There's Austin hiding with two escaped prisoners. Bert's gun in Catherine's pocket. Henry sick and his assistant running amok. Evelina trying to talk sense on the Hill. And not the least of his misgivings, Nettie waking up to find his note and being royally pissed off.

Footsteps thump on the wharf outside, and Ray steps into the shadows in the corner of the room, behind the door. Bert told him to keep out of sight. He left the lights off, but it never occurred to him to lock the door. The knob turns and the door opens a few inches.

"You there, Ray?"

It's Cyrus's voice. Ray hesitates. Cyrus is a Carter cousin too, his grandpa one of Margaret's twin brothers. Nettie's grandma had her kids spread way out, so the generations in their family are all cockamamie. Margaret was seventeen years older than the littlest and she probably spent her whole childhood raising her siblings. No wonder she ran away, or whatever she did.

He's always been curious about what's in those letters, though he has his suspicions. Now that Austin has read them, there's no way she'll let the secrets stay buried, and he admits it, he looks forward to that ancient history being out in the open. But at the moment he better concentrate on getting Austin out of this mess, or Nettie and he will have lots more to deal with than old letters and her strange kin. Makes his head hurt to try to figure out that tree, but family is family and Cyrus is part of it.

"Ray?" Cyrus calls out again.

"Yeah." Ray steps out of the shadows. "I'm here."

"Bert told me to come wait with you until he's done up the hill."

Ray returns to Bert's desk chair. "What else did he say?"

Bert must trust Cyrus if he's asking for his help, but Ray isn't so sure. All those years of following orders, it might be a hard habit to break. Ever since Vietnam, Ray doesn't have much use for career Army types, but Nettie is fond of Cyrus. Says he's the spitting image of her Uncle Tommy, with his soft blue eyes and round face smothered with freckles.

Cyrus perches on the edge of the desk. "I know your girl is missing. And I know she's got two high-profile detainees with her."

"You seen Henry Ames?"

"Negative." Cyrus says. "Seems he's missing too."

"What do you think is going on? Why's Tobias in charge?"

"Dunno. He's second in command."

Ray looks out the window. It's full dark now, and the hard rain drums against the glass. What's keeping Bert?

The phone on Bert's desk rings, splintering the silence. Both men stare at it for a second before Ray picks up.

"Hello?" Should he should try to disguise his voice, imitate Bert or something?

"Ray? It's Evelina."

"Oh. Hi." Better keep her involvement secret, just in case.

"Is my father there?"

"Nope."

"Is he okay?"

"Yup."

"You can't talk freely, is that it?"

"Yup."

Evelina's sigh travels unimpeded from the nation's capitol. "I spoke with that friend I mentioned. He's very interested and wants to help us."

"Good," Ray says.

"Okay. I'll call again later. But for now, just so you know, I've been in touch with the Human Rights Litigation Center, where Norah Levinsky works. They're working on a press conference for Monday in Manhattan. Your job, cousin, is to get those three women to New York. I talked to Reuben, and he'll give us a hand. Got it?"

"Yup," he says. That's good news. Reuben is solid, and it'll be good to have the sheriff on their side.

"One more thing," Evelina says. "I heard from that woman you mentioned, Jess Winterman, whose partner is the detainee who was . . . allegedly abused. Hopefully I was able to talk her out of going up there to rescue her partner."

When Ray hangs up, Cyrus doesn't ask who it was, and Ray doesn't offer. Five silent minutes pass slowly, and then Bert is in the doorway. He nods at Cyrus.

Ray can't help asking. "Catherine?"

"All set," Bert says.

"Catherine, Henry's wife?" Cyrus asks.

"Uh-huh," Bert says. "She's worried about her husband." He doesn't seem to want to talk in front of Cyrus either.

"Now what?" Ray asks.

Bert moves slowly around the small room, gathering life jackets hanging from nails knocked into the walls. "Well, we can't bring them out 'til after midnight, when the tide turns."

"I hate the idea of my girl and the other women out there alone, with that Tobias. At least we can wait with them."

"Sure," Bert says. "It'll take a while to get to the cove. My boat's ready, but we'll need two."

"I'll follow you in my boat," Ray says.

"Take Cyrus with you. It's rough out there."

Ray bristles. He can handle his own boat. These conditions will take his full concentration, and he doesn't need another worry on board. He searches Bert's face, and he looks bothered too. Maybe Bert wants him to keep an eye on Cyrus, make sure he doesn't sabotage their plan.

"Sure," Ray says reluctantly. "I can use a hand."

## 51. AUSTIN, 9:32 P.M.

Over the last hour, Austin has felt increasingly spooked. Partly it's the air in the cave—too thick to breathe and too thin to nourish. Partly the jittery fingers of dread on the back of her neck and that's not hard to interpret— Tobias must be insane with fury at her. If they're lucky, he'll wait for morning to search and by then they'll be away from here. But that's the kind of wishful thinking Pops always warns her against. Wanting doesn't make it so, he likes to say with a squeeze of her shoulder. And what can be taking Pops so long? Still, there's nothing to do but wait.

And read that last letter, from 1945, to take her mind off now.

> *Perhaps you moved away, darling Angelina, and never received my letters? Or maybe you hate me. In any case, I am writing this on your 30th birthday. I promise this is the last time I'll bother you, but I must finish my story and then I have two more things to tell you.*
>
> *I hope you have children of your own, a husband whom you adore. Angelo and I have two sons. We named Tommaso for my little brother Tommy, even though he has Angelo's dark skin and thick curls. Tonio's name comes from Angelo's father, but he could have been Tommy's twin, with fair skin and freckles he tried to scrub off when he was little. Children don't come out like you expect, do they? Still, these are your brothers, and they are soldiers.*
>
> *This evening I've been listening to the evening news on National Radio. The announcer didn't come right out and report that Mussolini is dead and his army surrendered. They never admit defeat. But*

*after 25 years, I've learned to listen between the words of my adopted language. Who knows what will happen to us now. If my boys survived the fighting, if their regiments are not stationed too far away, they could be home soon.*

Austin wished she knew more history. What happened to Italian citizens after their leader surrendered? Did Margaret's sons—Nettie's brothers, which would make them Austin's great uncles—return home safely?

*I promised just two more things.*
*The first is that five years after Angelo disappeared from my life, a letter from him arrived. He told me about the middle-of-the-night round up, the deportation center, the endless crossing home, the warships and disease. He sent money for the passage and begged me to join him in Carrara. I had to go to the school atlas to locate the small city in Tuscany, famous for its stone carvers since Roman times.*
*All these years later, I still question my choice to leave. I went without telling my family, without fighting to take you with me. I feared my parents would stop me. They might change my mind. How does a woman choose between a lover and a child? I don't know the answer. I don't know if Angelo would hate me if he knew I had his baby and allowed my parents to claim the girl, to raise you as their own.*

Austin rubs her eyes. This is so totally spooky. No wonder Gran sewed these letters away and won't discuss them. When she did read them, when Abby was a baby, could she have possibly guessed that her own daughter would do the same thing?

*The second thing is also a secret, but this one isn't mine. It's Angelo's secret and I'm not supposed to know it but I do. It's about the bombing of the quarry office the night after the European workers were sent away. The fire destroyed all the records, the week's payroll and the meager profits awaiting transport to the bank in Rockland. Angelo never discussed it with me, but in his desk I found a letter from a local member of the Storm Harbor stone carvers' union. Our plan worked, the man wrote. We couldn't stop the bosses from sending you away. But we didn't let the bastards win.*

*At that moment I knew that all the information I gave Angelo allowed him to make his plans. So I suppose it is partially my fault. And my secret.*

Austin pictures the bombed-out ruins of the quarry office, overrun by a century and covered by tangled vines. Every day she has walked past the place, never knowing the connection.

*After all these years, I have made my peace with my actions, my decision. I hope you understand. I hope you have kept the stone carving I left on your pillow. For five years it warmed the hollow of my hand, and my fingers wore smooth the jagged part. Maybe someday you will go to the cave and find your father's carving. Perhaps you will replace the broken piece to make it whole again. Possibly someday you'll come to Italy and meet your other family.*
*And maybe someday you will forgive me.*

*Love, Mama*

Austin closes her eyes. They're all ghosts now, Margaret and Angelo and Angelina. In the morning, or someday, she'll have to figure out what to do with these letters, how to talk to Gran about them. But now, she has one thing to do before Pops gets here. She needs to do it for Margaret and Angelina and for Nettie and Abby. And for herself—for a little girl abandoned early one morning at her grandparents' kitchen table with a bag of clothes and a scruffy toy giraffe.

Trying not to wake her companions, Austin inches her way along the clammy cave wall to the entrance. The sodden wind is softer now, barely whipping her hair. She leans her cheek against the damp chill of the stone. She sticks one hand out into the steady rain, then caresses the wreath of branches circling the initials. Her fingers find the broken place.

"Austin?" Gandalf is standing next to her, her whisper climbing above the rain and the waves. "Are you all right? What is your obsession with these initials?"

Austin lets her hand drop from the carving and looks at the older woman. After all they have been through together, why not tell her?

"Just don't laugh at me, okay?"

"Of course not," Gandalf says.

"I found this carving when I was a teenager. I was a lonely kid. Maybe that's why I cared about these people, whoever they were. Anyway, I've always wondered who MEC and AF were and what happened in 1914. I dreamed about them, made up stories about why they carved their initials here."

Gandalf traces her fingers along the intaglio carving, avoiding the broken place. "So who are they?"

"I just found out last night—reading these amazing letters from MEC. She's my grandmother's grandmother Margaret, and AF is Angelo. He was from Italy, a stone carver working here, in this very quarry. They loved each other and they used to meet in this cave. She writes about he how carved their initials and about the secret back entrance full of spiders and the little cove where they sometimes made love and how one day, he didn't show up." Austin rubs her eyes. "Margaret got pregnant, and Angelo was deported. He never knew they had a kid, my Gran's mother." Austin pauses. "It sounds like a soap opera, doesn't it?"

Gandalf smiles. "A little."

"But it's real and it's my family. When Angelo disappeared Margaret didn't know he was sent away, and she was pissed off and smashed the carving and broke a piece off."

Austin opens her hand and shows Gandalf the broken rock, warm in her palm. "Margaret's last letter asks her daughter—my Gran's mother—to put the broken part back."

"So what are you waiting for?" Gandalf asks.

"I can't believe you'd say that, Dr. Scientist. What difference would it make? MEC and AF have been dead for years. Even their baby is long gone."

"And we might not survive the night either." Gandalf touches something shiny at her neck, something Austin can't see. "But this matters to you."

It does matter, and the leaf fits perfectly in the chipped off spot—just like Austin knew it would. Her chest opens up and relaxes. Her fingers feel around the completed circle, along the interwoven twigs, around each sculpted leaf. She traces each letter, each number. Why does it matter so much to replace that stupid chunk of rock when there are more important things to fix? Generations of grudges. What did these ghosts do that was so awful, anyway? Margaret fell in love with a person her community didn't approve of. She chose him over their child—okay, that part's pretty awful. She gave her lover information that helped him fight back against a company that treated him and his buddies badly. He broke the law. Just like we're doing right now, she thinks. Then she is sobbing, and Gandalf is hugging her and pulling her back into the passageway. Together they make their way back to the inner cave.

Norah stirs and sits up. "Is something happening?" Her voice is thick with sleep.

"Just checking on the rain," Austin says, "and looking for Pops."

"And playing with your precious initials?" Norah asks.

"They are precious," Gandalf whispers.

"Waiting is what's so damned hard. Not being able to do anything. In my real life . . ." Norah's voice trails off.

"In your real life, what?" Austin asks after a few seconds.

"I wonder if I'll ever get my real life back. I'm used to making things happen. Bossy, some people would say. Not waiting around to be rescued."

"*Hoping* to be rescued," Austin says. "Tobias has more firepower at that facility than you can imagine. He could come after us with bombs and grenades and helicopters."

"He'll have to wait for the storm to die down for that," Norah says.

"The storm is dying down," Gandalf says.

Norah leans back. "So now your Ferret-man can send copters to bomb the quarry."

Austin blinks. Ripples of heat surge behind her eyes. No way will she cry again. She glances quickly at Norah, then down at her lap. "Aren't you scared?"

"Terrified. But that's how they want us to feel."

"It's working," Gandalf adds.

"That doesn't mean we cower in a corner and give up," Norah says.

Austin swallows hard. "We're not giving up."

"Let's think positively," Norah says. "What's the first thing you guys will do when you get home?

Gandalf laughs. "You mean after a hot bath and a long night in my own bed with Jess?"

"Yeah. After that."

"Get back to my research, I guess," Gandalf says. "Assuming we get off this island alive. Will you go back to suing the government? Who knows, you might end up here again someday."

"It's not my work that's the problem, Gandalf. Did your work land you here?"

"Of course not. I didn't do anything wrong."

"And I did? Come on, I work within the legal system."

Austin listens to their sparring until she can't take it anymore. She jabs her finger at Norah. The woman likes to push people, but how does she like being on the spot? "Still, it's a good question. Even if your work is legal and all, it did get you in a lot of trouble with the feds. What about your daughters? How can you do work that puts them at risk of losing you?"

"If we don't do this work, what kind of world do our kids inherit? I work with this lawyer at the Center, Emma. Her mother was an antiwar activist, framed for bombings she never did. She spent most of Emma's childhood in prison but Emma still believes we can make this country more just."

Norah pauses. "On the other hand, I've been having these nightmares."

"If you give up, that means they win," Austin says. She never really thought about that before Margaret and Angelo, because they usually win, don't they? She looks at Gandalf and Norah. "What if this Ahmed fellow really is a terrorist? Would you still protect him?"

Gandalf looks surprised. "I don't think so. Why?"

"But I might," Norah says. "Maybe Ahmed was just trying to get the U.S. out of his country's oilfields."

Austin points her finger at Norah. "Then you would be aiding a terrorist, right? So maybe you would belong at this camp."

"Stop arguing," Gandalf says. "Ahmed is not a terrorist, and no one belongs here. We need each other."

Norah nods and turns to Austin. "What will you do after this is over? Because you can probably consider yourself fired."

"At the very least." Austin tries to smile.

"Why did you take this sucky job anyway?"

"For the money. So I can go to Texas and find my dad."

"Texas might be a good idea," Norah says. "Far away from this place. I don't think the feds look kindly on people who help their enemies."

"We can talk more about it when we're out of here," Gandalf says to Austin. "But if you want to be in New York while you figure out what to do next, Jess and I have an extra bedroom. You can stay with us."

The hot waves come again behind Austin's eyes. She can't believe that Gandalf would invite her. For a moment she can see herself forgetting Texas, staying at Gandalf's place, maybe even looking for a job in New York City.

"I might do that, when we get out of here. Or . . . Or, maybe I'll travel, go to Italy. I think I have some family there."

Crazy stuff. Who's she fooling? Right now it seems unlikely that any of them will make it to Texas or New York or even Rockland. She closes her eyes and shakes her head.

"What's wrong?" Gandalf asks.

"Just a feeling that I better keep watch," Austin says. "Tobias is out there, already searching for us." She peers into the dark at the mouth of the cave, slips Tobias's revolver from her belt and checks again for bullets. Not that she for one single moment believes that she can protect three women in a blind cave from a well-armed and highly motivated bunch of federal jocks.

# 52. RAY, 9:42 P.M.

Above the roar of wind and water, the boat's engine is obscenely loud. Waiting to follow Bert into Hurricane Sound, Ray worries about someone hearing them. Then he worries if they can trust Cyrus. He wonders for a second what it's like on the open bay if conditions are this wild along the protected shoreline. He's anxious to get to the cove, to find his girl and bring her home. He is also deeply frightened. He has never seen the tide this high, the Bay so seismic, so threatening. Capsizing in these waters would be lethal.

When they finally leave the dock, it takes every molecule of concentration to follow the wildly heaving shadow of Bert's craft. Takes every ounce of strength to keep his boat steady as furious waves toss the small boats back and forth like bathtub toys. Turbulent and chaotic, rain and spray smash onto the deck from all directions.

Pulling himself hand over hand along the gunwale, Cyrus reaches Ray and grips his shoulder. "This is brutal," he says. "Can I help?"

"I'm okay," Ray shouts above the wind.

Actually, he's not okay, not at all. He is relieved when Cyrus ignores his response and joins him holding the boat steady. Even so, every muscle in his arms and back screams with the strain of staying on course. His eyes ache trying to keep track of Bert's boat while steering into relentless waves. Finally, the stern light ahead turns sharply to the left, and Ray follows.

"Hang on," he warns Cyrus. "Here we go." They catch the tide pushing through the narrow cut and are lifted up fifteen feet onto the swell. The boat hangs weightless atop the wave for an impossibly elongated moment, then rides the rush into the cove. With a spine-jarring slap, they hit the calmer water. Ray wipes his face with his wet hand and rolls his shoulders to relax the kinks.

Cyrus aims his flashlight at the shore, then back at the inlet. "I've never seen anything like this. No way we'll get back through that cut until she turns."

"It'll take us a while to find the women and get everyone down the cliff and into the boats."

In the relative hush of the protected cove, the rumble of the motor sounds even louder. Still, both men hear Bert's yell.

"Tie up here," he calls. They secure their lines to a spruce trunk that seems to grow from stone. Bert points to a steep hill. "Trail's up there. Somewhere."

"And you're going to find it how?" Cyrus asks.

"My unfailing instinct."

Ray grins. "And dumb luck."

Bert holds up his hand. "From here on, we move quietly. Tobias might have decided not to wait for morning."

Their boots squish and slurp in the swampy weeds at the edge of the cove, sinking into the mud and pulling out with thick sucking sounds. Ray slips and falls. His knees sink deep into the muck, and he needs Bert's help to stand. They skid across the seaweed-covered rocks at the shoreline, then walk one by one onto the narrow path and start up the rocky hill.

At the top, Ray leans against the granite wall. "Gotta rest."

Cyrus throws him a glance. "Sure, old man."

"Watch your mouth," Bert says. "Ray's got just two years on me."

Ray tries to slow his breathing. It's louder in his ears than the wind zipping along the ridge or the splatter of rain on his hood. He'll be fine if he can keep the guys talking for a minute or two, just so he can catch his breath. Talking about anything at all will do.

"Hey. We're the three musketeer cousins. On a mission of mercy."

"Speaking of mercy," Bert says to Ray. "You said Nettie goes ballistic about the east rim cave. So how come your granddaughter's hiding out there?"

"Nettie doesn't know. Besides, it's not my idea. It's Austin's and a good one. Can you think of any other place out here that locals know and the damned feds don't? Austin and Gabe discovered the initials years ago, but until now she's never been inside the cave."

The minute the boy's name falls out of his mouth, Ray wishes he could reel it back. Bert doesn't need to be reminded of his dead son, not with so much danger ahead of them.

"What initials?" Cyrus asks.

"Ha," Ray says. "Maybe you young twerps don't know everything, after all."

Bert shushes them. "You know how sound travels out here. Ready to move on?"

"Yup." Ray pushes off the granite wall and peers along its surface. "How far do you think? I've never come from this direction."

"Ten minutes," Bert says. "But this part will be slick. Single file and take it slow. No more flashlights from here on. Makes us too easy a target."

"So what are the initials?" Cyrus whispers as they began inching their way along the cliff face.

"Just lovers' stuff," Bert says.

## 53. HENRY, 10:02 P.M.

Henry loses his grip on the slick surface of Cat's raincoat and repositions his arm across her shoulder. No way he could have done this alone. Even with Cat's help, it's taken forever with him needing to stop and rest. They haven't seen a soul since leaving the facility, but he would have been useless if they had. He feels marginally safer once they reach the woods, even with all the downed branches and tree roots trying to trip him, but the hardest part of the trip is still to come. Just up ahead looms the quarry rim. To get to the place Cat described, they have to follow the narrow granite ledge between the water and the cliff. He shudders.

Cat stops. "What's wrong?"

"Nothing that two aspirin and twenty-four hours uninterrupted sleep won't fix."

"And those cardiac tests, right?"

"Anything you want." Henry leans his face against Cat's. She is beautiful, even sopping wet with hair plastered against her forehead.

Cat touches his cheek. "I guess we'd better survive this, because we have a lot to talk about."

"Like Melissa."

Cat doesn't answer. As Henry tries to frame his question, his hope, he hears a sound—a footstep, a broken twig?—behind them. "What's that?"

"I didn't hear anything."

He steps into a thicket, pulling Catherine with him, and switches off the flashlight. "I think someone's following us." Henry reaches for his holster. "Damn. Tobias must've taken my gun when I was unconscious."

"That's taken care of." Cat guides his hand into her slicker pocket.

"How?"

"Bert."

He owes Cat's cousin big time. Family relations with Bert have always been cordial, but they have little in common and rarely socialize. Hardly ever since Cat's and Bert's mothers died. "Is Bert the one we're meeting?"

"Yes. Ray Coombs too."

Damn. He'll be in debt to the whole clan, and it's his own fault for hiring the Coombs girl. Not that there are all that many choices on the islands, and no way on earth to follow the Bureau's anti-nepotism regulations. After all this, he can certainly stand holidays with the Carter clan. That is, if he gets out of this alive. If he isn't sent to prison for dereliction of duty or something worse. If Cat doesn't leave him. He sticks his hand into his pocket, and fingers the black silk. It would be like cutting off an arm, but maybe he can give it up, if he must.

"We have to talk," he says.

"Oh, we will, but later." She pauses. "Listen, Henry, There's something else you should know, and you're not going to like it. One other person knows about all this, and that's Evelina."

"No!"

Cat touches his lips. "Shh. Somebody might be out there, remember?"

"Why? What does she have to do with this?"

"Ray called her," Cat says. "He said that even if he and Bert can get everyone off the island, there'll be political hell to pay. He says we'll all need her help."

Okay, first they get to safety and then he'll worry about what comes next. But spare him Evelina with her bleeding heart liberalism. "What can *she* do?"

"I'm not sure. Ray mentioned some kind of investigation, maybe a Congressional inquiry. She says the only way to stop the abuse is to make it public." Abuse. The word makes Henry wince. But he can't argue with it, not after that tape of Tobias with the math professor. And it's not the first time Tobias has been out of line with detainees. Henry has tried to convince himself that the guy is just overenthusiastic, a little heavy-handed, but he has known for a long time that isn't the whole story.

He looks at his hands, barely visible in the dark. These hands didn't personally turn down the AC and almost freeze the woman to death. They didn't cut her face and slice her clothing from her body. They certainly didn't push themselves down Austin's pants and grope her breasts. But those things happened on his watch and that makes it his fault.

"I've been thinking," Cat says slowly. "Whatever Evelina sets up, you can testify, make things right. You know, talk about what's going on, what Tobias did."

Testify? That would be a betrayal of the Bureau, after all his years of loyalty. "How can I do that?" he whispers.

The Cohen woman's image materializes in the darkness of the thicket. She yells: *I'll tell you how. Remember me? Naked, with my underwear sliced off by a knife-wielding federal agent. Your people almost killed me, Henry.* Then Norah's image, diminutive but fierce, adds her accusation: *Don't forget me. How your "guys" taunted and terrified and humiliated me. Is that the way your beloved Bureau operates? Is that what you're loyal to?*

And the Bureau is probably sending armed agents after him at this very moment. Henry shakes his head hard, trying to dislodge the thought, the women, to expel his guilt. He'll think about this later, once they are safe. He peers out of the thicket and listens intently. "Okay. It's quiet now. Let's get going. Bert will be waiting for us."

She doesn't move for a moment. "One question. Will you testify against Tobias? And when did you decide, by the way, to do the right thing?"

"That's two questions." He shakes his head. "I didn't really decide. It just happened."

"That's bull, dear."

"Okay, you want an answer? I decided the night I woke you up wearing a dress." He steps out of the thicket. "Now come on. Let's go."

She still doesn't move.

"I'll think about testifying." And he will, for Cat and Melissa. But later, because now they have to keep moving. Tobias is somewhere out there.

# 54. TOBIAS, 10:15 P.M.

He must have been imagining things, because now the voices are silent. It sounded like Henry and another person in response, but the words have been swallowed by the rain and wind or maybe they were never there at all. Now he hears nothing human except his own breath. He slings the canvas bag across his shoulders and resumes jogging along the trail, through the rain. He dodges broken branches, climbs over downed trees, avoids the biggest puddles. At the quarry he turns left and hurries up the steep slope.

Hiking up to check the airstrip was a total waste of time. On the way back Tobias slipped on the path and skidded down the hill on his butt, yelling and cursing. The dock guardhouse was empty too and Bert's boat was missing. Looking around the small room, he saw nothing suspicious, but he kicked Bert's desk, splintering the cheap wood veneer.

With each failed search, his mood grows progressively darker. But other than the airstrip and the dock, there is no other way to get off island. So the women have got to be trapped on the island overnight, most likely in the quarry caves everyone talks about. He has never been there, but has a good idea of where they are. He knows how to set up surveillance of the area and find Henry and the women.

At the top of the cliff, he sets the canvas bag under a stunted pine and spreads his slicker on the rain-soaked ground. This is a good place: the branches offer some cover from the constant rain and the root system provides additional structural support to the pebbly overhang. He stretches out prone on the ground with the rifle, resting his elbows on the wet matted weeds at the cliff edge. Squinting through the night scope towards the shoreline, he gets a good look at two boats bobbing and tossing in the wild tide. From this distance he can't identify the figures, but one of the boats could be Bert's. The caves should be below him, at least fifty feet down. Their entrances are hidden by the cut of the rock face, but thanks to the technology he doesn't need to see his prey to locate them.

Balancing the rifle against the tree trunk, he dons the thermal goggles and adjusts the position of the rubber eyecups. Mentally dividing the visual field into a grid, he scans the ground the way he was trained: systematically, searching from top to bottom of the visual field, column by column from left to right. After a storm like this, any beast dumb enough to risk the slippery rocks is likely to be human. As his eyes adjust to the eerie green glow of the heat-sensing mechanism, he recognizes the increase in his heart rate, the quickening of his breaths. He is getting close. He can feel it.

Henry is out there somewhere. Most likely with someone else because of the other voice he heard, though Tobias can't imagine who on the staff would risk his career to help him. Somehow the boss lucked out and eluded him on the path through the woods, but he won't get far. Not in his condition. Not with Tobias's skills as a tracker and with Cyrus's help. Cyrus hasn't actually done anything yet, but Tobias saw the way the soldier's eyes lit up at the mention of a job with the Bureau.

Problem is, Tobias hasn't decided what to do with Henry when he finds him. All things being equal, the best career move would be to bring him in as a fugitive. Turn him over to the Bureau honchos to face charges. Only it isn't clear exactly what those charges might be, or how a recounting of recent events might reflect on Tobias. Before he keeled over, didn't Henry say something about a tape? Tobias will have to find that and destroy it. All things considered, it might be better to just kill him. Tobias can see the headlines: rogue agent taken down in the act of escaping with two high-interest prisoners.

But the idea of shooting Henry . . . well, it feels different from just letting him die of natural causes. Tobias has never been queasy, never disobeyed an order, not even when one of those little doubt-niggles made him question his superiors' wisdom. He feels himself wavering just a little but no! Those soft memories are trying to undermine his resolve, to obscure his target. Silly memories of hanging out at the Bangor Tavern after work, of the first time Henry brought his infant daughter to the office. He pushes the images out of mind, because there's no way Tobias Sampson is about to start shirking now, when there's so much at stake. Henry is no longer his friend and mentor. He is now a traitor and when the time comes, Tobias will do what he was trained to do.

And in the meantime, no shortcuts. Just careful surveillance, each section in turn, not jumping ahead.

On the fourth sweep down the grid, he finds them. Three man-sized shapes. Estimating their location from the visible landmarks, the men are moving slowly in a northeast direction along the path cut into the granite between the quarry lake and the cliffs. They must have come from those boats because there's nothing else on the south end of the island, even without the storm. One is probably Bert. The second has to be Cyrus, embedded with the enemy. But who's the third?

He tightens the head-mount straps on the goggles, pushes himself two inches further over the cliff edge, and looks down towards the quarry water. Sweeping along the path, he identifies a second source of heat-image about fifty feet ahead of the men. It's large and formless, not shaped like a person. He recognizes the pattern from training. It matches the type of heat dispersal made by warm-blooded bodies, either people or large animals, in a room with an open door. Or a cave opening. The three men will get there in a few minutes.

Working quickly, he pulls the two rope coils from the bag and ties one around the nearby pine. He walks along the cliff top to the southern rim, in case they try to escape in that direction. He wraps the second rope around a spruce and ties it tight. The tree's not as sturdy as he'd like, but he's got to cover that direction. If Bert is helping them escape, he'll certainly know the best getaway routes.

He checks his belt for the four sets of handcuffs, wishing he'd brought more. He'll need to Subdue, Disarm, Immobilize the three females plus Henry, in addition to Bert and whoever else is out helping them. With Cyrus's help, he can bring them all in. Removing the smoke grenade from its packing, he places it within easy reach. Hopefully he won't need it. Anything that makes it harder to see is of dubious value, especially with the reduced visibility from this damned rain. But he's trained to be maximally prepared, to have all options available.

Replanting his elbows in the soggy earth at the very edge of the cliff, he scoots his body forward another inch and positions the rifle. He's pretty sure what that green-glowing amorphous shape represents and he plans to be ready. He will not let Henry get away again. Or the women. Now he waits for the shoot signal from Cyrus's flashlight.

# 55. AUSTIN, 10:34 P.M.

Someone's coming.

Standing sentry just inside the narrow cave opening, Austin hears a noise along the path, coming from the direction of the detention center. Hopefully it's Pops, but it could just as easily be Tobias. She eases her head outside and listens hard. Silence. The air is softer now. How can such violent weather bring such fresh-smelling air?

Retreating into the cave, Austin calls a whispered warning to Norah and Gandalf. Then she takes Tobias's gun from her pocket and holds it out, butt first, to the two women, though it's probably too much to hope for. This whole thing is a mess and it isn't going to end well. Whatever was she thinking, that she could rescue anyone?

"Someone's coming. Either one of you know how to use this?"

Gandalf leans back, hands splayed chest high with palms out. "Not me."

"I could try," Norah says. "I've never shot a gun, but my husband's a cop and I'm a good bluff."

Gandalf stares at her. "You're married to a cop?"

"Separated."

"Sleeping with a person who knows how to use a gun doesn't count," Austin says with disgust.

"If that someone coming is Tobias," Gandalf says, "he is going to be furious out of his mind that he was overpowered by two women."

"But it could also be my Pops." Austin returns the gun to her pocket. She steps into the passage, leans against the carving.

"Anyone in there?" a male voice calls. "It's Henry and Catherine."

Austin's shoulders sag in relief. She didn't really expect Henry to make it. How could he possibly walk so far, given how bad he looked in the hallway? But Pops must have called Catherine and of course she would find a way to help Henry.

She touches the initials. Someday, someone will love her enough to help her like that. Until these last few days, she always thought her dad would be that person. Stepping outside, Austin guides Henry and Catherine through the narrow opening into the deep chamber, where Norah and Gandalf sit silently against the wall. Gandalf's neck is tight with tension and Norah holds her arms stiffly, hands thrust into her jacket pockets. It probably would have been a mistake to give a gun to two angry women facing their jailor.

Jailors, she reminds herself. *She* was one of them.

In the flickering light from the candle stubs, Henry looks pasty and grim. He leans hard on his wife, his arm draped over her shoulder. Austin doesn't know Catherine well, just enough to say hello in the supermarket aisles or wave as their cars pass on the road. She wasn't that friendly with their daughter either. Lissa was three years ahead in school and she hung out with the girls who wore jeans with sparkles on the hip pockets and went shopping with their mothers in Boston on school vacations. Mostly Austin can't forgive Lissa for being the person Gabe wrote to from Iraq.

What's the introduction etiquette in this situation? "Catherine, these ladies are Norah and Gandalf," she mumbles. "I'm going out to watch for Pops."

Sticking her face back into the wet night and breathing deeply, Austin admits she's a coward for leaving the four of them alone. She fingers the crinkly pages in her pocket and admits she'd rather face the unknown forces lurking outside than the emotions brewing in the stuffy cave room. Closing her eyes, she tries to block out the sound of waves smashing against rocks in the angry bay beyond the quarry. She listens for voices, for footsteps.

What's keeping Pops?

If not for the slippery rock, she might have missed them in the racket of the rain. A sharp cry comes from the left, followed by a thud and the murmur of voices—more than one. With a skeleton staff on duty, Tobias will most likely be alone, so this is probably—hopefully—Pops and Bert. Still, she stays hidden in the narrow opening, hoping the three adult-sized silhouettes moving along the path are Pops and Bert. And who else?

"Austin?" Pops's voice draws her out of her hiding place. She throws her arms around him and presses her face against his wet slicker.

Bert rests his hand briefly on Austin's shoulder. "Thank God you're okay. Tobias said . . ."

"Better not talk out here," Pops says. "Let's see if these ladies are ready to travel."

"Henry and Catherine too," Austin says.

Bert turns to Cyrus and points to the path beyond the cave. "Walk north twenty feet or so, and keep a look-out, okay? We'll hold everyone in the cave for another ten, fifteen minutes. Got to time this right, so we get down to the boats just after the tide turns."

Austin waits until they are inside the passageway before asking Pops, "What's Cyrus doing here?"

"Bert asked him to help. Why?"

"He's Army."

"Bert trusts him," Pops says. "And he's family."

"That's your answer for everything." She smiles. "Did you find Margaret's cove?"

"Yup. The boats are tied up there. The tide'll turn pretty soon, and we'll be able to get home. Let's get these folks moving."

Austin turns to the carving, just for a moment. Thank you, Margaret, she whispers. She traces the letters and numbers first, and then around the twisted wreath of branches and leaves. Her fingers find the thin line where the broken piece makes the circle whole. She leans against the stone, letting the initials press into her body.

She wishes she could tell Gabe about Margaret's letters. He would be so excited about having family spread over the world. And he could help her understand all the emotions warring inside her. Because if it was wrong to deport AF a hundred years ago for being Italian, for being in a union and believing in something the government didn't like, what does that mean about what her government is doing now?

She sticks her head into the rainy night outside and looks around. Just Cyrus, leaning against the granite wall. Watching her.

# 56. GANDALF, 10:58 P.M.

Gandalf watches every move Henry Ames makes. Not that he stirs much after his wife helps him sit back against the cave wall, with Norah's duffle as a cushion. The wife feeds him sips of water from a plastic bottle. She seems kind; how can she love someone who tortures people? Even if he doesn't actually do the torture himself, even if he reprimands Ferret for his excesses, he still accepts the principle of aggressive questioning. Regardless if a person is innocent and telling the truth. At least about all the relevant issues.

But she cannot contemplate the state of Catherine's conscience right now because it is hard to think straight. Her shakiness might be due to exhaustion, or hunger, or the lingering effects from the deep-freeze treatment. It feels like with chemo when her fever spiked and she hallucinated cloud people with suction-cup feet walking upside down on the apartment ceiling.

She leans closer to Norah. "How long does it take to get warm again?"

Norah squeezes her arm. "I'm still cold."

A new voice echoes in the cave entrance and an older man enters. Henry's wife jumps up and hugs him. "Bert! Thank God you're here. Can you get us home?"

"I think so." Bert squats in front of Henry, and the three of them talk in low voices. Gandalf listens intently, but cannot deconstruct the sounds into words or sentences. Then the new arrival turns to Norah and Gandalf. He sticks out his hand.

"Bert Carter. I captain the ferry between Storm Harbor and Hurricane. Ray and I have boats to get you folks out of here."

Norah takes his hand. "Are you Austin's grandfather?"

Bert tilts his head and closes one eye, which makes him look incongruously clownish in the candlelight. "That would be Ray. I'm his cousin."

"What are we waiting for?" Norah asks.

"The tide. Can't get the boats out of the cove until it turns. It's safer waiting here. Down by the water there's no shelter, no place to hide. But it'll take a while to get us all down the cliff and into the boats. We'll start pretty soon." Bert turns back and resumes his conversation with Catherine and Henry as another man walks into the cave, followed by Austin a moment later.

"This is Ray Coombs, my Pops," she tells Gandalf and Norah.

"Thank you so much," Gandalf says.

"Thank me when we've got you to safety," he says.

Bert joins them. "We'll head down in two groups. To attract less attention, in case Tobias is watching. You're sick, Henry. I want you coming with me in the first group. My boat has a closed cabin."

"Norah's hurt," Austin says. "She should go with you too."

"Makes sense." Bert helps Norah stand, then checks his watch. "The rest of you wait ten, fifteen minutes. By the time both boats are loaded in, the tide will carry us out."

"Cyrus will keep watch until the last minute," Ray says. "Then he'll come down with us."

"Who is Cyrus?" Gandalf asks Austin.

"Another cousin. He's Army, works at the facility. He's outside now on lookout."

Terrific. Another man she would much rather not depend on.

Norah hugs Gandalf and Austin. "See you back in civilization."

Leaning heavily on his wife, Henry walks slowly towards the cave mouth. He stops halfway and looks across the shadowy space at Gandalf. His expression is hard to read, both crushed and expectant.

"I'm sorry," he says.

Catherine brushes her finger along the line of his jaw. "Tell her the rest."

Henry looks down at his feet. "If there's an inquiry, I'll testify in your favor," he says, then continues to the cave entrance.

Gandalf nods, not knowing how to respond. As they disappear into the narrow corridor, she misses Norah dreadfully, even her rigid opinions.

Austin hands her a bottle of water and an energy bar. She unwraps one for herself. "You've had almost nothing to eat. No wonder you can't stop shaking."

Ten minutes later, Austin says it's time. Gandalf's heart tumbles into her belly. It beats wildly, churning the energy bar.

"I'll help you," Austin says, handing the flashlight to Gandalf. "Hold this."

"It's still raining," Ray says, "but less. We'll hug the rock wall and take it slow and easy. And quiet."

Ray goes first, then Austin and Gandalf. A man stands sentry outside the cave entrance; he must be the Army guy Austin mentioned, the cousin. Gandalf glances in his direction, to whisper thank you, but here's something familiar about him. Something awful. She switches on the flashlight and shines it on his face.

His eyes are cornflower blue. She knows those eyes.

Her brain flashes back to a white metal room barefoot at the airport, and two men come in. One man has a raspy voice and he stands behind her and grabs both her arms, binding her wrists together, and she kicks back at him. This man, with blue eyes, stomps his boot on her bare feet, just before he smothers her face with a black hood, a hood of fabric so close against her mouth and nose that she knows she will suffocate. Troll and Blue Eyes.

Gandalf stares into the man's cornflower blue eyes and screams.

## 57. RAY, 11:27 P.M.

When the professor screams, Ray whips around in time to see Austin grab the flashlight. The beam splashes through rain, breaks up into sparkling reflections against the shiny granite wall, then pierces the sky.

"Turn that off," Cyrus shouts.

A second light shines down on them from the cliff top. It seems instantaneous, it happens so fast. A loud noise blasts Ray's ears, and they are all inside the noise. Pieces of rock jump up from the path and skitter in the gray smoke. For a moment he can't see Austin and he panics because it's his job to protect her, and then it's okay because she is right here.

"Get down." Cyrus pushes Gandalf and Austin towards the wall, shoving them into the narrow "V" where cliff meets ledge. They curl up close into stone.

Smart man. Maybe Cyrus isn't as Army as he thought. Ray moves closer to the women. "Are you both okay?"

Austin nods. "Get down here with us."

Ray steps closer. But he can't move fast enough, and there's more loud noise, a series of booms coming from above, and there's Austin screaming "Pops" and then a hollow, empty-sounding thump. The cliff tilts, and Ray is in the air. He sees Nettie's face, her mouth smiling, and she's telling him to be careful, to protect his head and so he does, curling his arms around his face and neck. Then she's saying something else, telling him something else, it's about Austin, and he gets worried again because where is Austin and then he remembers he wants to talk to her about the carved initials. He wants to ask her about the letters, about what was in them. She's a smart girl, Austin is, and has probably figured it out without him. But she'll have questions about Aunt Margaret and Angelina, and it will be good to finally talk about it openly and maybe after all of this, Nettie will find peace about the grandmother she never knew.

But he has lost Austin again, and then Nettie's face is gone too, and the noise is gone, and the lights are no longer reflecting against the cliffs, and everything is red then black, and where is Austin, and he is falling.

## 58. AUSTIN, 11:32 P.M.

"Pops!" Austin screams.

Right in front of her, Pops flies apart into pieces, and everything turns red. Bright crimson parts of him arc into the air and then tumble silently off the smoky cliff. They fall towards the quarry water below, pursued by streaks of fire, splashes and the echoes of gunfire.

She falls to her knees and leans forward over the edge. She stares down through smoke to the place where he disappeared. The quarry water is deep, Gabe told her that summer day. Bottomless. Raindrops make small ripples in the red puddle around her on the ledge.

Cyrus fires three shots into the air, up towards the cliff top.

"Everyone down. Get close to the wall and stay low," he orders. "That's Tobias up there and he's aiming for you ladies."

Austin feels a tug on her hand. It pulls her through the rain and wisps of smoke and scorched smell into the shadow of the cliff.

In the wet and the smoke and the fear, Austin huddles with Gandalf, feeling the older woman tremble. Austin is here, her body pushing into rock, and at the same time she isn't here at all. How can Pops be blown apart, pieces falling through the quarry water? He has always been right next to her, sticking close, even all the times she pushed him away.

Her first childhood memory is sitting with Pops on the rocks behind the house, at the cusp of coastline and bay. It could have been the day her mother dumped her with Gran and Pops and took off, though Austin doesn't actually remember that part. Gran was a teacher and had to go to work, but Pops stayed home from fishing that day. He told her a rambling story about the island wood fairies, and they built their first fairy house together.

Over the next weeks and years, they built many tiny dwellings among tree roots. Pops insisted that the dwellings had to be made entirely of natural materials—of sticks and bark, pebbles and twigs and seaweed and pinecones. When they finished each one, Austin would lean against his scratchy wool shirt, smelling of pinesap mixed with rotting sea life, and he would reward her with a lesson in seagull talk. "I never went to college," he told her, "so seagull is the only foreign language I speak." He did seem to converse with them, though he refused to translate the nasty parts. "They're pretty raunchy, those gulls," he confided to her little-girl self.

She wipes her eyes. He still has that green wool shirt, although the body inside it has softened and drooped. Why hasn't she hugged him more, why hasn't she been nicer these past few years, instead of making fun of his weather watching? Instead of always talking about leaving Maine. Leaving him.

She looks past Gandalf's arms, past Cyrus's body shielding them, to the water. How can Pops be down there, when he was just next to her? The sorrow in her throat swells, squeezing her windpipe and stealing her breath. Gandalf seems to know and hugs her tighter. Austin tries to look past her own memories into the now, at what she has to do. But it is all too huge, too impossible, without Pops.

"Listen up," Cyrus says. "Tobias is up there and he has totally lost it. I reckon that Henry and the others got by safely, since I didn't hear gunfire before. We need to move back into the cave, away from Tobias's line of sight. Come. We'll figure something out." He holds his hands out to the women.

## 59. GANDALF, 11:46 P.M.

"Now what?" Austin asks Cyrus between sobs when they have retreated back into the cave.

Gandalf still cannot quite grasp who Blue Eyes is. Except that she remembers Austin was *there*, too, and she was Apricot then. Right now it is hard to think beyond the shaking and the pounding of her heart, and the fear clogging her throat.

"We need a way to get past Tobias," he says.

There is something, Gandalf thinks. Something Austin said, back before her grandfather exploded into pieces. It was something Margaret said and then she remembers.

"The back entrance," Gandalf says. "It was in Margaret's letter, remember? Perhaps Tobias does not know about it."

"Where is it? Where does it go?" Cyrus asks.

"Spiders," Austin hiccups, and points to the back of the cave.

Cyrus follows his flashlight beam into the dark shadows and returns a moment later. "I found the back exit. I'm not sure exactly where it comes out, but it's better than . . ." He doesn't finish his sentence, but Austin and Gandalf follow him.

Standing outside, Cyrus peers through the rain in one direction and then the other. He points. "I think it's this way. Let's go quickly. Tobias has heat-sensing equipment and he could find us again at any moment."

Walking along the narrow ledge and holding onto Austin, Gandalf estimates that even if they're going in the right direction, the back entrance only gained them fifty yards or so, but hopefully that's enough. Thank you, Margaret.

She presses tight against the wet wall, but images of Austin's grandfather in pieces materialize in her path, threatening to trip her. It is colder now. Needles of rain prick her face, then become frigid snakes twisting down her neck and lopsided chest. That makes her miss her breast prosthesis, and her laptop too, but it doesn't matter because the shivering is back, bigger than anything, bigger than the quarry and the storm and her fear. Shivering has taken over her whole self, freezing her heart and squeezing water out of her eyes. She is so cold and so tired. She cannot walk another step. She cannot hold the groaning inside anymore, and a sound comes out. She slumps against the cliff.

"Come on," Cyrus urges. "We're almost at the end and then it's downhill to the cove."

Gandalf hears rumbling above them. Pebbles tumble down, slowly at first, then faster. Bigger rocks follow, plunging around them with more force.

"The cliff's collapsing," Cyrus yells. "Press yourselves tight against the rock."

Austin again curls up and makes herself small. Gandalf nudges her into the space between her own body and the cliff wall. She wants to close her eyes but she cannot and she watches rocks slam onto the ledge, stone crashing into stone. Some bounce and splash into the quarry water below. Clumps of earth follow. Three large branches and a rifle plummet through air onto stone.

Finally a large figure pinwheels down. He drags a rope and broken spruce trunk with him, all flailing limbs and howling screams. He smacks onto the ledge, bouncing once. Gandalf winces at the crack of his head against granite.

"Stay back, ladies." Cyrus points his gun at Tobias. "He might just be stunned."

Now the rumbling is inside Gandalf's chest. It roars up into her throat and explodes from her mouth. When she howls, Austin lets go and stares at her. Gandalf stands up, anger flooding her veins. She steps closer, next to the blue-eyed Cyrus with the gun.

Tobias is sprawled prone on the rock, head turned towards her, his eyes closed. Rain falls on his exposed cheek and the back of his neck. His right leg is bent at an impossible angle, clearly broken, so he can't run even if he wakes up. Both arms stick out above his head, and his hands hang off the ledge into the empty black air. Those rattlesnake hands, compact and square and swift when he smacked her face, are flaccid now. She trembles, remembering those squared-off fingers holding the knife. She touches the scabbed slash across her cheek. Even now, when his hands are not coiled to strike, are unable to hurt her, they hold power.

He lifts one shoulder, opens his eyes for a few seconds, then moans.

One push would do it. One firm push or better yet a kick to his side would roll him off the cliff. It would be payback for Austin's grandfather, for Norah assaulted by the misogynist jeers of the guys, for the cold and the fear and the ice and the face slaps and the knife. For his foul mouth on Austin's breast and his ugly hand shoved down her pants. For his threats to Jess and his lies about Ahmed. She pictures Ahmed's face. She has to think about that, when she can once again think analytically. About the past and about the email she sent. Did she get Ahmed in trouble, and was she willing to do that because of their history? No, it is the fault of the evil man lying in front of her.

Hatred mixes with the anger in her bloodstream and it is the most potent and toxic cocktail she has ever felt. She steps closer.

From behind, strong arms wrap around her shoulders and pull her close. A chest is soft against her back and sweet apricot hair wet against her face. Austin probably wants to help push him off the cliff.

"Don't," Austin says.

"He deserves it."

"He does." Austin pulls Gandalf back. "But let Cyrus take him in. Tobias will face charges for what he's done."

"I doubt it," Gandalf says. When did she become so cynical? No, it is not cynicism that she feels; it is fury.

"Yeah," Austin says. "What he's done is probably legal, even though it's horribly wrong. But we'll expose it. All of us will."

Maybe they will. But it isn't enough. This is personal. Gandalf shrugs away Austin's arms and steps forward. She nudges Tobias's ribs with her foot. He grimaces and opens his eyes. He looks half-dead and probably couldn't understand, even if she could translate her anger into sentences. She has never spit on anyone in her life, but she tries it and it's both repulsive and oddly satisfying.

"That's for Pops. For hitting me. For the cold. For Norah."

Still pointing his gun, Cyrus steps forward and unclips plastic handcuffs from Tobias's belt. He gives them to Austin. "Cuff him, then get the two of you down to the boat. I'll stay and guard this bastard until Reuben gets here."

"Reuben?" Gandalf asks

"The sheriff," Austin says. "Pops must've called him."

"Can you handle his boat?" Cyrus asks Austin.

Austin nods, looking stunned. Gandalf takes Austin's hand. She is probably thinking that Pops will never again drive his boat.

"Bert's waiting at the cove." He flicks his head towards Gandalf. "This is over now. Take her and go home."

# SUNDAY
## SEPTEMBER 11

# 60. AUSTIN, 12:47 A.M.

It's rough going down the rocky trail to the cove. The stone is slippery, and Austin sees Pops's blood, everywhere—in the puddles, in the raindrops, in the rivulets weeping along the ancient cracks in her slicker.

They make slow progress, pressed along the wet rock. Austin walks without feeling her feet move. She breathes without knowing how air can move in and out of her body, past the thick lump of sorrow wedged in her throat. Gandalf's hand is a lifeline, and Austin squeezes hard to banish the words she must say to Gran when she gets home. Words about Pops and how he saved her life, and Margaret's words too.

At the bottom of the hill, she and Gandalf follow their flashlight beam over seaweed-shrouded rocks. They hang onto each other, staggering through the muck. Mud grabs their boots and won't let go. Finally they reach the boats where Henry and Catherine huddle in the cabin and Bert and Norah wait in the stern. Their faces are pale and worried, yellow raincoats glowing in the rainy light.

"You guys okay? We heard shots," Norah calls out. "You look awful."

"Where's Cyrus?" Bert asks. "And Ray?"

Austin opens her mouth but can't speak. Pops. Pops. Pops. She squeezes Gandalf's arm.

"Tobias shot Ray. He's gone. Into the quarry." Gandalf's chattering teeth chop the words into sharp pieces. "Then Tobias . . . fell. From the top of the cliff."

"Is he dead?" Norah leans forward to reach for Austin. She grabs her injured leg, and the boat tilts sharply. Bert pulls her back to steady the rocking.

"Pops is dead, and Tobias looks seriously injured," Gandalf says. "Cyrus is guarding him until your sheriff comes." She and Austin help each other into Pops's boat.

"Cyrus?" Norah grabs Bert's arm. "Can we trust him? He works for Tobias."

"Don't worry," Bert says. "Ray and Cyrus are kin."

That family thing again. Austin closes her eyes. She refuses to cry. Yet. Not until she can sink into Gran's arms—then she can wail and howl. Arms pull her close, and Gandalf is shivering so hard it's a vibrating hug. Must be from the cold. Austin makes a mental note to look up the aftereffects of cold torture, so she'll know how to help her friend, and what to expect in the future. Except that she's done with this stuff.

"You're in shock or something," Austin whispers. She removes Gandalf's oilskin and cocoons her in the ratty blanket Pops keeps in the boat for emergencies. Hooking the hood over Gandalf's head, she spreads the slicker back around her, over the blanket. The empty sleeves flap in the wind like the yellow wings of some exotic bird never before seen in mid-coast Maine.

"You okay driving the boat?" Bert asks her. "It's wild out here."

Austin nods. "I just aim for the outlet, right?"

"Don't even need to aim." Bert starts his motor and shines his light towards the opening. "The tide'll suck you out."

The cove outlet appears as a narrow slice of darker night in the wet wall of rocks and forest. Austin pushes the ignition button. Pops just had it replaced. Omigod. Pops. Pops. Reversing slowly, she avoids the rocks and follows Bert across the small cove.

Next to her, Gandalf shivers, and the yellow wings tremble.

"You cold?" Austin asks.

"I feel like I've been cold forever."

"A hot bath will help," Austin says. "At Gran's."

Gran. How is she going to tell Gran? She wipes her eyes, because first she has to get them home. She steers behind Bert's boat towards the cove outlet, aware of Gandalf sitting stiffly behind her, drawing the yellow sleeves tight around her body against the wet cold. Austin's eyes fill again because there's this thought, on top of losing Pops. Even if they make it safely across the angry sea and even if Gandalf manages to get away, she might never again see this odd woman.

And then she can't think about anything except what's happening in front of them—Bert's boat swells up onto a mountain of water and hovers.

A moment later, Bert and his boat drop away and disappear over the edge of the barely visible world.

"Maybe we should reconsider . . ." Gandalf says but it is too late.

Already they're sucked by the storm-swollen tide towards the dark tunnel cut through forest and rock. Riding the mammoth bulge of water, they rise and rush through the narrow outlet. Slapped by branches and sprayed by sea fury, they are delivered into the salty-wet wind of the bay.

Furious waves pelt the boat, and Austin tightens her grip on the wheel. She half-sees Gandalf grab hold of an empty sleeve flailing in the wind and pull it close, wrapping the slicker tighter around her body. Then the next wave hits the boat head on and shatters over them. Gandalf leans closer to Austin and hangs onto her arm. They follow Bert's boat along the dark outline of Hurricane's coast, through the final shudders of the storm.

By the time the two boats reach the protected waters of the Sound, there are lights in buildings along Main Street.

"Power is back," Gandalf says. "Maybe the phone service is restored too."

She's probably thinking about calling Jess. Once Gandalf gets home to Jess, she'll most likely forget she invited Austin to visit.

The boats enter the harbor and turn in to shore beyond the town pier, at her grandparents' place. They tie up on either side of the small wooden dock. Two silhouettes stand at the cusp of rocky shoreline and angry water.

The taller shape steps forward. Sheriff Reuben helps Henry, Catherine, and Norah onto the dock. The second person is shrouded by an oversized slicker with the hood up even though the rain has passed into drizzle. As if she already knows what happened, she doesn't move from the rocks.

"Is that your Gran?" Gandalf asks.

Austin tries to speak. She wants Gandalf to understand everything she's feeling. But it's no use because she's already weeping, and she doesn't understand it herself, except that Pops is gone, and it's all her fault. She climbs out of his boat and walks up his dock and onto the jumbled rocks of his yard into Gran's arms. A dozen seagulls circle and squawk their complaints.

"Pops is gone." Austin sobs into Gran's neck. "Dead."

Gran leans back to stare into Austin's face. "What happened?"

"He was shot. Trying to get me out of there. And it happened so fast— there was no time to say goodbye. To tell him how much I love him."

Gran cups Austin's face between her hands. "Don't you think he knows that?" she sobs.

"But it's my fault. He was trying to rescue me."

"Looks like he succeeded."

The two women rock sideways, back and forth in the ancient dance of comfort. Gran's tears are warm on her neck, soaking her hair. Austin wants to tell her how grateful she is that they rescued her childhood. She wants to ask how they can live without Pops's seagull talk and his Weather Channel commentary and his Fig Newtons.

And the letters. She wants to talk with Gran about the letters, about what happened to Margaret and why she disappeared, and who Angelina really is, and the Italian branch of their family.

"Pops told me about the packet of letters from Margaret. I found them, Gran. I took them and read them."

"I know." Gran smoothes a strand of wet hair from Austin's forehead and tucks it behind her ear.

She wants to talk with Gran—if only she could tell Pops too—about the bombing and Angelo not letting the bad guys win, even if some people thought that Margaret's own father was a bad guy.

"Can we talk about them?"

"I can't."

"I don't get it," Austin says. Then she remembers that Gran read the letters too and she knows what happened. Maybe she's ashamed, and that's why she hates Hurricane so much. It's so complicated, but maybe Gran will feel differently if she sees the initials, the carving, all whole again. And Pops can help sort it all out, but no. He can't. Not ever. And it's no use trying to figure it out now because the ache is so big it fills her chest and squeezes the words. She squeezes her eyes shut and tucks her face in Gran's hair.

"Someday," Gran says. "Someday we'll talk about them. I promise."

# 61. HENRY, 2:15 A.M.

He huddles with Cat and Gandalf under the corrugated metal carport. Norah leans against the wet shingles of the house, her mouth a straight line of pain. No one speaks. They watch Reuben and Bert talk on the dock, then Bert turns his boat towards the town harbor to begin the early ferry run out to Hurricane Island. They try not to look at Nettie and Austin on the rocks, their sorrow barely audible over the screeching lament of the seagulls.

But Sheriff Reuben must have something more important than private grief in mind, because he joins Nettie and Austin on the rocks, putting an arm around each. Henry can see his mouth moving. Nettie breaks away and hurries into the house, but Reuben and Austin join them in the carport.

Sheriff Reuben looks at each of them and breaks the silence.

"The Congresswoman asked me to get you folks to the airport right away. She's arranged a plane to take you to New York. There's a press conference tomorrow, and she wants all of you to testify."

"What about my family?" Gandalf interrupts. "Jess is on her way up here."

The sheriff shakes his head. "You'll have to ask Evelina about that. You can call her from the plane."

"I guess we can't wait until morning," Henry says. He doesn't like the serious way the sheriff looks at them, as if he holds bad news in his jaw. Henry knows unspoken ruin when he sees it and he can guess the rumors the sheriff isn't sharing. Most likely, the Bureau has already dispatched a team to clean up the mess in Maine.

Across the Sound, Hurricane Island is shrouded in morning fog and drizzle. After everything that has happened, how can he feel conflicted about the camp closing?

"How much trouble are we in?" Henry asks.

The sheriff shrugs. "I'm not sure. But Evelina thinks you're in a lot of danger. Two federal agents who recently tried to testify about, uh, unconventional interrogation techniques—"

"Say it," Norah interrupts. "Torture."

"Whatever. Both men met with unfortunate accidents. Fatal ones."

The Regional Chief—somehow it doesn't feel right to call him JR any more—doesn't mess around, does he? How easy it would be for Henry to suffer a similar accident. There are so many possibilities: brake failure on a twisty road, a barely noticeable nudge on a crowded subway platform, polonium-spiked sushi or a poison syringe in an umbrella tip.

"The press conference is critical," Norah says. "We need to educate people, make this a Watergate moment. I'm sure the Center will host it."

Henry isn't sure he wants anything to do with her Center.

Reuben turns to Norah. "Evelina said your Center was raided late last night. A lawyer, Emma Something, was arrested, charged with giving material aid to terrorists."

Norah sways and steadies herself against Gandalf.

"Isn't Emma the work friend you told us about?" Gandalf asks.

Norah nods. "The press conference is even more important now. The government will try to blame everything on Tobias, to spin this as a story about one bad apple."

Cat squeezes his hand again. "One bad apple and a whistleblower."

"A whistleblower with compelling taped evidence." Henry opens his jacket to reveal the mini-disk in his pocket.

"That's great." Norah steps forward to high-five Henry and grimaces in pain.

"Don't forget Norah is hurt," Gandalf says. "She needs a doctor."

"There are doctors in New York," Reuben says. "Let's go."

"Good idea," Henry says. It's probably healthier for all of them to get off these islands now. Before the Regional Chief sends reinforcements to arrest them. Or worse.

"I'll be there in a minute," Austin says, opening the kitchen door. "Got to say goodbye to Gran. And get something."

# 62. GANDALF, 3:08 A.M.

"Hunker down," Reuben orders as they arrive at the airport. He points to two dun-colored airplanes. "Those are military. I'm driving onto the tarmac." Gandalf hears him talking on the phone about take-off clearance and a quick departure.

The rain has stopped. With her last ounce of energy, Gandalf helps Norah stumble towards the plane.

"Can you believe this?" Norah asks. "I mean, what fucking just happened? Did we just escape from a secret federal prison, with the help of a sheriff and an FBI agent?"

"You tell me. You're the political one." Gandalf steps in a puddle, and the cold rainwater splashes onto her sweatpants. The ugly gray sweatpants she put on so many hours ago in the supply room. How many more hours before she can soak in her own deep bathtub, wear her own clothes?

The propellers are already spinning as they clamber up the portable metal steps. Someone slams the door and pulls the stairs away as they fasten seat belts. Henry sits with the pilot, Catherine and Norah behind him, Austin and Gandalf in back.

"I feel so bad leaving Gran," Austin says over the increasing engine noise. "She wouldn't come?"

"Says she has to make arrangements for Pops." Austin buries her face in a green wool shirt cradled in her arms. "I should be with her."

"You can't," Gandalf says. "It is not safe for you here."

The plane rises steeply into the morning sky. The three women lean together and press their faces against the scratched plastic windows. Gandalf looks at the three islands clustered in the empty bay. "What a location," she says. "Perfect to catch every storm coming up the coast."

Austin's face crumbles. "That's what Pops always said. He loved these islands." She points at the shrinking shapes. "That's Lily Haven to the north and Storm Harbor below. Hurricane is the runt to the east. If you squint, she looks like a girl running away from her sisters, hair blowing in the wind."

"I think she is running towards them," Gandalf says. Like us, she thinks.

Catherine passes back a canvas bag. "This is from Evelina."

Inside, along with granola bars and apples and juice boxes, pens and yellow pads, are cell phone chargers. Gandalf plugs her phone into the outlet on the armrest and turns it on. Scrolling through her inbox, she finds the most recent message from Jess.

*Just got a call from the Congresswoman. She says you're coming home. See you at JFK. I miss you, sweetheart.*

*On my way*, Gandalf writes back. *I love you.*

She opens one other message. *Hello, Gee*, Ahmed writes, *Thanks for your message. It is good to hear from you. Sorry I can't help with your problem. Cassidy sends his love to Sundance.*

Relief sends a wave of warmth to her chest. Or maybe it's from Jess's message. Whatever the reason, Gandalf takes off the oilcloth jacket and one layer of fleece. Leaning back into the seat, she fingers the gold wizard charm around her neck. She does not believe in wizards or any other superstition, but the piece of precious metal signifies something about her and Jess, something new. Pushing into the sky in a fragile metal cylinder, time stands still, and she is calm, and almost warm, in a moment that she does not want to leave. A moment of feeling stretched, yet torn apart. She hungers for this misbegotten adventure to be over and yearns for the return of her life with Jess. But now she also has Austin and Norah, and she can't go back to the way it was before. She brings the gold charm to her lips. Maybe it offers a reprieve, a new beginning.

"Listen up," Henry says from the front of the plane. "I just spoke with Evelina. The press conference is tomorrow afternoon in New York. Since Norah and Gandalf are his constituents, her bigwig friend on the Homeland Security subcommittee agreed to hold it in his district office in Brooklyn. Evelina wants us each to write a statement to read. She asks us to write down everything that happened, the whole and honest truth. Right now, she says, while it's fresh in our minds."

"The whole truth?" Austin murmurs. "Which one? The truth is different from what I thought four days ago."

Gandalf closes her eyes. Can she bear to relive publicly everything that happened? Starting with the white room and blue eyes? And does the whole truth mean the other thing, that she has never told Jess. The thing she hardly ever even thought about until Ferret made her remember. Because honestly it is nothing; just the fumbling sort of non-event that started at a party when people are lubricated by too many margaritas and the exhilaration of talking mathematics late into the night. It only lasted the week of the symposium, and Ahmed knew it meant nothing. Still, it was cheating, and she has been dishonest. She will make that right with Jess. And she will start right now, before she can change her mind.

"Speaking of the truth," Gandalf whispers, leaning close to Austin. "You told me your secret. I have one too. I lied during the interrogation."

"You did?" Austin stares at her. "About what?"

This is a mistake, Gandalf thinks, but then she looks at Austin's face. It is dear and surprised and so young.

"About not having a personal relationship with Ahmed. I had a brief thing with him once, for a few days at a conference."

"Oh." Austin looks embarrassed. "That's between you and Jess, you know. You didn't lie about him being a terrorist, did you?"

"Of course not."

Austin shrugs. "That's the story here, isn't it? Hurricane Island and torture."

Gandalf could hug Austin. Oh, yes, she does want to tell this story. She takes a pen and yellow pad from Evelina's bag.

# MONDAY
## SEPTEMBER 12

Henry sops up the last of the yolk with a crust of rye toast and smiles at Cat. Eating a very late, room service breakfast in a nondescript mid-town hotel is worlds away from storm-ravaged islands and cold torture. It probably wasn't necessary last night to register under a false name and have Cat pay with cash, but he can't help it. Even well rested, his brain cycles round and round between hotel surveillance cameras and facial recognition software, heart-racing images of ex-federal agents dying in mysterious and unexplained circumstances, and the memory of his daughter's shameful accusations.

His thoughts must show on his face.

"You nervous?" Cat puts down her newspaper and pours more coffee.

"A little." He checks his watch. Two hours until the press conference. He points to the newspaper. "Anything bad happen on the anniversary yesterday? Any acts of terrorism?"

Cat shakes her head. "Not according to the *Times*."

Damn JR and all his hype about high-profile detainees. None of this would have happened if the Regional Director hadn't been so paranoid. He might still have his job.

No, this was coming down the pike anyway. And he probably made it worse for himself early this morning when he went down to the lobby and logged on remotely to his work computer. It was amazing that he remembered all Tobias's passwords, and that the system didn't lock him out. But he did, and, it didn't, and he wrote a scathing press release about the use of cold torture on civilians and sent it out to his distribution list.

He raises his cup to Cat, in salute. Things between them aren't resolved, not by a long shot, but after last night maybe they've got a future. Barring poisoned umbrella tips.

In two hours he'll gather in Brooklyn with Gandalf and Austin and Norah. Melissa will be there too, and he'll try to be civil to Evelina because she really came through, big-time. He'll tell the press his story, about the torture of civilians, specifically about how they interrogated Professor Gandalf Cohen. He'll show the DVD and publically resign from the Bureau. Then he'll schedule those cardiac tests, meet with the lawyers from Norah's Center, and start looking for another job in which he can serve his country and keep it free.

"I'll wash up." Austin carries the lunch dishes into the kitchen. She likes being in Jess and Gandalf's apartment and wants to be a good guest. When they arrived at JFK yesterday, Henry warned them that staying at a known address wasn't safe. Said they should get a hotel room under a fake name, like he and Cat were planning. But Gandalf insisted on coming home, and the three of them wanted to stay together. Norah's ex brought her kids for a visit yesterday afternoon, but then Norah insisted he take them to a friend's house and keep away from the press conference.

Her twins are great—smart and funny—and Austin can't believe how Norah goes all maternal when they show up, much less strident and bossy. Austin turns Norah's offer of an afterschool babysitting job over and over in her brain, examining it from every angle. She might just do that, after this mess is over. Because after she spends some time with Gran, she's going to move to New York, stay here with Gandalf and Jess and find a job. Maybe even go to Italy and look for her relatives, the descendants of Margaret and Angelo. Pops would laugh, and point out that she was running away from family to look for family. But he would approve.

Gandalf pokes her head into the kitchen. "Leave the dishes," she says. "We need to leave soon."

"I'll be ready in a minute," Austin says. "Got to call Gran."

"I'm sure she's safe," Gandalf says. "They have Tobias locked up in a secure hospital ward, with a brain injury."

"She's staying with Cyrus and Jeannette for a few days." Austin touches Gandalf's arm. "But I've got to check on her."

Tobias rings for the nurse. He demands his phone, again.

"Against the rules," she says, again.

"Then take these off." He tugs his wrist restraints against the bedrail.

"They're for your own safety. Confusion and disorientation are common after head injury. Now, rest," she commands as she leaves the room.

The restraints are just for show. They don't mean anything. "Trust me," the Regional Chief promised on the phone, "and everything will be fine."

Tobias will play along but he doesn't trust JR or anyone, not completely. No way he's going to let the DC guys scapegoat him for this mess. JR claims they transferred him to Portland for the expert neurosurgeon, but the doc says that the injury was minor. Tobias suspects they want him away from his people. Sure, the doc is first-rate. His brain is working good as new under all the wrapped, white gauze. And the ribs will heal, no biggie. Even his leg—it makes him queasy to look at those pins sticking through the bones—will mend. The hard part is being cut off from the action. Especially since rumor has it that JR himself is in New York for the press conference. That's great, because he'll get to see the fruits of Tobias's planning first hand.

Luckily, Tobias is first-rate at his job too. He's still officially in charge and he has all the bases covered. So he's expecting it when the nurse sticks her head back in.

"You've got a visitor," she says. "Ten-minute limit."

Stanley Mason's eyes widen when he sees the bandages and metal contraptions, but Tobias waves his hand dismissively, as much as the restraints will allow.

"I'm fine," Tobias says. "What about you? Are you on board?"

"As long as you do what you promised, about getting me into the Bureau."

"Soon as this job is done. Are you sure you understand your assignment?"

Mason grins. "You bet."

"There'll be heavy security," Tobias says. "Take the letter from my top drawer. It will get you in, but you'll have to get yourself out. There'll be back stairs, behind the stage."

His head throbs. Tobias hates relying on the sergeant for such an important assignment, but his personnel choices are severely limited. At least Mason will get the job done. He hopes.

"Bring me the disk tomorrow." Tobias gestures the sergeant to leave and closes his eyes. He pushes the pain med button pinned to the blanket and soon he's floating again. There are clouds. Funny that the Cohen bitch studies them. He has always dreamt of leaning out of an airplane and touching them. One of these days, when the torture device comes off his leg, maybe he'll do just that. He'll learn to sky dive. Once the DVD is in his hands, once Henry and the three bitches are paid back, he can do anything.

Gandalf climbs the stairs from the subway. She is grateful that Austin and Norah went ahead early and astounded that she is holding hands with Jess in public and not feeling overwhelmed with awkwardness. Then she laughs at herself. After being held naked for who-knows-how-many strangers to gawk at on the surveillance system, she may never worry about exposure again.

No, that's not entirely true. There is the DVD Henry plans to show at the press conference in less than an hour. She wonders if she is naked and breastless on the section he plans to show, or modestly wrapped in the blanket. She touches the scab across her cheek and pictures her scraped knees under her slacks; she does not look her best in any case. How absurd to worry about vanity at a time like this. She squeezes Jess's hand and leans closer.

"I'm not sure I can do this," she murmurs, stepping over a downed branch on the sidewalk.

"Don't lose courage now, sweetheart."

They turn the corner onto Court Street, and Gandalf stops. The district office is four, five blocks away but the crowds are already visible. Television trucks block traffic and uniformed police hold people back behind striped sawhorse barriers.

Jess checks the directions Evelina texted and leads Gandalf past a caravan of SWAT Team vans into an alley. They avoid a deep puddle and give their names to the armed guard with a clipboard at the side door. "Elevator to the fourth floor," he says. "Auditorium on the left."

"SWAT Teams? Auditorium?" Gandalf whispers to Jess when they're inside.

Jess squeezes her hand. "Primetime, sweetheart."

Upstairs there are more guards, and then they are inside the auditorium. The front dozen rows are crowded with people adjusting television cameras and recorders; fleece-covered microphones hang in the air from metal pole extensions. Flanking the doors, burly men in suits talk into tiny microphones attached with twisty cord to earbuds.

The auditorium doors open, and people flood in. They fill the room with loud voices and storm clouds of anticipation. They are just concerned citizens, Gandalf tells herself. Harmless civilians with press passes or other official identification.

A large woman with owl glasses steps forward and takes Gandalf's elbow. "Dr. Cohen? I'm Evelina Carter. Thank you so much for doing this."

Reluctantly, Gandalf releases Jess's hand and lets herself be escorted onto the stage, where metal folding chairs are arranged in a semi-circle behind a large wooden podium. Evelina points to the empty seat between Austin and Norah, who holds a black cane. Henry, looking pale and anxious, studies a paper in his hand. On a wheeled cart behind the curtain on the other end of the stage, a large flat-screen monitor glows blue.

Gandalf points to Norah's cane. "You doing okay?"

"Better. Thanks to antibiotics and painkillers. You?"

"Scared to death." Gandalf looks out at the crush of reporters and photographers, searching for Jess. She locates her sitting next to Catherine, who Jess met briefly at the airport, and a young woman with matching dusty brown hair. Lissa.

Gandalf meets Jess's gaze. She has not yet found the right time to tell Jess about Ahmed's email, about Ahmed. Tonight, when this is over, she will explain.

Will this ever be over?

She looks at her notes. Her usual method of banishing stage fright, a combination of physics mnemonics and mathematical equations, fails her. She lowers her hand, letting it drift until it touches Norah's arm. She remembers to breathe.

The buzzing quiets as Evelina steps up to the podium and taps the microphone for attention. Gandalf barely registers the congresswoman's introductory remarks. She turns to watch Henry walk to the podium. He clears his throat and looks down at his papers.

Austin's shout breaks the silence. "No!" She stands and points towards the shadowy off-stage area to their right. "Stop him."

Henry swivels around to face the man squatting at the DVD player. The man jumps up and turns, holding a disk in one hand and a gun in the other. Under his gray sweatshirt hood, his face is vaguely familiar.

"Mason?" Henry shouts.

For a split second they all stand frozen. Then things happen all at once. The shooter points his gun at Henry. Austin tackles the shooter who fires twice. Two police officers run from the other side of the stage. More shots explode. Norah, Evelina, and Gandalf dive from their chairs onto the floor.

Gandalf covers her head with her arms. Screams from the audience bounce off the walls. A gun skittles across the worn wooden planks. Henry collapses onto the floor. The stage fills with SWAT team officers with bulletproof vests, guns and shields, poker faces.

When it's quiet, Gandalf combat crawls to Henry, lying behind the podium.

"Henry?" Gandalf touches his shoulder.

He lifts his head. "Is it over?"

Gandalf peers around the podium. The shooter is holding his shoulder, where a red stain seeps through his sweatshirt. Cops flank him, pinning his arms behind his back.

"Yes," Gandalf says. "I think so."

It takes a few minutes for the SWAT team to drag the shooter away and escort the speakers off stage to a small room with sofas. Henry refuses the ambulance. "I'm fine," he insists. "Just let our families know we're okay. They'll be frantic."

Evelina joins them, waving the disk. "Who was that guy?" she asks.

"Stanley Mason," Henry says. "An army sergeant assigned to the facility. Sent by Tobias, no doubt."

"Do you remember Mason?" Austin asks Gandalf. "He was one of the guys who picked you up at JFK."

Not Blue Eyes; that was Cyrus. So Mason is Troll, with the gravelly voice. She nods. "At least they got him."

"There'll be others," Norah says.

"Smarter ones," Henry adds.

"Listen," Evelina says. "Maybe we should postpone the press conference."

The three women exchange glances, then look at Henry. He shakes his head.

"No," Gandalf says. "We want to do this, today."

"Before they send someone else to stop us," Norah says.

They return to their semicircle of chairs, with SWAT team members visible in the wings. The audience takes a long time to quiet. This time, Evelina introduces Gandalf first.

Standing at the podium, Gandalf looks out at the crowd of reporters and elected officials and citizens. The audience seems even larger than before and it pulses with anticipation, turbulent and electric. She finds Jess in the crowd and touches her gold wizard charm. She feels Austin and Norah and Henry sitting strong behind her.

"My name," she begins, "is Gandalf Cohen. Four days ago federal agents kidnapped me at JFK Airport and transported me against my will to Hurricane Island."

# THE END

# BIOGRAPHICAL NOTE

Ellen Meeropol's characters live on the fault lines of political turmoil and human connection. She is the author of one previous novel, *House Arrest* (Red Hen Press, 2011). A literary late bloomer, she began seriously writing fiction in her fifties. Her short fiction and essays have been published in *Bridges, DoveTales, Pedestal, The Rumpus, Portland Magazine, Beyond the Margins, The Drum,* and *The Writer's Chronicle.* A former pediatric nurse practitioner and part-time bookseller, Ellen holds an MFA in Creative Writing from the Stonecoast program at the University of Southern Maine. She lives in Western Massachusetts.